Parables Reimagined

Stories of God's Kingdom
for Today's World

Christian Fiction
Short Stories Omnibus

by

Natalie Vellacott

Copyright
Natalie Vellacott 2023
Cover design images: Freepik.com
All rights reserved.

CONTENTS

I DID IT MY WAY

Chapter 1 4
Chapter 2 20
Chapter 3 34
Chapter 4 44
Note to Reader 46

THE RETURN

Chapter 1 48
Chapter 2 52
Chapter 3 55
Chapter 4 58
Chapter 5 60
Chapter 6 65
Chapter 7 70
Chapter 8 72
Chapter 9 74
Chapter 10 78
Chapter 11 80
Chapter 12 82
Chapter 13 85
Chapter 14 87
Chapter 15 88
Chapter 16 92
Chapter 17 94
Note to Reader 97

A PILLAR OF THE COMMUNITY

Chapter 1 99
Chapter 2 104
Chapter 3 106
Chapter 4 109
Chapter 5 112
Chapter 6 117

Chapter 7 120
Chapter 8 123
Chapter 9 125
Chapter 10 127
Chapter 11 130
Chapter 12 134
Chapter 13 135
Chapter 14 137
Chapter 15 139
Note to Reader 143

DARE TO BE DIFFERENT

Chapter 1 145
Chapter 2 148
Chapter 3 150
Chapter 4 152
Chapter 5 155
Chapter 6 158
Chapter 7 161
Chapter 8 165
Chapter 9 168
Chapter 10 171
Chapter 11 174
Chapter 12 177
Chapter 13 181
Chapter 14 184
Chapter 15 187
Chapter 16 189
Note To Reader 192

EAT, DRINK AND BE MERRY

Chapter 1 194
Chapter 2 197
Chapter 3 200
Chapter 4 202
Chapter 5 204
Chapter 6 207

Chapter 7 211
Chapter 8 213
Chapter 9 216
Chapter 10 218
Chapter 11 221
Chapter 12 223
Chapter 13 225
Chapter 14 227
Chapter 15 229
Chapter 16 231
Note To Reader 234

Chapter 1

Annie realises that she is lying face down on the ground. As she takes a quick glance around, all she can see is a dazzlingly bright light. There is something dreadful and brilliant about the light that makes Annie afraid to look directly at it.

Where is she? The last thing she can remember is that she had been lying in a hospital bed. That's right, it was a routine operation to remove a cyst. Her family had come to visit her before she had been put to sleep.

Am I still being operated on? Is this what it's meant to be like? Annie isn't sure and she feels uneasy.

A loud voice sounds, "Rise up Annie Yale. We have business to do."

Annie puts her hands over her ears. She can't stand the awesomeness of the voice. It's almost painful. *Just a strange dream probably caused by the hospital drugs. Nothing to worry about. I wish it would end, though. It's pretty realistic.*

"It's not a dream Annie, something went wrong during the operation." The voice again, pure, perfect and awesome.

"How can that be? I'm still young and have a lot of time left. It was a routine operation. That's what they said." Annie starts to panic as she realises what the voice is telling her.

I'm dead?!

She plucks up the courage to lift her head and look at the figure standing in front of her. All she can see is the light and the outline of a man.

"You know Who I am, don't you Annie?" The man speaks to her, His voice is stern but there is a hint of sadness.

"You are Jesus." The clarity hits Annie. She knows exactly Who this man is.

"You're wondering how you recognise Me," Jesus says. The sadness is unmistakeable this time. "I've always been there but you never trusted Me."

Annie now recalls falling to the ground and being dazzled by the bright light on arrival. "Where is that light coming from? It's almost blinding."

Jesus shakes His head sadly, "Oh Annie, I know the light is making you a little uncomfortable, but I'm afraid that's the least of your problems."

"What? What do you mean?" Annie is shaken by His words. They have the ring of truth. She is afraid. "Is this heaven?"

"What do you think?" Jesus asks as He gazes at her sorrowfully.

"It doesn't seem like it as I didn't think I would feel afraid in heaven." Annie hadn't realised that she even believed in a place called heaven until now.

"This isn't heaven. It's Judgement Day. You are standing before My throne and we're about to look at your life in detail," Jesus explains.

"What will happen at the end?" Annie whispers. She's almost afraid to ask the question.

"Everything depends on whether the things you did wrong on earth have been dealt with," Jesus is patient.

Annie thinks of the good things she has done in comparison with the bad.

"No, not like that," Jesus clarifies.

"How do you know what I'm thinking?" Annie feels exposed. She doesn't like it.

"Everything is about to be revealed," Jesus says.

Annie now finds herself sitting on a small chair. Two brightly coloured beings are either side of her. She guesses they must be angels. Glancing to her side, she can see the big throne with the brilliant light and the man called Jesus, that she'd immediately recognised.

A big screen is in front of them.

A movie? Annie is still thinking about Jesus' words but she doesn't really understand what is happening.

The screen flashes as images appear. Annie is horrified as she reads the title: *"The life of Annie Yale (1971-2017)"*. *We aren't seriously going to watch a movie of my whole life? I wonder how much detail there will be.*

She doesn't have to wonder about this for long as the first scene begins with clips of Annie as a baby. She is gurgling, laughing and throwing food around. Annie smiles. *Well, at least this part is good.* The thought has only just left her mind when the images change. Annie is now a toddler. She's screaming and shouting at her parents.

Then, deliberately tearing a book to pieces and thumping her younger brother David. Annie turns her head away in shame and embarrassment. Then, she thinks better of it. *I was just a small child. We all do things wrong at that age.* She reassures herself.

Jesus and the angels are silent as the movie continues.

Annie feels uncomfortable and has the sudden urge to speak, "Where did you get this footage from?" Even as she says it, she realises the foolish nature of her question.

"I am everywhere and see everything," Jesus answers.

One of the angels pauses the movie.

Are we really going to sit here and watch the whole of my life? Annie wonders.

"Yes, Annie." Jesus is still patient. Annie knows that this is His nature.

"Can't we just skip to the end so that I know what will happen to me?" Annie feels desperate. She has a horrible feeling about the whole situation.

"Annie," Jesus says sadly, "you've never trusted Me with your life or had your sin forgiven. You can't enter heaven."

"So what are we doing this for? Isn't it pointless?" Annie asks although she has a feeling that nothing that is done in this place is ever pointless.

"We are reviewing your life so that you can see why you can't go to heaven and so that you can also see that your punishment is fair," Jesus tells her.

"Punishment? What punishment? How long will it last?" Annie still doesn't understand.

"Oh Annie, it's forever. You rejected the only way for your sins to be forgiven whilst you were on earth." A tear appears in Jesus' eye as He explains.

"Forever? But surely there's something I can do?" Annie starts to cry, softly at first. She wants to believe that this Man is lying but deep down she knows that He cannot lie. *Perhaps I can reason with Him.* "I didn't reject God on earth, well not completely," she submits.

"Let's look at the evidence, shall we?" Jesus replies in a way that causes Annie to fall silent once more.

They turn back to the movie.

Annie is now about four and is trotting into a Sunday school class. She sits and listens as the elderly lady tells the story of *Jonah and the*

Big Fish to a group of about ten children.

"See, look, I did learn about God. I didn't reject Him." Annie stops crying, temporarily feeling vindicated by the discovery. She'd forgotten that she went to Sunday school all those years ago. *Phew, that was close. Now I know why my mum forced me to go. Thanks, Mum!*

There is no response from those watching the movie with her. They don't seem to be impressed by her Sunday school attendance. As they continue watching, a bubble appears above Annie's head on the screen. In it is written, "I wonder which dolly mummy will buy me. I like the pink Barbie one best. Oh, this is really boring. I hope it will finish soon."

Annie flushes red. She wants to run to the screen and flick off the monitor. *Surely, they can't be planning to watch all of my thoughts as well as my actions? I don't even remember playing with Barbies. Maybe it's just a guess based on what other children were doing at the time. It can't be my real thoughts, can it?*

"It's much more accurate than that Annie. I told you, I see everything." Jesus tells her whilst keeping focused on the movie.

Annie hangs her head in shame and dreads what's coming next.

Annie sees images of herself at about seven. She is dashing around with other children at a park. Her mum is standing nearby with adults she vaguely recognises as some of the parents of her school friends.

"So, Annie got tired of Sunday school in the end?" one of the ladies asks her mother.

"Yes, I don't think she was really into it anyway. I only sent her as it seemed like the right thing to do, and it gave me a chance to get some house stuff done," Annie's mum replies.

"It's a nice story for kids, but then they reach a certain age." Another lady has joined the conversation.

"At least you tried it. Got to be open-minded and let them look into all the religions." A fourth voice is heard.

The angels look dismayed. "Shall we move this forward?" they address Jesus.

"Yes, but first. I just want Annie to see a little of her friend Jessica," Jesus says. "You remember Jessica, don't you Annie?"

"Sort of, she was one of the other kids from church and we also went to school together. I don't remember seeing her much after the first few years at school, though." Now, Annie is curious.

"No, she took a very different path to you." One of the angels speaks to Annie for the first time.

Jesus looks at the angel. "Let her see for herself. That's the best way."

A small girl with dark hair and plaits appears on the screen. She is kneeling by her bed and it looks like she is praying. "Dear God, please forgive my sin. I know you will because Jesus died for me and made me clean. Help me to do what's right. Also, please get Annie to come back to Sunday school and to be my friend again. Amen." The little girl gets up and into bed where she picks up a book and starts reading.

Annie is astounded. "She prayed for me. Why? I don't even really remember her."

"She prayed for you a lot for a few years. You moved away from her as you found new friends. Jessica's name is in here." The angel speaking pats a huge book on a table that Annie hadn't even noticed until now.

She looks at the cover, *The Book of Life*. "What is that?"

"It's where the names of all those who have trusted Me for forgiveness of their sin are recorded." Jesus has been listening to the conversation and now He speaks.

"So, what happens to people whose names aren't there?" Annie asks. She knows her name won't be there but she keeps hoping there is a way out of the mess she is in.

"We spoke about this before Annie, their sin must be dealt with. Let's watch some more of the film," Jesus instructs.

Jessica wanted to be a good friend and cared about me. I wish I'd paid more attention. Things could've been so different. Annie realises that even at a young age she had been given a friend who could have helped her onto the right path.

Annie cringes as the film has now moved on to her late teenage years. *This is where the bad stuff will really come out. It seems so much worse when I'm not with my friends. It was funny when we were all together.*

The movie skips through drunken nights out and a number of sexual relationships, the details of which aren't shown on the screen. Annie covers her face with her hands and the angels look away.

Suddenly, the camera zooms in, Annie can be seen walking with two girls.

"I'm Agnostic," Annie tells them.

"Really what is that?" one of the girls asks.

"It means I'm not sure if God is there or not. I guess I'll find out when I die."

There is a stunned silence in the Throne Room as those present absorb her words. "I didn't mean that, I didn't realise." Annie weeps at the realisation that her flippancy and pride seem to have cost her her soul.

"Don't you think that's a bit risky?" Annie's head snaps up as her friend replies. *Is that Helen? I don't even remember this conversation.*

"Why? It's not like I'm an Atheist. I'm leaving room for God to prove Himself, but so far He hasn't." Annie challenges her friend in a mocking tone.

Annie cringes once more and wishes herself far away..

"Isn't the Bible proof enough?" Helen responds. "Really, Annie, I still think it's risky. We're talking about life and death after all. Have you seriously looked into it? Don't you think it's worth just a little of your time?"

How on earth did I respond to that? Annie wonders, but she knows it won't be good.

"Since when have you been part of the Bible-bashing brigade? Life and death, huh! I prefer to live for now. I'll think about that later, like when I'm ninety!" Annie looks triumphantly at her friend.

Helen doesn't even look slightly angry, just terribly sad. She opens her mouth to say something but closes it again. A bubble appears above her head. *This is turning into a pointless discussion that won't be helpful for Annie. I'd better stop. Oh Lord, please open her eyes to the truth, before it's too late. Forgive her foolishness and careless words.*

Now, Annie recognises the expression on Helen's face, she can see the same thing in the eyes of Jesus and the angels, pity mingled with compassion.

The angels have lifted up their wings and covered their faces to shield themselves from the harsh words coming from the screen.

The scene shifts. Helen is alone in a bedroom. There are pieces of coloured paper on the walls. The camera zooms in and Annie can see lists of names. One of the lists is headed "salvation." Annie sees her name, it is number three on the list. The movie shows Helen praying on her bed, then she is praying in church, then a meeting with a group of people, then in her bedroom again. The various clips continue for a long time.

Is the video stuck? Annie again forgets that her thoughts are basically audible.

"No, Annie. Helen prayed for you every day for years even after you lost touch. She also had all her church group praying for you," one of the angels explains.

"Why were they praying for me?" Annie still doesn't get it.

"They were praying for your eyes to be opened to the Truth," the angel explains.

Hmm, it doesn't seem like the prayers worked. Annie wishes there was a way to stop herself thinking or at least to shield her thoughts from Jesus and the angels.

"God heard the many prayers of your friends. He prompted you to listen, but you ignored Him and put it off for later. Your heart became a little harder every time. We don't force anyone to believe, you have a choice," Jesus tells her.

"I don't remember being "prompted," as you call it. Are you sure it was me and not just someone who looks like me?" Annie knows her suggestion is ridiculous. She is sure that Jesus knows everything about her, and that mistakes in this place would be impossible.

"Well, let's see, shall we?" Jesus replies as the video moves on.

Annie watches herself walking alone through a park. She still looks to be in her late teens. In fact, she is wearing the same clothes she was wearing when walking with her friends before. She is listening to some music and humming cheerfully. She stops and sits on a bench. She reaches into a bag and takes out a sandwich.

I do remember eating my lunch in that park quite a lot. It was always very peaceful. I wonder why they are showing me this, it doesn't seem relevant.

Annie eats her sandwich, then closes her eyes apparently enjoying the late afternoon sun on her face. A breeze is blowing and gently lifts up some leaves. It carries them towards Annie. The leaves land near to her feet. Annie opens her eyes as she feels the leaves brush against her leg. She looks down and notices a small screwed up piece of paper in the middle of the leaves. Curious, she picks it up and opens it.

Watching her younger self on the screen, Annie can see the picture of a fence across the front of the piece of paper and the words, "Are you sitting on the fence?" She holds her breath as she waits to see what she did with this paper.

Annie opens the paper, which turns out to be a leaflet, and she is reading it. She looks worried, then irritated, but she keeps on reading. Then, she looks around suspiciously. There is no one there. She tears up the leaflet and puts it into a bin nearby. She shakes her head as she walks away.

Watching her own hostile reaction, and swift disposal of the seemingly innocuous paper, Annie is confused. "What was that paper? Why did I react like that?"

"It was a Christian leaflet explaining why failing to make a decision about God is the same as rejecting Him," Jesus says. "You sat on the fence for too long Annie and that leaflet was a warning."

"But it was just some rubbish that was blowing around in the wind and happened to land near me. What if I hadn't even picked it up?" Annie can't understand how her response to reading this leaflet can add to her catalogue of woes.

"It wasn't random at all, watch," Jesus replies.

He looks at one of the angels who nods. The video is rewound slightly. A room appears on the screen, a small group of three ladies and three men have their heads bowed as they sit in a circle.

More praying. Great. Annie is beginning to see how things work around here.

"Prayer makes things happen." The angel responds to Annie as if she has spoken aloud.

The small group finish praying, then head out of the building which, from the outside, looks like a church. They are carrying leaflets in their hands. They break away from each other as they head along the street. Annie thinks she can see the front of the leaflet that she had torn up in the hand of one of the group. They start offering the leaflets to people as they pass by. Many refuse to take them but others accept and stuff them into pockets. Some are seen putting them in nearby bins after checking that no one is watching. Annie is relieved that she isn't the only one to have done this.

A man takes a leaflet from one of the church group and continues along the road. Annie recognises the road as the one that leads towards the park. The man is reading the leaflet as he walks but then he grunts, screws it up and throws it into a hedgerow as he walks past the edge of the park.

The video is paused. "Now, do you see, Annie? It wasn't random at all."

Annie shakes her head. She doesn't see. It still seems like pure chance to her.

"I think she needs to see, and hear, the prayer meeting at the beginning," Jesus tells the angel controlling the video.

The video is again rewound and the small group are back inside the church, in their circle, with heads bowed. Annie forces herself not to smile as the people rush back along the pavement in reverse. *It's all so bizarre. To think that every detail of every person's life was being recorded.*

"Lord, I pray that souls might be saved through our outreach today. I pray that each leaflet will reach the right person and that You will prepare their hearts before-hand to receive the Message. Amen." A lady with a light green coat and dark hair.

"I pray that none of these leaflets would be wasted. That even if a person should discard one, it might be found and read by someone else....."

Annie gasps as the video is paused again. "That's exactly what happened. That man threw the leaflet in the hedgerow and then the wind blew it to me and I read it!"

"Who do you think controls the wind, Annie?" Jesus asks.

"So that was really You bringing the leaflet to my attention?" Annie still can't believe it.

"It was in answer to the prayers of Jessica, Helen and all the other people who were praying for you." Jesus wants her to see how things really are.

"I didn't know how important it was though. If I'd known....how can You expect me to pay attention to one small piece of paper? That's not really fair." Annie is full of regrets but what she is saying seems reasonable, in her mind anyway.

"I'm afraid, Annie, that this is just one of fifteen Christian leaflets that you were offered in the street over the years. You took just five of them and, of these, four ended up in the nearest bin." An angel with a large book reads documented statistics.

Annie knows she is grasping at straws as she asks, "What

happened to the fifth one?"

"You put it in your pocket and took it home," the angel says.

"And what happened to it?" Annie can't remember there ever being any Christian stuff in her house.

"Should we show her?" The angel looks at Jesus.

Jesus nods.

This time the scene is a living room in somebody's house.

"That's my house!" Annie exclaims. The familiarity is strangely comforting for a few seconds. "I thought you were going to show me what happened to the leaflet, though?"

"That's right," an angel confirms.

"But, this isn't the house I was living in when I was young. It's my house now...I mean....before I..." Annie can't bring herself to actually say the D word.

"Yes, Annie. The last leaflet you were offered was the one you took home," Jesus confirms.

Annie trembles, "How long ago was this?"

"I'm sorry Annie, it was just three months ago," Jesus says soberly.

Annie falls silent as she absorbs the shocking news. She had been given one last chance as recently as three months ago. "I did take the leaflet home, though. That's what you said, right?"

"Yes, that's right," Jesus answers. "Don't you remember this, Annie?"

Annie pales as she starts thinking about it. "Actually, I remember being given a leaflet. Yes, it was whilst I was wandering around in town. I was very upset about something. A young boy, only about fifteen, or sixteen, offered me the leaflet. When I refused it, he followed me along the street trying to give it to me. In the end, I decided it was easier just to take it to get rid of him."

"That's the one. That boy's name is Peter. He grew up in a care home, his parents both died in a car accident when he was only seven. Some Christians adopted him, when he was eleven, and taught him about Me," Jesus explains.

"So, if the leaflet ended up actually *in* my house, as You said, what happened to it?" Annie keeps coming back to this as she feels it must be significant somehow.

"You know this is important, don't you Annie?" Jesus asks.

"I think so, I don't really know why, I just sense that there's something special about that leaflet," Annie replies.

"You're right about that," an angel agrees.

The movie returns to the living room in Annie's family home. Annie's estranged husband Dean is sitting watching TV.

Annie flinches on seeing him, "Oh, so it's before the split. This could be awkward."

"We're looking for that leaflet remember Annie," Jesus reminds her.

A teenage girl comes racing down the stairs and into the living room. "Bye, Dad, I'm going out, okay?"

"Make sure you're back before ten, love." Dean pauses and looks at his daughter before fixing his gaze back on the TV.

Annie sees herself walk into the room. She sits down on a chair at a distance from her husband and picks up the remote. "Let's watch something else," she says as she flips the channel.

Dean's face tenses. He gets up and leaves the room.

"This was the difficult patch." Annie has no desire to rehash the bad memories but she doesn't seem to have a choice. "I thought this was about the leaflet?"

"Watch and see," an angel says.

The camera moves upstairs. A teenage boy is lounging on his bed. He's reading a book and listening to loud music at the same time.

"Grant, always listening to music. Could never get those headphones off him," Annie speaks wistfully as she thinks of her children. "I don't think I've ever seen him pick up a book, though. What is that?"

The camera zooms in and, as it pans around, the book cover is in focus. The title of the book is *Ultimate Questions*.

Is that a religious book? Where did he get it from and why would he read it? Grant was never interested in anything like that....

As they continue to watch Grant, he becomes sleepy and eventually, the small book falls on the floor as he leans back against the pillows and dozes off. A piece of paper also flutters to the floor and lands near the book.

That's more like Grant. The religious stuff obviously put him to sleep. Annie isn't surprised.

The camera zooms in again and the lens focuses on the floor.

Firstly, it hovers over the book and then moves to the paper lying nearby.

"The leaflet?" Annie whispers. She is stunned. *Grant had it?*

A short clip appears on the screen at this point and shows Grant apparently creeping around the house at night. He goes downstairs and into a walk-in cupboard where the family hang their coats.

Annie again gasps as her son finds her black handbag, opens it and starts rummaging around. He pulls out her purse and takes several five-pound notes.

"He was stealing from me?" Annie asks.

"Afraid so, Annie. A lot of children steal from their parents these days. They seem to think it's their right to do so," an angel shakes his head sadly.

"Why are you showing me this, though?" Annie asks.

Grant puts the bag back on the hook but then hesitates. He gets the bag again and slides his hand into the large black pocket at the side of the bag.

"Crafty little…..that's where I kept loose change," Annie comments as if the angels need an explanation.

Grant pulls out a piece of paper and some coins. He glances at the paper then folds the coins inside it. He sneaks back upstairs to his room. He walks across to a small desk, switches on the light and tips the coins onto the table. He adds the five-pound notes and starts counting the money. The light shines on the slightly screwed up piece of paper and Annie reads the words, 'Where will you spend eternity?'

So, that's how the leaflet got there! I remember it now. I don't think I ever actually read it though, Annie tries to think back. *How did that lead to Grant reading religious books, though?*

As if she has again spoken out loud, the movie shows Grant at his desk writing something. Annie wants to see what it is, but it is obscured by his head and shoulders. He finishes writing and seals an envelope.

A few days later, a small parcel, addressed to Grant, arrives in the post.

Oh, did he write to someone to send it to him? Annie can't believe her son would have done this. He was only ever interested in music and football.

"Perhaps, you didn't know him as well as you thought, Annie?" an angel says.

Annie again thinks back, she remembers Grant disappearing on Sundays for the few weeks before her operation. She also recalls an odd conversation with him:

"Where are you going? It's pretty early for you to be up at the weekend, isn't it?" Annie had asked him.

"Just to see a few friends. No big deal Mum," Grant had answered.

Annie had been suspicious. It wasn't like Grant to get up early for anything or to be vague about where he was going. He tended to be honest about what he was up to even if his parents didn't like it.

She persisted, "Football friends?"

"Well, um, some of them play football, so yes, I guess so."

"Okay, well, remember that your father wanted to take you out this afternoon. You'd better be back in time as I really don't want any problems."

Annie winces as she realises how she had drawn her son into her marital struggles.

"Where did he go?" Annie snaps out of her daze and addresses the angels.

"Where do you think, Annie? You've seen that he was reading Christian books. Where do Christians go on Sundays?" The explanation is given in a patient tone.

"But, surely, Grant didn't seriously buy into all that, did he? Just from reading a piece of paper with a few words on it…." Annie is finding the whole thing hard to comprehend.

"It wasn't just a piece of paper Annie, it contained words from the Bible, words that God Himself wrote using human authors. When people read the Bible, God works in their hearts to convince them of its truth and importance," Jesus tells her.

"But, I've read bits of the Bible at school and in Sunday school. How come that didn't happen to me?" Annie is starting to move past the initial shock and now she wants explanations.

"Were you ever really paying attention, Annie? Did you ever read it in a sincere search for the truth?" Jesus prompts her.

"I guess not, but if the Bible is so powerful, then surely it would have got my attention anyway...." Annie trails off as she realises that her argument is weak.

"There were times when you thought about what you were reading more seriously, and We began to show you truths, but as soon as you realised what was happening, you resisted and hardened your heart," Jesus reminds her.

Annie looks miserable. "Wait, so Grant actually became a Christian?"

"Let's see what happens," Jesus directs the angel towards the video controls once again.

The movie resumes. Grant is walking along a corridor with another boy who is carrying a football. They are laughing and joking. The other boy suddenly slaps Grant on the back in a friendly way and says, "You know what bro, you should come to the youth meeting on Friday."

Grant hesitates and flushes slightly red, "Is that a church thing? You know I'm not really into all that."

"It is at my church, yes, but the other kids are just like us. We'll probably just play football and then listen to a short talk."

"How long is the talk?" Grant looks suspiciously at his friend.

"Maybe five or ten minutes. You might learn something. What are you afraid of anyway? If you don't like it, then don't listen. At least you'll get to play football and the other kids are cool."

"Well, I guess it might be okay and if I don't like it I don't have to go again." Grant still sounds unsure.

"Great, I'll call round at your house on Friday and we can walk."

"Wait, what should I wear?" Grant suddenly asks.

"Doh, your kit, obviously."

"Oh, I thought it might be a suit and tie job." Grant feels a bit stupid but he really doesn't know what to expect.

The friend looks amused and a bubble appears above his head. *People's expectations of church are really strange...playing football in a suit and tie?!*

"See you Friday."

They part company.

"So, it wasn't just the leaflet," Annie says.

"Well, the leaflet got Grant's attention. Notice, though, that he didn't say anything to his friend about it," the angel observes.

"Why didn't he?" Annie is curious.

"Did you feel comfortable talking about religion with your friends?" Jesus asks. "It's one of the ways Satan keeps people away from the truth."

"What do you mean?" Annie is confused.

"He creates an environment where talking about religion is culturally inappropriate," Jesus explains.

"and death," an angel mutters.

"Yes, actually, that's true. People don't talk about these things anymore. It's incredible really when they are so important and so much is at stake. Wait, though, who is Satan?"

"It's one of the names for the devil," Jesus tells her.

"You mean the red creature with horns and a pitch fork? You can't expect me to believe that he's real." Annie stares, incredulous.

"It's one of his best tricks. To make people think of him as a fictional creature akin to a fairy or goblin. Then he can do his best, or worst, work undetected. Believe me, he definitely exists and he is responsible for a lot of the destruction and pain in the world."

"But, why don't you stop him then?" Annie asks an obvious question.

"He will be stopped, but not until the end," Jesus answers.

Chapter 2

Annie jumps as a loud sound startles her. She turns towards the sound and sees some more angels emerging from a small door. They are busily arranging another screen that has dropped down from the ceiling. That must have caused the loud noise. Annie looks questioningly towards those she had been speaking to.

"You asked whether Grant became a Christian. I thought it might be helpful for you to see what is happening on Earth now. There is no time here, so we can see what is happening at any point in the present or the future, but your eyes will be restricted to the present, Annie," Jesus informs her.

A picture appears on the screen. A church full of people wearing black, many are crying and a coffin is making its way down the centre aisle.

Annie gasps, "Grant died?! But he was even younger than me."

"No, Annie," an angel assures her. "Look, there's Grant."

Annie sees Grant and Sophie, her two children, and sighs with relief. Then she sees her estranged husband Dean. The three of them are sitting together at the front of the church. All are sobbing.

"Whose funeral is it then? It must be someone that was close to us as a family." Annie can't figure it out. The family tended to keep themselves to themselves as far as possible. "Oh, it must be one of Dean's parents, but then, why would Grant be crying, he never got on well with them. One of my parents, then? But, Dean couldn't stand them, especially since the separation, and he's crying too." Annie looks blankly at the angels.

"Come on, Annie. Remember there's no time here. Whose death would impact your family in this way?" Jesus prompts.

"Oh….," Annie says softly as the truth hits her. "It's my funeral. I'm not sure I want to watch this. It could be very weird."

"It's important for you to see the legacy you left," Jesus tells her.

Annie senses that it isn't optional, and she is happy to delay the inevitable end of this examination of her life.

"Look, Annie, do you see who else is there," an angel asks. He pauses the video and points to several figures towards the back of the church.

Annie doesn't recognise the two ladies but one of them looks vaguely familiar. "Who are they?" she eventually asks after staring and racking her brain, for a short time.

"You've already seen them today, on the other video, Annie," the angel prompts. "But they were a little younger then."

"Wait, oh, I guess it must be Helen and, um, is it Jessica?" Annie asks, she still isn't sure.

"Yes, that's right."

"I lost touch with them years ago, why would they even bother coming to my funeral?" Annie is surprised, she knows that she wouldn't have shown such concern for her former friends had things been the other way around.

"Grant found some details in an old diary of yours and decided they might want to come," Jesus tells her. "Right, let's watch this part."

Silence reigns and every eye is fixed on the screen as a man in black robes and a clerical collar moves to the front of the church and stands behind the lectern which holds a large black Bible. He begins to pray in a loud voice and everyone in the church bows their heads. Most close their eyes, apart from a few wide-eyed children who glance around. The prayer is long and full of words that Annie doesn't understand.

"Bless our sister Annabelle Yale and receive her soul into Thy heavenly dwelling places. Remove the curse of Satan and purge her of all uncleanness. Bring comfort to her remaining family and surround them with love, peace and unity in the Spirit......" The minister drones on and heads start to nod around the church.

"No wonder I didn't get on with this religious stuff, it doesn't make any sense to me, even now," Annie whispers.

Jesus nods. He looks disappointed.

The minister finishes his lengthy prayer with an 'amen' which is dutifully repeated by most people in the congregation.

"Now, we are going to sing a special request from some members of Annabelle's family. Please turn to page four in your service sheet."

I wonder which song they chose. Annie feels an inexplicable dread as the camera zooms in on one of the service sheets and she reads the words:

> "For what is a man, what has he got
> If not himself, then he has naught
> To say the things he truly feels
> And not the words of one who kneels
> The record shows I took the blows
> And did it my way.
>
> Yes, it was my way."

She immediately recognises the final lyrics of her favourite song, *My Way* by Frank Sinatra, and the irony isn't lost on her.

"Are they really going to sing this in a church?" Annie is ashamed and embarrassed, despite having nothing to do with the decision. She hangs her head as the congregation sing the favourite song with gusto, seemingly oblivious to the atheistic lyrics. Annie raises her head slightly as the song draws to a close, she looks at the body of people. She notices that a few aren't singing. These people, although few in number, are significant to Annie as they include Grant, Jessica and Helen. Their heads are bowed as if in silent prayer, and the expressions on their faces are sombre.

At the end of the song, the minister, who had been singing along cheerfully, announces that a few people will be saying some words before the sermon. He promises to keep his message brief, as he knows people probably have other things planned for later in the day. On hearing these words, there is almost an audible sigh of relief from the large body of people.

Dean walks to the front of the church and reads a loving tribute to his "fun-loving, hard-working, wife, who died far too young."

Annie snorts as she hears his words. "Who does he think he's fooling, we'd been separated for two months already and he'd already served the papers." Annie feels a strong desire to justify herself as if this will somehow make a difference to her predicament. She realises, at the same time, that a lot of the people in attendance probably didn't yet know about their marriage struggles. Dean's behaviour still seems fake and insincere. However, Annie knows deep down that she would most likely have done the same thing had circumstances been reversed. *I mean, who wants personal struggles to be dredged up when someone has already died. Don't speak ill of the dead...or something like that.*

Dean concludes with the words, "May my dear wife, Annie, be carried away with the angels to heaven and rest in peace."

Annie blinks, *If only they knew.*

"Isn't anyone going to say something religious? After all, they are in church!" she asks a little desperately.

Jesus and the angels remain silent.

The minister resumes his position behind the lectern. The Bible remains closed. He begins speaking, "We are gathered here today to remember the life of Annabelle Yale who was suddenly taken from us last week. We know that she lived a good, moral life and was married to Dean until the day of her death. She blessed many of those around her and was involved in charity work. She followed the example of Jesus who took pity on the poor and destitute."

"Wait, when did I do charity work?" Annie is astonished. She can't recall any such thing. In fact, she had always thought that voluntary work was a waste of time and that people only did it because they couldn't get proper jobs.

"Dean told him about the time you worked in Oxfam," an angel says after examining a large scroll.

"That was paid, I managed the shop and it was only for a few weeks!!" Annie is horrified by the misrepresentation. "And, I left because the money wasn't good enough," her voice has become a whisper.

Annie listens as her list of positive attributes continues to be embellished by the minister who is doing his best to make people remember Annie fondly.

She feels sick to her stomach. The façade is truly appalling and she wants it to stop. She spins away from the screen, falls to her knees and tries to hide her face.

"We know that God accepts those who are sincere and try to live a good life. Annie did this and we can be sure she will be celebrating in heaven with Jesus at this moment." The minister speaks boldly and seems to be full of confidence.

Annie crawls away from the screen sobbing.

There is a murmur in the congregation as Grant stands up. He moves towards the minister, who has just finished speaking and appears about to announce another song. There is tension and determination on Grant's face. His fists are clenched by his side. He whispers a few words to the minister who nods and quickly steps aside. He pales slightly.

Grant steps in front of the lectern and opens the large black Bible.

"Annie, I think you should watch this," Jesus tells her.

Annie is strangely compelled to crawl back to the screen.

Grant begins reading, his voice is shaky but the words are clear, "Jesus said, 'I am the way, the truth and the life, no one comes to the Father except through Me.' These are the words of Jesus, from the Bible, and they apply to each one of us. None of us can approach God in our current state because He is perfectly holy and we are full of sin. Thankfully, God had a rescue plan. He sent Jesus, His Son, to live a perfect life and to die in our place and for our sin. Believing this is the only way to get to heaven. Living a good life and being sincere won't cut it because none of us could do enough good things or be sincere enough. We aren't perfect. Without Jesus, we will be punished for our sin when we die in a place called hell, forever."

There is complete silence as people hang on every word from the son of the lady lying in the coffin at the front of the church.

A chair loudly scrapes as Dean stands then storms down the aisle and out of the church. He casts a disgusted glance at his son as he makes his dramatic exit.

Grant hesitates, just for a second, before continuing his speech. "Perhaps, some of you are thinking this is completely inappropriate. To bring religion into the mix at a time when people are grieving. Let me ask you, though. What is more loving, for me to warn you before it's too late for you as well, or to hold off for fear of being culturally inappropriate? I'm convinced that my mum would want me to do this. I only wish I had warned her and I will have to live with that guilt for the rest of my life." Tears stream down Grant's face as he retakes his seat. Sophie sits rigidly beside him, a mixture of fear and shock frozen on her face.

Annie wants to reach out to her son and wipe the tears away, but she knows it's too late. She feels pain, and regret, at what might have been.

The minister, who had taken a seat after Grant's interruption, suddenly realises that he is expected to continue the service. He is now a whiter shade of pale as he moves awkwardly towards the platform. Should he acknowledge the complete contradiction of all he had said, or just breeze past it and carry on? He decides on the latter, anything for an easy life.

"Well, that was quite a speech. Thankyou for your honesty, young man. I'm sure you are hurting and grieving the loss of your mother, as are many others here. Right, let's sing our final song, number one on your sheet, *Amazing Grace*."

The familiar music begins, but the congregation are subdued as they sing. Gone is the joyful enthusiasm that had been evident for Sinatra's most famous song. They are now collectively forced to think about their own eternal destiny in the words of John Newton:

> *"Amazing grace! How sweet the sound*
> *That saved a wretch like me.*
> *I once was lost, but now am found,*
> *Was blind, but now I see.*
>
> *'Twas grace that taught my heart to fear,*
> *And grace my fears relieved.*
> *How precious did that grace appear*
> *The hour I first believed.*
>
> *Through many dangers, toils and snares*
> *I have already come;*
> *'Tis grace hath brought me safe thus far*
> *And grace will lead me home.*
>
> *The Lord has promised good to me*
> *His word my hope secures;*
> *He will my shield and portion be,*
> *As long as life endures.*
>
> *Yea, when this flesh and heart shall fail,*
> *and mortal life shall cease,*
> *I shall possess within the veil*

A life of joy and peace.

*When we've been there ten thousand years
Bright shining as the sun,
We've no less days to sing God's praise
Than when we've first begun."*

Grant's sobering message has brought sudden clarity to these lyrics for many in the congregation for the first time. They find they are unable to sing as the words don't apply to them. They stutter and stumble and feel utterly miserable, desperate for any type of distraction...and for the service to end. Even for those who happily go along to carol services at Christmas, and sing lustily at Easter, it now feels hypocritical to utter such significant things without the sincerity to back it up.

Heads go down as the minister prays the final prayer, then most people jump up and quickly head for the exit. A few remain seated as if held by glue. They look stunned.

Grant looks around, having composed himself and wishes he had ensured a Christian minister would be taking the service and not just someone paid to do a job. He feels inadequate to deal with the few remaining people who are most likely in need of some advice, and help, relating to what they've heard. Gratefully, he watches Helen and Jessica and a few others as they approach them.

There is an older man still sitting alone at the back of the church. Grant braces himself as he begins the long walk down the aisle. It is only when he is beyond the point of being able to turn back that he realises it's his paternal grandfather. *Oh no, they never really liked me and now I've probably seriously offended them. Perhaps, I shouldn't talk to him.* Grant pauses as his grandfather looks up and, as if seeing him for the first time, beckons for him to approach.

Grant prepares for a serious telling off, or disinheritance, or any other likely scenario, but his feet propel him forward. He slides into the pew next to his grandfather and notices the tear tracks on his weary face. They sit in silence for a minute.

Annie is now watching the film earnestly. She has no idea how Dean's father will respond to Grant. Their relationship had always been difficult, but strange things have already happened and anything is possible.

"I just want to know one thing," the older man finally speaks.
"What is it, Granddad?" Grant asks with trepidation.
"Why?"
"I felt I had to do it," Grant answers as best he can.
"I don't understand. There's nothing in it for you. You risked losing your family and friends to comment on the life of someone who's already died. Why would you do that?" He seems genuinely perplexed.
"It wasn't for my mum, it's too late for her. It's because I really believe it's true and that all people will one day stand before God and will have to give an account of their life. Then they will be sent to heaven or hell, forever, depending on whether or not their sin has been dealt with," Grant finishes and holds his breath, waiting for the rebuke that he knows must be coming. His grandfather is of a generation where it is considered disrespectful to talk down to elders.
"Hmm, so what you're saying is that you're willing to sacrifice your own reputation and relationships for the sake of your beliefs because you care more for these people than you do about yourself."
Grant can see the wheels turning in his grandfather's head. A Bible verse suddenly pops into his mind, "The Bible puts it like this, *'For what shall it profit a man if he gains the whole world yet loses his own soul,'* Most people think in terms of giving up money or things, but it can apply to anything we have on Earth, including our reputations and relationships."
"I remembered some of the things you said in your speech today from when I was a child. It struck an odd nerve in me. Could it be true?"
"Darling, are you coming, we're going to be late…." the shrill sound of Grant's grandmother cuts through the reverie.
Grant remains silent as his grandfather jumps in response to his wife's call, then stands, and, shaking his head in bewilderment, makes his way out of the church. Grant bows his head in prayer.
Annie watches the scene in amazement. She feels a mixture of pride on witnessing the behaviour of her son, and sorrow at her own impending doom. "At least some good came out of my death," she comments.
"There are numerous funerals every day without a mention of

God, and plenty of others where He is central in name only. That would have been the case at your funeral as well if it weren't for Grant. It's another trick of the devil, convincing people they can pay lip service to God, or just acknowledge Him at weddings and funerals, or Christmas and Easter, then forget about Him for the rest of the year. What kind of Deity accepts that kind of haphazard and insincere worship, though?" Jesus' words force Annie to think.

"A pathetic, powerless one, desperate for attention," Annie mumbles.

"Right, and you've touched on another of the enemy's tactics; he presents God as a weakling more in need of people than they are of Him. He convinces them that they can behave how they like and do whatever they want because God's love will over-ride their every failure without the need for repentance on their part."

"Yes, I can see that now. I guess that's why I sat on the fence for so long. I had no real understanding, or fear, of God, and Who He truly is," Annie speaks wistfully. "Wait, though, you said that hearing the truth doesn't guarantee a positive response from people. What happened to Dean's father after he left the church?"

"What do you mean, what happened?" Jesus asks her.

"Well, he heard the Message and it touched his heart, he even asked whether it could be true." Annie increasingly senses the urgency of the task on Earth despite being unable to rescue herself.

"Rewind the film slightly," Jesus instructs.

The film is rewound. It shows the old man standing up, about to leave.

"Just pause it there," Jesus says.

"Did you see that Annie?"

"What, you mean, when he shook his head?" Annie asks puzzled.

"That was his dismissal of everything he had just heard and seen. He basically thought about it whilst he was sitting there, but then pushed it out of his mind and heart, once and for all, with that shake of his head. Then he walked away from the light, which was attempting to bring the Truth home to him, by walking away from Grant, and out of the church. Notice that he doesn't even look back. He won't think about that service or anything that happened that day, again," Jesus solemnly tells her.

"How can a person do that, though?" Annie asks.

"Years of deliberately hardening his heart to the Truth. It would truly take a miracle to break through all those layers and sadly he doesn't want to hear it. He will make sure now that he doesn't put himself in a position again where he hears about Me," Jesus says.

"There's more, Annie. Every time the Word of God is clearly preached, there will be responses, some positive and some negative. Grant had the courage to present the whole Message, we are watching the responses. Look...."

Annie looks again at the big screen as the images move forward. Dean's grandfather walks out of the church and they again watch Grant bow his head in prayer. As he lifts his head a few minutes later, there is a soft whimper coming from nearer the front of the church. Grant looks perplexed as he stands and hurries back to his former seat. Sophie is leaning forward and has her head in her hands. She is crying softly.

"Oh, I thought you'd left already..." Grant looks slightly awkward as he hovers over his younger sister.

Her head snaps up as she hears his voice, "I didn't know you were still here," Sophie says.

"I was talking to grand-dad at the back of the church, but he's gone now," Grant explains. "Are you okay? Just sad about Mum?"

"I am sad about Mum, but what you said and did shocked me," Sophie cries.

"Why? You've heard the things I said before," Grant replies.

"I know, I just didn't realise how serious you were about it all or that it might actually be true. It made me think about my own life and whether I could be in danger. What made you start to take it all so seriously?"

"It's a long story, but basically, I read a leaflet that made me think, then a friend at school invited me to a youth group. I kept hearing the same things about Jesus and in time I realised it must be true. Then, I knew that I needed God to forgive the things I'd done wrong that had been troubling me for a long time. I asked God to forgive me for those things and trusted that He would because Jesus was punished for them on the cross. Then, I started to live a new life following Jesus."

"What, just like that?" Sophie sounds amazed. "It can't be that simple, can it?"

"Well, yes, it's simple in one way, but life as a Christian is difficult because you'll always be going in the opposite direction to everyone else. You have to really believe in your heart that it's true, that Jesus died on the cross to pay the price for your sin. Otherwise, when things get difficult, you'll just give up." Grant sits down next to his sister.

"So, if I tell God I'm sorry for my sin and follow Jesus, I'll go to heaven one day? That's what you said, right?" Sophie asks somewhat shyly.

"Yes, that's what the Bible teaches," Grant is surprised by his sister's sudden interest in Christianity.

"Seems like there's nothing to lose." Sophie wipes away her tears and starts to smile. "What do I need to do?"

"Take some time to pray to God, ask forgiveness for the things you've done wrong, then resolve to try not to do those things again, then live a new life following Jesus," Grant says carefully.

A bubble appears above his head, *It's great that she's showing so much interest, but I wonder how sincere she is and whether it's just surface level due to her emotional state right now.*

Annie watches the scene curiously. "Sophie too? Wow, that's great!"

"I'm sorry, Annie. Not all those who seem to profess faith actually follow it through," an angel explains.

The video skips forward and another scene appears. There are three girls walking together along a school corridor. Sophie is heading towards them from the other direction. As she walks past the girls one of them sticks out a foot and she trips over. Her books fall to the floor.

"Bible-basher," one of the three girls sneers at her.

"Think you're better than us, Little Miss Holy," another of the girls stands over her as she collects her books.

A bubble appears above Sophie's head, *I wish I could just fit in, it's too hard all this Christian stuff. I'd rather be popular with lots of friends. Perhaps, it's not too late as I've only just started this school and not many of them know I've been going to church.*

The scene ends and the monitor powers down.

"What? That's it?" Annie exclaims. "Surely, it took more than that for my daughter to abandon something she seemed so sure about only a few weeks before."

"I'm afraid Sophie wasn't prepared for the trouble that comes to people who believe in Me," Jesus says. "When she first heard that her sin could be forgiven and she could have a new start, she was excited and happy to go along with what Grant said. However, she didn't really count the cost of following Me. In the end, she chose the easier path preferring to blend in with her friends. She is still young, though, and there may be other opportunities for her."

"Can I see what happens to her?" Annie asks almost desperately.

"No, Annie. I said that your view will be limited to the present. This exercise is not to satisfy your curiosity, but to help you to see that your punishment is just and fair. In relation to Sophie, you were responsible for teaching her the right path in life, but sadly you failed. You didn't teach her about Me or the Bible and God wasn't even mentioned in your house until Grant started his investigation."

Annie knows that this failure will be added to her growing list. How she wishes she had looked at life differently and paid attention to those who were trying to tell her how things really were. Instead, she had sneered at, and shunned, everyone who had tried to help her.

"Okay, Annie, there was another person impacted by your funeral. Shall we look at what happened there?" an angel asks.

Annie likes the idea of a subject change and knows the angel is referring to Dean, "I guess so, Dean looked pretty furious when he left the church."

Images again appear on the screen. Dean is storming out of the church and heading for his car in the car park outside. His face is red and his fists clenched by his side. He gets in the driver's seat and puts his foot down. A bubble appears above the vehicle as he speeds along. *How dare he? Who does he think he is to judge us? I can't believe Grant is my son. Well, not anymore. That's the last time I speak to him.* He continues along the road and just manages to stop for a red light. *I'd better calm down a little, if I want to get home in one piece.* He waits at the light. *What if Grant was right?, I've heard those things about Jesus before, a long time ago. Wait, where did that thought come from?*

Dean accelerates and immediately spots an Off Licence. *I need a drink.* He pulls the car over, heads inside and grabs a case of beer. The thought of a few drinks cheers him up as he continues his journey.

He arrives home and adds the lager to the fridge which is already full of alcohol. He pops open a drink and takes a big swig feeling slightly better straight away. *I'll show them, I won't turn up for the burial, then they'll wonder where I am and he'll be sorry. I did my best not to embarrass the family or air our dirty laundry in public but I shouldn't have bothered. Grant ruined everything anyway.* **HOW DARE HE!**

Dean finishes his first beer and grabs another one from the fridge. He lies down on the sofa and flicks on the TV. He can't focus, though, as thoughts continue running through his head. *How did Grant get so involved in all of this stuff anyway? It seemed like he was really serious about it….what if it is true?*

The film abruptly ends.

"Wait, I want to see what happens next," Annie exclaims.

Jesus looks at the angel holding the remote and nods. The film starts up again.

Dean glances down at a pile of paperwork on the coffee table in front of him. He picks it up and starts sorting through it absent-mindedly. He casts his eyes over the divorce papers and Annie's will. *Well, at least now I'll own the whole house and both cars. It was definitely a good idea to take out that life insurance policy last year. I need to check how much it was for. Might be enough to have a few extra holidays this year and to build an extension. I could even go on that cruise I've been wanting to do for years. If I did it with a singles group, I might even meet someone. Perhaps, it's not so bad after all. In fact, it might be the easiest way out of this whole situation as people won't even need to know our marriage was in trouble. I can walk away and start again with more money and a lot more freedom, no more nagging and complaining…..*

The film freezes with the thought bubble over Dean's head.

"What? So, he didn't do anything about what he heard at the funeral. Surely he would have wanted to look into it to see whether or not it was true?!" Annie can't believe it.

"He considered it, but the desire for money and other material things distracted him and then became his immediate focus….." Jesus says.

"Did he ever become a Christian?" Annie isn't sure why she is asking the question about her estranged husband, or why she even cares, but she is becoming increasingly aware that the only thing that really matters about a person's time on Earth is whether or not they trusted Jesus by the time of their death.

"That's not for you to know Annie," Jesus reminds her. "We are reviewing your life, not the life of others. Only I know the future."

Chapter 3

We're going to continue looking at your life now," Jesus announces.

Annie falls silent. She doesn't want to watch any more humiliating experiences on the big screen. She has long since realised that any good that she thought she had done was minute, and mostly selfishly motivated.

"I want to address some of the things you've said so far, Annie," Jesus says. "We've already looked at the opportunities you had to learn about Me through your childhood friends, and leaflets being given to you in the street. Actually, though, that's the tip of the iceberg. Don't you remember the period you went to church for a while?" Jesus already knows the answer, of course, but wants Annie to remember.

"Not really, why would I have done that?" Annie asks. "Oh, do you mean at Christmas and Easter? Of course, I went then, with everyone else."

"I know you went then, but there was also a time where you went every week for a while. It was when you were at university," Jesus gives her a few more details.

"Oh yeah, now I remember, I somehow got involved in the Christian Union and went to church as I thought it might look good on my CV," Annie admits

"That was one of the reasons, but do you remember the real reason you went along?" Jesus replies.

"Not really," Annie knows it can't be good as the angels start shifting uncomfortably as if preparing for something terrible that's about to be exposed. "Hold on, though, I thought from all that's been said so far that church attendance isn't enough." The thought suddenly occurs to Annie and she blurts it out hoping for a subject change.

"You're right, Annie. Being a Christian isn't about church attendance, but we are looking at the opportunities you had to hear and respond to Me," Jesus says.

"If the main message is the same thing Grant said at my funeral, I don't remember hearing that before," Annie comments.

"You have heard the Truth many times, Annie," Jesus tells her. "Let's watch."

The original screen comes to life again. Annie is now in her early twenties and is sitting on a sofa in a house. She is earnestly talking to a man.

"That's Daniel. What's he got to do with this?" Annie asks.

"Oh good, you remember him. Unfortunately, he wasn't a good influence on you," Jesus says. "The devil used him to manipulate you."

Daniel says to Annie, "If you really like him, you'll have to convince him you're into in all that religious stuff. That's the only way. It's all he's interested in these days."

"But, I'm really not interested in religion, isn't that wrong?" Annie asks.

"Depends how much you want to be with him, I'm telling you, Annie, he won't date a non-believer."

"I don't think I can fake it, though," Annie protests.

"Of course you can, we're all wearing masks. You can be whoever you want to be. Just do some research and learn enough to convince him. Then go to church for a while and throw a few Bible verses in. He'll be smitten," Daniel grins.

"What happens when he finds out?" Annie asks.

"By then, he'll be in love and he won't care," Daniel says cruelly. "Besides you'll be doing him, and me, a favour, as all that religion stuff is nonsense anyway and it's taken over his life. He's such a bore now."

The angels shake their heads, "It catches so many people out," one of them says.

"You're right, I'll do it. I do really like him," Annie says as she gives in.

I can't believe I agreed to do that. To try and derail someone's sincere beliefs for my own selfish gain. What's wrong with me?

"I guess it didn't work?" she asks Jesus, almost pleadingly.

"Watch and see," Jesus says. "You're right, that this is not your finest hour, Annie, by anyone's standards."

The movie flashes through clips of Annie attending church and CU meetings, making a big show of being involved in Christian charity work, and publicly giving money. Annie is totally humiliated as she knows the motivations of her heart are on display for all to see. The video also catches the sideways glances at Jason, the object of her affection, to see if he is watching her religious sincerity and good deeds.

Once again, Annie feels ill.

"I think we've seen enough of that," Jesus instructs.

The movie jumps forward a few months. Jason is walking towards Annie with an odd expression on his face. She waits expectantly.

"Annie, I've been praying about this for a while now and have spoken to our pastor about it. I wondered if you wanted to go out to dinner with me later this week?"

Annie's face flushes and a bright smile lights up her face, "I've been praying too and I think this is exactly what God wants. Yes, I'd love to go."

Jason smiles back, "Great, how about Friday? I can pick you up?"

"Yes, sounds good," Annie replies.

Watching her younger self, Annie remembers the twinge of guilt she felt at that very moment, how she suppressed it and convinced herself it would be worth it in the end. She remembers rushing off shopping to make sure she had a new outfit for the date with Jason. She remembers buying the most revealing clothes that she could get away with as a 'Christian'. Clothes that would really show off her body and make Jason like her even more. Her friends encouraged her as they tried clothes on together and laughed at the thought of poor Jason having taken on more than he could handle. Looking back, it all seems so wrong. Annie can't quite remember what happened on the actual date, though.

The video shows Annie, on the eve of their date, opening the front door in response to the bell. Jason is standing there with a bunch of flowers and a big smile. He looks her up and down briefly, then averts his eyes as his smile falters and he hides behind the flowers.

"These are for you," he mumbles, thrusting them towards her and stepping backwards. "You should grab a coat, it's cold outside."

"It's not too cold, besides, I want to show off my new dress," Annie answers. She wants Jason to know that she's made a special effort for him.

Jason doesn't look at her as they head out of the door and Annie notices that he is keeping his distance. She feels a little uncomfortable but shakes it off as first date nerves.

"I thought we'd go somewhere relaxed and informal. I hope that's okay?" Jason says this in a way that makes it clear he's already decided.

"As long as I'm not going to stand out like a sore thumb in these clothes," Annie comments.

Jason bites his lip and says nothing.

Annie notices that Jason is smartly dressed but looks similar to how he always looks at church.

They pause outside Nando's. Annie blinks. *Surely not?* She breathes a sigh of relief as Jason keeps driving, he's barely said a word to her.

"Right, here we are," he speaks brightly but his voice falters.

Annie looks up and sees the Nando's sign, closer now. Jason must've spun the car around and entered from the other side.

Jason jumps out and heads for the front door of the restaurant as Annie is forced to scramble to catch up with him.

What on earth is wrong?

Jason waits for Annie at the entrance and holds the door for her stiffly as if they are strangers. He has an odd expression plastered on his face, one that Annie doesn't recognise.

They find a table and order their food. Jason barely says a word and Annie grows increasingly uncomfortable….

"I think we've seen enough of this. Annie, do you remember the date now?" Jesus asks.

"Yes, it was terrible. I don't want to watch any more," Annie replies softly.

"We don't need to see any more of the actual date, but I think you need to know why Jason behaved like that," Jesus says.

The screen flickers. Jason is now huddled with two of his friends, Matt and Simon, in a booth, in a restaurant..

"I didn't know what to do, honestly. It was our first date, but when she showed up looking like that and refused to even wear a coat, it was like she was a different person. I realised straight away that it would never work between us if she thinks it's okay to go out dressed like that." Jason looks miserable as he explains to his friends what happened on his first date with Annie.

"Woah, man. That's a bit hasty. Couldn't you just tell her how it makes you feel?" Matt advises.

"I might have done, but I've got the horrible feeling that she did it on purpose knowing exactly how it would make me feel." Jason looks at his two friends. "In fact, I'm starting to wonder whether that was her goal all along."

"What do you mean?" Simon is confused.

"Well, she hasn't been in church long and she was very keen when I asked her out," Jason says. "What if she's been making a play for me the whole time...."

"Really, do you think she would go to that much trouble, for a date with you?" Matt looks doubtful.

"The devil works in subtle ways," Jason says in a subdued tone.

"Why don't you give her the benefit of the doubt?" Simon suggests.

"I just don't think I can trust her now. I think I'll see whether she sticks around at church even if I don't ask her out again," Jason says thoughtfully. *How could I have been so stupid?*

Annie watches the rest of the clip with her hands partially covering her face. *Oh no, I'm so embarrassed.*

"You stopped going to church and CU when you realised he wasn't interested," an angel tells her.

"I know, I remember it well now. I just thought Jason wasn't sure how to conduct himself on the date, or that he was nervous, or something," Annie still can't believe what she's just seen.

"I'm afraid it gets worse Annie. Jason had been honestly praying about you, as he said. You lied to him when you told him you had also been praying. We actually stepped in and prevented things going any further to protect Jason, and to put an end to your deception," Jesus gives her the final details.

"A willing tool in the enemy's hands," an angel sighs.

"So, I guess that was my last appearance in church?" Annie asks.

"Where did you get married, Annie?" Jesus reminds her.

"Oh, of course. I meant when I didn't *have* to be there," Annie flushes as she realises what she's just said.

"It's not an excuse, Annie, but sadly, most people think of church in the same way. Just somewhere to go for official occasions rather than a place to worship God," Jesus tells her.

"We did look at a humanist wedding, or just having the registry office ceremony, but it didn't seem like it would be a real wedding if it wasn't in a church," Annie reminisces.

"It probably would have been better if you hadn't got married in a church seeing as neither of you believed in God," an angel comments sternly. "Actually, it's not the building that matters but the fact that you made vows before a God you didn't believe in, and your service included Bible verses that you didn't believe were true. It was insincere from the outset."

"I didn't think about it like that," Annie says soberly.

"Why not? Would you think it was okay to sign a contract clearly stating principles you didn't agree with? Or make a vow that you knew you couldn't keep?" an angel asks her.

"But, we changed our vows to make them more relevant to us," Annie protests.

"Yes, you cut out the requirement for you to obey your husband, but do you remember what you vowed to do instead?"

"Um, I think I said I would love, honour and cherish," Annie guesses.

"Actually, you just said, love and cherish," an angel reads from a scroll.

Annie wonders how many scrolls there are if her every word has been recorded. Then she considers how many scrolls there must be if every word ever said by every person has been taken down for later scrutiny. It's a scary thought.

"That's right, now I remember," Annie agrees. *What's wrong with that? I just got rid of the sexist, dated language. Surely, they don't object to that.*

"Annie, what was the rest of the sentence?" the angel asks.

"I don't really remember, something about, 'til death do us part?" Annie doesn't understand why this is so significant. She hadn't intended her marriage to break down and had been sincere when she made her vows....

"You actually said this;

I, Annie, take you, Dean, to be my husband, to have and to hold from this day forward, for better, for worse, for richer, for poorer, in sickness and in health, to love and to cherish, till death us do part, according to God's holy law, and this is my solemn vow,"

Jesus tells her.

"Yes, that sounds familiar. What's the problem, though? Is this about our separation? That wasn't our intention. We just had irreconcilable differences in the end," Annie says.

"Whilst it's sad that your marriage broke down, that's not the point that's being made here Annie. Look closely at your wedding vow," an angel points to the screen as the words appear in big letters.

The angel produces a long wooden stick and moves it along under the words as Annie reads aloud. When he gets to the last line, he pauses.

"Oh!" Annie exclaims. "I made the vow to do all these things according to God's holy law but I didn't even believe in God! My whole marriage was a sham...."

"Right, Annie. The Bible is routinely used as an instrument to ensure the appearance of truth as people swear on it in court rooms up and down the land, yet these same people abhor the content. Don't you see the hypocrisy and meaninglessness of all of these procedures?" Jesus asks her.

"I do, now. Why doesn't someone say something? Why don't they realise that it's all so wrong?" Annie's eyes have suddenly been opened to the lunacy on Earth; empty rituals in the name of a God that most either never believed in in the first place, have long since abandoned, or have given up as a fairy story.

"I hate hypocrisy, Annie; people that honour Me with their lips when their hearts are far from Me," Jesus says.

"Do you remember how you managed to secure your church wedding in the first place?" an angel asks.

Oh no, it can't get any worse, can it?

"Unfortunately, yes," an angel says.

"I remember going to a few services at the church before the wedding," Annie is vague again as it's all a bit of a blur.

"Yes, you did marriage classes and lied your way through the vicar's questions. You even became members of the church," an angel says.

"I hadn't realised there would be so many questions, or so much involved in getting married. I remember that I felt uncomfortable, but it felt like it was too late to back out and that we should just keep going and get through the procedure," Annie finishes lamely, "Oh, and I asked a few of my friends who said they had gone through the same thing, and that the church expected people to lie. They said it didn't matter as long as I was sincere in wanting to get married....." Annie trails off completely as she realises how utterly ridiculous her excuses now sound.

"Annie, this vicar, who is a real servant of Mine, a Christian, asked you whether you were sleeping together and various other relevant questions about your faith and intentions. You were actually living together, and you were several weeks pregnant when you started the classes, you had no intention of being involved in church beyond the wedding, and you had no faith to speak of. How can you possibly reconcile any of that with the answers you and Dean gave to the vicar? Would you have lied like that in any other area of your life?" Jesus asks and waits for an answer.

"It didn't feel like it was really lying, just that we had to do what was necessary so that we could get married. Every situation is different after all," Annie squirms in her chair.

"Do you think the vicar would have married you if he had known the reality?" Jesus asks her.

"I don't know," Annie says softly.

Jesus shakes his head. "Oh, Annie. I can see I'm going to have to make things crystal clear. Let me show you what happened after your wedding."

The screen flickers to life. They are watching the vicar alone in his office at the back of his church. He is praying. A book is open in front of him on the desk. The camera zooms in and Annie sees that it contains lists of names with dates and contact details. She sees her own name listed along with her former husband's. The page is headed 'weddings'. There is an empty column at the edge of the page and at the top of the column is written 'church attendance'. Annie watches as the vicar scans the list and shakes his head before closing his eyes once more, and resuming his solitary prayer.

"I don't get it, "Annie says.

"Annie, you and Dean became members of this vicar's church when he agreed to conduct your wedding. You signed a membership agreement stating that you would regularly attend services and take part in the life of the church. You even submitted a written testimony explaining how you became a Christian which reassured the vicar that you were genuine," an angel says.

"But, how did I know what to say?" Annie is increasingly horrified by the way she has duped this sincere old man.

"You copied a testimony off the internet and found one for Dean as well," Jesus says. "Again, I have to ask whether you would have done this in any other area of your life. Doesn't it seem wrong, Annie?"

"I don't remember this. I guess, though, that others did the same thing as the 'church attendance' box is empty all the way down the page," Annie hopes she can redeem herself slightly by blending in with the crowd.

"Do you think that those who commit fraud and are never caught by the police are any better than those who get caught and are punished?" Jesus asks her.

"Oh....." the point hits home.

"The old man must've realised that people would just say what he wanted to hear, though, surely," Annie grasps at a straw.

"There are a lot of vicars who just want to go through the motions, yes. However, this man sincerely wanted to do the right thing and only to marry those who were genuine Christians, and wanted to join his church. He was devastated to find a whole batch of people willing to lie and dupe him into conducting their ceremonies. In fact, he spent a long time wondering where he had gone wrong when the various couples didn't show up at his church. In the end, he withdrew completely and resigned from the ministry," an angel is reading again from a scroll.

"What happened to him in the end?" Annie asks dreading the answer.

"He became disillusioned for a while, and depressed, but after a few years, he picked himself back up and found a job in a shop. He started going to a different church and his relationship with Me was restored," Jesus tells her.

"I can't believe my actions could have such a big effect on someone," Annie is appalled by her behaviour and full of regret.

"As this man was a true believer, he wasn't ever in danger of falling away from Me completely, he just took a knock, but he's safe forever now," Jesus adds. "He died a few years after your wedding."

Annie feels strangely relieved that her devious behaviour hadn't managed to derail the sincere man of God. However, her anxiety increases as she senses that the discussion about her wedding may have brought the review of her life to a close.

Chapter 4

Annie's worst fears are realised as Jesus speaks,

"We've watched enough, now, Annie. You can see that every one of your actions had consequences either for you or for others. Most people only think about earthly consequences or the things they can see, but there is a spiritual battle going on all of the time, and those who aren't for Me are against Me."

"I never really thought about that," Annie admits.

"There are those who hear the Word but it is snatched away by the devil before it can take root, like Dean's father. Then, there are some who receive the Word with joy but only last a little while, they fall away when trouble or problems come because of the Word, like Sophie. There are others who listen to the Word but the cares of the world and the deceitfulness of wealth choke it, making it unfruitful….."

"Like Dean…." Annie finishes.

"Yes, but there are also those who sit on the fence, Annie. These people think that by failing to make a decision about Me, they can live their lives as they please. They put off a sincere search for the truth until it's too late. They assume they will live to old age and they can deal with things then…but some die young and meet Me before they are ready."

"If I had only taken the time to search for the Truth, I can't believe I gambled with my soul like that," Annie is terrified as she knows her punishment awaits. After the examination of her life, she also knows she deserves nothing less. She is full of regret which she knows will last for eternity.

Annie feels desperate as she thinks about her family, friends and neighbours; all those she knew and loved on Earth. She has nothing to lose and decides to make one last request of Jesus who is waiting for her final words. Gathering all the sincerity and fervency she can muster, she falls to her knees in front of Him, "Please can someone go from here to warn them?" she begs.

Jesus replies,

"There was a rich man who was clothed in purple and fine linen and who feasted sumptuously every day. And at his gate was laid a poor man named Lazarus, covered with sores, who desired to be fed with what fell from the rich man's table. Moreover, even the dogs came and licked his sores. The poor man died and was carried by the angels to Abraham's side. The rich man also died and was buried, and in Hades, being in torment, he lifted up his eyes and saw Abraham far off and Lazarus at his side. And he called out, 'Father Abraham, have mercy on me, and send Lazarus to dip the end of his finger in water and cool my tongue, for I am in anguish in this flame.' But Abraham said, 'Child, remember that you in your lifetime received your good things, and Lazarus in like manner bad things; but now he is comforted here, and you are in anguish. And besides all this, between us and you, a great chasm has been fixed, in order that those who would pass from here to you may not be able, and none may cross from there to us.' And he said, 'Then I beg you, father, to send him to my father's house— for I have five brothers—so that he may warn them, lest they also come into this place of torment.' But Abraham said, 'They have Moses and the Prophets; let them hear them.' And he said, 'No, father Abraham, but if someone goes to them from the dead, they will repent.' He said to him, 'If they do not hear Moses and the Prophets, neither will they be convinced if someone should rise from the dead.'" (Luke 16 vs 19-30 ESV)

Note to Reader

This is a work of fiction. Timings and events surrounding a possible Judgement Day scenario have been depicted. I am not suggesting that my dramatic reconstruction is what will happen, or attempting to reach beyond the detail given in the Bible. My purpose in writing is to make people stop and think about their own lives, and souls, in the context of the story.

From the Bible, we know that each person will one day die and then face judgement. They will have to give an account of their life to God and everything has already been recorded (although probably not on video tape!) They will then spend eternity in either heaven or hell depending on whether or not their sin has been forgiven. Sin can only be forgiven if someone pays the price for it. The price is death. Jesus is the only One able to deal with our sin because He is the only One who lived a perfect life, and therefore has no sin of His own. Jesus can therefore act as a substitute, and our sinful lives can be exchanged for his perfect life, if we trust that He died for us on the cross. Jesus is a bridge between us in our sin and a holy God. These are the things we can be sure about.

Annie Yale and her family do not exist in reality. However, they are representative of many people living on earth without giving God a second thought.

Our society has collectively turned its back on Christianity deciding that the Bible is a collection of myths and sneering at anyone who dares to suggest otherwise.

Please, stop and think. What if the Bible is true? What if our sin has separated us from God and one day we will stand in front of Him to give an account of our lives. What if God loves us so much that He has already provided a way of escape by sending His Son Jesus to die on the cross for our sins? What if trusting Jesus is the only way to reach heaven and to avoid eternal punishment in hell?

Annie was unprepared when she met with Jesus. The truth is that any one of us could die at any time, none of us is guaranteed tomorrow. It is too late for Annie but as long as you are still alive, it is not too late for you.

The Bible says, *"If you confess with your mouth that Jesus is Lord and believe in your heart that God raised Him from the dead. You will be saved."* (Romans 10 vs 9 ESV.)

THE RETURN
A Short Story of Lies and Deceit

NATALIE VELLACOTT

Chapter 1

Grant feels the rush of adrenaline as Pete puts his foot to the floor and yells, "Wahoo!"

The others chatter away in the back as the beer is alternately chugged and spilled. The music is loud and the night is still young.

The car lurches from side to side and throws them around as Pete takes the bends of the country road at high speed.

"This is great," Grant enthuses, "But maybe you should slow down a little. We've plenty of time to get there."

"You're kidding, aren't you? I wanna see how fast this thing can go." Pete is flushed and breathless, and Grant wonders whether he has taken something.

The vehicle veers over the central white line. Headlights from an oncoming van flash brightly several times. A horn is heard but already it seems far off as they are going so fast.

"Seriously, slow down, mate," Grant says, more urgently this time.

The others are oblivious and concentrating on the joint that is being passed around.

Pete leans on the steering wheel, the bass kicks in and the vibrations can be felt as the music reaches an intolerable volume.

"What are you doing?"

"Hey, turn that down."

"Whoops, I'll just fix it." Pete leans forward fiddling with the radio.

"WATCH OUT!" Grant yells as they again veer across the white line. He leans over and grabs the steering wheel. "Are you trying to get us all killed?" Grant feels angry and wishes he hadn't agreed to this trip.

"Hands off," Pete snarls as he wrenches the wheel back and revs the engine.

"What's going on?" Scott asks from the back, as a haze of smoke drifts forward and settles in the air.

"Hey, I can't see properly, keep that in the……..WHAT'S

THAT?" Pete shouts.

The car thuds on impact and something heavy bounces off the side of the bumper.

Pete brakes sharply and there is a screech of tires as the car comes to a juddering stop a little further down the road. The boys in the back loudly complain as they hit their heads on the seats in front. None of them are wearing seatbelts.

Grant pales. "What was that?" he shouts above the continuing music. But he already knows the answer. He had seen the red car, stopped in a layby with its hazard lights flashing lethargically.

Leaving the engine running, Pete is the first to get out. He walks around to the front of his car and surveys the damage.

Grant unbuckles and starts to open his door. He hesitates for a second and apprehensively glances in the wing mirror. His fears are confirmed as he can just make out a large mound in the road behind them. A person is running from the red vehicle towards the mound.

Pete is now at the back of his car but before Grant can get out he returns. He quickly shuts Grant's half open door on his leg, then runs around to the driver's side and jumps back in. He is deathly white; panic and fear are written on his face.

"We need to get out of here," Pete mumbles as he turns the volume up impossibly high.

The boys in the back are now alert but they can't see anything due to the steamed up windows.

"What did we hit?" asks Daniel. "Turn that racket down, won't you?"

"I reckon it was a deer," yells Alex. "At least, it felt like something heavy."

"Is there a lot of damage?"

"Was it dead?"

The unanswered questions hang in the air then fade into obscurity as Pete quickly drives away from the scene, tyres squealing as they spin on the surface of the road.

The girl lies on the tarmac. She can't feel anything. She can't hear anything. She can see the blackness of the sky. Then everything goes dark.

The running person reaches the girl. Horrified, she had seen everything; her friend run down and thrown to the road surface like a rag-doll. Then, the young guy emerging from the vehicle. She had imagined help not being far away but she saw him hesitate before retreating to the safety of his car and speeding away.

Still in shock, she had just clocked part of the retreating vehicle's registration number but now she must focus on her friend who is dying in front of her. She is unconscious but breathing, with a faint pulse, but she is bleeding profusely from a nasty injury to her leg.

She feels sick but knows that she has to take control. Her friend's life depends on it. She gently moves her into the recovery position, ties a jumper around the injured leg, and makes sure she can still breathe.

Next, she retrieves a bright orange rain-jacket and a torch from their car. Putting the jacket on and flashing the torch, she stands in the road, protecting her friend. She waits.

She is crying and hyperventilating when, twenty minutes later, and after a few near misses, a passing motorist finally stops.

An ambulance is called and when the paramedics arrive shortly after, the girl is still alive.

Chapter 2

Two days earlier.

Grant rolls over in bed and groans as his alarm goes off. He presses snooze for the tenth time before his father's loud reminder that he'll be late for college.

He yawns and falls out of bed wishing for an extra few hours sleep. He just feels so tired all the time. He knows it's his own fault having got in at 2am from a football party the night before, and a similar time the night before that. In fact, he can't remember getting to bed before midnight on any day in the last few months.

Throwing on his clothes, he quickly rubs some toothpaste around his mouth and glances in the mirror as he heads for his bedroom door. The dark circles are still around his eyes and he also notices the emptiness, the sparkle has gone.

Pausing just for a second, he glances at the Bible on a shelf in the corner. He hasn't read it for months, he feels a little guilty but he doesn't have time to think about it right now. There's a test in his physics class today and football practice later on.

"Hi Dad, bye Dad," he mutters as he runs down the stairs and heads towards the front door.

"Wait a minute, you still haven't said anything about the holiday to Costa. There's not much time left and I need to make the final payment. Come on son, it'll be great," Dean encourages.

Grant looks back briefly and nods. "I'll let you know tonight."

He heads out of the door and starts jogging towards his college. *I wish my dad would stop behaving like one of my mates. It's weird.*

Arriving for class a few seconds before the lecturer walks in, Grant finds his mates and sits down. They are passing around a magazine with a naked woman on the front. Grant knows there is worse inside the cover. He smirks for their benefit but feels uncomfortable.

"Put that away mate, you'll get us all in trouble," he whispers to his friend Pete and is relieved when for once Pete complies.

The test paper is handed out and everyone falls silent as the exam begins. Grant hasn't really studied but he isn't worried as he usually gets by. His head is pounding though, and he feels a little ill. He glances at the others, they were all with him last night but seem fine. He wishes he could hold his drink and keep up with them, they won't stick around otherwise. They're only really hanging around with him because of his ability on the football pitch. Oh, and because he has money now that his late mum's life insurance came through.

He shakes his head and tries to focus on the paper. If he can just make it through this day, tomorrow will be better, he feels sure of it.

Finally, a bell sounds and the teacher collects the papers. She looks at Grant with concern and tries to catch his eye, but he carefully avoids looking at her so she doesn't say anything. She has already asked if he is okay more than once but received a sneer from one of his friends. She still prays that she will see him back in church.

Grant quickly exits the classroom, trailing after Pete and his other friends. They wander outside, lighting up one by one. Grant still feels unwell and lies down under a tree on the grassy field as the others sit around chatting.

"What's with you?" Scott asks him. "You look terrible."

"I'm fine. I just couldn't sleep," Grant lies.

"At least that teacher has stopped harassing you now. Did you see how she looked at you all sympathetic and that?" Pete scoffs.

"Yeah, I know. She's alright really," Grant replies.

"How do you know her anyway? She's one of those religious nutters, isn't she?" Daniel mocks.

"I don't know, I don't do that any more." Grant doesn't want to get into this with his mates as he knows they won't get it.

"Hey, my Uncle got into all that stuff when his wife died, you needed a crutch for a bit, don't sweat it man," Scott says condescendingly.

Grant isn't going to tell them that he had "got into it" *before* his mum had died. He falls silent then goes for a subject change. "Do you guys think I should go to Costa with my dad?"

"Yeah, why not? It'll be fun and the night life's great, if you know what I mean." Pete winks.

"I just wish my dad would be, well, more dad like. He's been weird ever since my mum died. It's like he wants to be my pal, or buddy. He's not like it with Sophie...." Grant doesn't really expect a response.

The others look awkwardly at each other. Death and religion in one conversation, far too heavy and there are more interesting things to be thinking about.

"Hey, look at that girl, I'm gonna ask her out!" Pete leers at a petite blonde girl. She quickens her pace and looks slightly frightened as she notices his interest.

Pete laughs and yells at her fast retreating figure, "Hey, don't worry honey, I was just looking."

Grant is miserable. He hates this. Hanging out with these guys seemed like fun at first. They honed in on him soon after his mum died and he was grateful for a change as it took his mind off the grief for a while.

Now, he is stuck and trapped in a life that often feels empty and meaningless. He doesn't like the topics of conversation, or the attitudes of these guys to the people around them, especially Pete. He doesn't know what to do about it though, as he hasn't the strength to make any changes and wouldn't know where to start if he did.

Chapter 3

One year earlier.

Grant makes his own way home from his mum's funeral. He reckons it'll be a long time before his dad speaks to him again.

He had to say something; he couldn't bear the hypocrisy and meaningless ceremony of the vicar's religious rituals. Yes, his speech was bold, probably too bold and it must've seemed judgemental, but that wasn't what he wanted to convey. He honestly just wanted people to know the truth, so he spoke from his heart, and out of love for them, although guilt over his failure to share his faith with his late mother had perhaps made him seem a little fanatical.

At least his younger sister Sophie was interested and perhaps, more astonishingly, his grandfather who he's never really got on that well with.

He arrives home and, as he lets himself in, braces for what he knows will be an onslaught. However, the house is deathly quiet.

In the kitchen, he sees empty beer bottles and, on the table, paperwork with pen marks all over it, as if a child has scribbled all over the pages. Taking a closer look, he sees it is his parent's divorce, not yet finalised. He's a little surprised to see it displayed so prominently as, after his father's speech at the funeral pretending everything was okay in their marriage, he assumed that evidence to the contrary would have been hidden away, or destroyed. A bottle has been smashed on the floor and left for someone else to deal with.

Wearily, he picks up a dustpan and brush and clears up the mess. His father must be sleeping it off. He's relieved that the confrontation will be delayed. He climbs the stairs and sticks his head into his dad's bedroom. He is slumped face down on the bed. Grant checks his dad is breathing, then softly closes the door and heads for his own room.

He collapses on his bed and lies in the dark thinking over the events of the past few weeks. It's been an emotional whirlwind and he hasn't really had proper time to grieve for his mother as he's been too busy taking care of everyone else. Then, the exhaustion of grief kicks in and he's asleep before he knows it.

He wakes early the following morning and lies in bed thinking. It's Sunday and usually he'd be going to church. He knows he won't be expected due to the tragedy in his family. His church friends have been avoiding him since it happened. A few have sent texts offering condolences but they don't seem to know what else to say. Grant doesn't hold it against them knowing that he would probably be the same if he was in their situation. I mean, what do you say to someone who has just become a Christian and then immediately lost their mum?

An old lady from the church had been to visit Grant but, when she started quoting Bible verses, his dad had asked her politely to leave. This had happened *before* the funeral and now his father will, no doubt, be even more anti-God. For now, so as not to wind his dad up even further, Grant has decided that he must keep his church friends away from his house at all costs. Also, he doesn't want his father to be given the opportunity to confront him with the legitimate question: "Why did God let your mother die?" as he doesn't have an answer.

Someone else from church had sent a card with Romans 8 vs 28 in large letters on the front. Grant does love God, but it doesn't feel like anything is working for good at the moment. His friends mean well, but he wants to be left alone for now. The whole thing has shaken his faith but he is determined to persevere. *Isn't there something about blessing for those who are persecuted?*

Grant's reflection is interrupted by his sister, Sophie, clattering around in the bathroom. He wants to speak to her about the conversation they'd had at the funeral. At 14, she is a bit flaky, but she had seemed genuine in her desire to know more about his faith, so he wants to strike while the iron is hot. He ventures out of his room and nearly bumps into her in the hall.

"Oh, it's you!" she says, startled.

"Well, who else did you think it would be?" Grant asks.

"Is Dad awake yet?" she whispers.

"I don't think so, he was out like a light when I got back yesterday." Grant hopes she hadn't seen the state he was in, but her expression tells him she probably had.

He changes the subject. "Did you want to come to church with me this morning?"

"Actually, I'm going to go with my friend Joanne. After the funeral she told me she's a Christian, she didn't say anything before as she thought I wouldn't want to know. She said there's lots of young people and a band. They have coffee and stuff after…." Sophie trails off realising that she hasn't taken a breath.

"Oh, that sounds good. I really think God can help us deal with stuff at the mo, you know?" Grant replies.

Sophie nods. She does know.

Grant notices her puffy eyes and dark circles and realises he isn't the only one struggling with tiredness and grief.

"Alright, I'll see you later then," Sophie heads into her room and Grant backs into his, to get ready for church.

Chapter 4

6 months later...

It's a Sunday evening and Grant has just arrived home from a football match. As soon as he's inside, he starts tidying the kitchen and lounge. It's been six months, but his father still hasn't completely forgiven him for his "inappropriate outburst" at the funeral. Therefore, Grant is still on his best behaviour. Really, you would've thought he had committed some awful crime the way he's effectively been sentenced.

Dean emerges from another room, "How was the game? Did you win?"

"Of course, and I scored as well." Grant grins, he's on safe ground with football and is hoping that his dad might soon come to one of his matches.

Dean, though, has other things on his mind. Since Annie's death and the huge insurance payout, he's spent a fortune on re-doing the house, jetting off on luxury holidays; mostly without his children, and just accumulating more and more stuff.

Coincidentally, or so he thinks, he's also found himself surrounded by lots of new friends who are more than happy to take advantage of his generosity. He's also developed an addiction to drink, more so than before the death of his late wife, and gambling. So, when he is around his head is elsewhere.

Grant wants to try and rescue his father from himself by getting him interested in football.

"Just going out actually," Dean is out of the door before Grant can say anything else.

Grant flops onto the sofa and starts channel hopping. His phone rings.

"Hey Grant, just wondered if you were okay, haven't seen you for a while?" Adam's voice, bright and cheerful, as usual.

"Hey matey, I'm doing okay, just had lots on. I'll catch up with you soon though?" Grant stays vague and deliberately non-committal.

He needs to keep his church friends separate from his football buddies. Adam wouldn't approve if he knew Grant had skipped church for a football match. Grant is irritated by this intrusion and the questions, it's as if they are keeping tabs on him.

"What about pizza on Friday? A bunch of us are meeting at 7. Fancy it?" Adam persists.

"Yeah sure, I'll see you then." Grant will likely cancel on the day, or just not show up. He doesn't owe them anything and, in recent months, they've kind of gotten used to him doing that anyway. He feels a little guilty as he knows Adam probably means well.

After the call, he briefly thinks back to his original decision to become a Christian. It all made sense at the time and he had been on fire for God, wanting to tell anyone and everyone. Now, he feels embarrassed about his actions at his mum's funeral. He had been convinced it was the right thing to do but afterwards, no one seemed to agree with him. Even the Christians, who he's sure overlooked his behaviour because he was grieving, felt he had gone overboard and that it wasn't the right time, or place. He cringes as he thinks of the vicar that had been put in his place and of all the non-religious people that he had out-rightly condemned without a second thought. Now, he can't even remember why he felt so strongly in the first place. Looking back it all seems so unnecessary.

Grant knows he is drifting from God. He hasn't been to church in months, often because it clashes with the football but even when it doesn't, he can't make the effort to get out of bed. His Bible stays on the shelf accumulating dust. He sometimes prays, but usually just a half-hearted, "God help me win the football match." *Well God cares about the small things in our lives, right?* He smirks as he knows this isn't how the verses should be applied.

Shaking his head, he goes to the fridge and helps himself to his dad's beer pushing thoughts of God, church and Adam from his mind.

Chapter 5

The present....

Grant has had a sleepless night, he wonders if the others are suffering too. He knows Pete saw the body in the road and the person running towards it. The others in the back were stoned so probably not aware of much. Grant hadn't touched the joint and had only had a few pints after the football game. They had been heading for another party but after the incident, Pete had taken them straight home as he apparently wasn't feeling well.

Grant reaches for his phone to call Pete but hesitates, he's not sure if he's ready for the conversation about what happened. It feels like something out of a dream rather than anything real that actually occurred.

He dials Pete's number but there is no answer. He feels lonelier than ever. He keeps replaying the events in his mind. He knows they should have stopped. He knows they should have checked if anyone was hurt. He knows that even if panic had caused them to lose their senses at the time, they still should have gone to the police afterwards. Now it's too late.

What if he knows the person? What if they blame him forever and refuse to forgive him. What if they have relatives who insist on taking revenge? What if the person could have been saved if they had stopped? What if...? What if...? The questions and possibilities torment his conscience.

In his desperation, Grant prays for the first time in months.

"God, please don't let someone be seriously injured. Please don't let anyone die. Please don't let anyone find out it was us." His prayer is motivated by fear; fear of the consequences.

His prayer is interrupted by his phone ringing. Holding his breath in case it's about the accident, he answers it.

"Hey mate, any chance of grabbing a lift to college today? I can't get hold of Pete," Scott asks. He sounds normal.

"Um, yeah sure," Grant answers automatically. He was planning to skip lectures today, it doesn't feel right to just carry on as if nothing has happened. "I'll be a few minutes late, though."

"No probs, I'm only just getting up myself. What's happened to Pete, do you know?" Scott doesn't sound at all worried.

"No idea, he said he wasn't feeling that well last night, didn't he?" Grant suggests.

"Oh, did he, I don't remember, I was pretty wrecked." Scott laughs. "I'll see you in half an hour."

They hang up and Grant tries Pete again. Still no response and now his phone goes straight to voice mail. *That's odd.*

Grant collects Scott and they head towards their college with Scott chattering away. Grant nods every so often and tries to engage in conversation but he can't stop thinking about the accident. Scott clearly has no idea that there had even been an accident, let alone that they'd hit someone.

They arrive and head to class. Someone taps Grant on the shoulder and he jumps.

"Woah, jumpy. What's up with you?" asks Gemma, a girl that he's been getting to know.

"Nothing, have you seen Pete?" Grant responds. He can't think about much else and needs to talk to Pete.

"No, he wasn't in class today," Gemma answers.

Pete sometimes takes an odd day off to help his older brother Darren with his second hand car business. Usually, he shows up a day or two later boasting about his side income and flashing a wad of cash. So, no one is especially worried that Pete is off grid.

Grant stays silent, lost in his thoughts as he walks along with Gemma.

"Are you okay? You don't seem yourself?" She gazes at him.

It's obvious she's interested and Grant had been thinking of asking her out, but somehow, he doesn't really know why, the accident has changed things.

Fortunately, Alex and Daniel join them allowing Grant to temporarily avoid Gemma's questions.

"Hey, what's up?" Daniel asks.

"Great game last night," Alex comments.

"Have you guys seen or heard from Pete?" Grant asks.

"No, isn't he around?" Alex isn't bothered and Daniel doesn't even respond to the question.

"Hey, shall we go out after training later?" Daniel asks.

"Oh no, training." Grant had forgotten the scheduled football training session later in the day. "I'm not sure I can hack it, I'm really tired."

"You're turning into a light weight. Pete said he wasn't feeling well too. What's wrong with the pair of you?" Alex laughs.

"I'll come for a few drinks later," Gemma says, looking hopefully at Grant.

"Sorry guys, last night was enough for me. I need to get home." Grant can't be persuaded and their pleas fall on deaf ears.

He won't be able to focus on anything until he finds out what happened to the victim of their hit and run. Even as he thinks of it, he realises that it's gone from an incident, to an accident, to a hit and run in his mind. Well, that is what it was, they hit a person and then ran.

Grant leaves his friends and abandons his final class. There's no point in him being at college anyway as he can't think straight. He's on tenter-hooks and just waiting for his role in the hit and run to be exposed. The not knowing is a mild form of torture. The mind does terrible things when it's stressed and anxious, working overtime to imagine all sorts of unpleasant and unlikely scenarios.

Grant heads to his car and drives to Pete's place. He knocks and Pete's brother Darren answers the door. He gives Grant a slightly odd look; Pete must've told him.

"Hey Darren, is Pete about?" Grant asks forcing a casual tone.

"He's upstairs, wasn't feeling well," Darren grunts. He's never particularly communicative. He doesn't invite him in.

"Can I speak to him? His phone's off." Grant can't leave without talking to Pete.

"Well, okay, but don't stay too long, I want him fit for work tomorrow," Darren replies.

Grant takes the familiar stairs two at a time. "Pete, you alright?" he calls.

"Who's that? Is that you, Grant?" Rather than the usual brash and confident, Pete's voice sounds weak and strained.

"Yeah, can I come in?"

"Give me a sec," Pete says.

Grant pushes the door open to find Pete standing awkwardly in the middle of the room in his boxers.

"Guess I ate something I shouldn't have," Pete offers.

"Maybe, but we need to talk about what happened last night." Grant gets straight to the point.

"Whaddya mean?" Pete's stance is defiant as he crosses his arms over his chest.

"I know you know we hit someone," Grant says. "And I guess you told Darren about it?"

"What? Did he say something to you?" Pete asks, surprised.

"No, he just gave me an odd look," Grant admits.

"I think we hit a deer as it caused a fair bit of damage and I had to get rid of my car," Pete says firmly.

"It definitely wasn't a deer. I saw a lump in the road with clothes on it and a person running towards it. How many wild animals do you know that wear clothes?" Grant insists.

"No, it wasn't clothes. You were only looking through the wing mirror. I reckon you couldn't see properly," Pete says. He's sticking to his story.

"Wait, did you say you had to get rid of your car? As in, you've already done it??" Grant registers the earlier comment.

"Yeah, Darren took care of it earlier," Pete admits with a slight flush of his cheeks.

"Why the rush? Why didn't Darren fix it? I thought that's what he does?" Grant asks.

He is shocked by Pete's attitude and is realising with horror that a large cover up appears to be on the cards. He feels sick.

"Time for a change. I'd had it for a while." Pete heads for the bathroom. "I'm feeling better now, wanna go to the pub?"

Without bothering to reply, Grant reels around and walks straight out. He feels very small and alone as, determined to do the right thing, he heads for the police station.

"You want to know if any accidents were reported on the B265 last night?" The desk clerk looks at him with a bored expression. "I can't really give out any information unless you tell me why you want to know."

"I think I might have witnessed something," Grant says calmly.

The clerk, a middle aged man looks at him with a little more interest as he scans his computer screen.

"Nope, nothing that I can see." The clerk looks up having resumed his disinterested posture.

Grant stops himself from looking too surprised. "Can you check again?" he manages.

The clerk is fast becoming irritated, but humours him with another tap on his keyboard. He spins the screen around to face Grant. "Quiet night, you see. Nothing much happened."

Grant sees a virtually empty screen with just a couple of shopliftings and minor traffic violations earlier in the day. It looks like nothing at all has happened overnight.

Bemused, Grant thanks the clerk and heads for the door. He thought he would be relieved to learn that no accident has been reported. Instead, he feels bewildered and more guilty than ever.

Chapter 6

A week later...

"Did you hear, did you hear?" the students whisper to each other as they head to class.

"What, what's going on?" Pete asks as he, Grant, and their group head to football practice.

"Police came in earlier and now there's an email asking for witnesses to a crash. Some girl across town is in a coma, might not make it...." A passing guy fills them in and then heads off, laughing about something else.

Grant and Pete exchange glances, both have paled noticeably.

"I'll see you guys later, I need to go see my brother." Pete rushes off.

Grant stares after him.

The other guys are naturally curious.

"I wonder who the girl is and where it happened."

"I hope they got the driver."

Perhaps, it's a different accident. After all, he did go to the police station and they definitely told him that no accidents had been reported. Surely one that ended up with a girl in a coma would have been reported?

"I need to go too." Grant heads off, keen to read the email.

"Something I said?" Alex laughs. The rest of the group are oblivious having not yet connected their friends' weird behaviour to their road trip last week.

As soon as Grant is by himself at home, he opens the email. He's almost afraid to read it but he knows what he will find:

"To all staff and students

Today, we had a visit from the police. They are investigating an accident that occurred on the B265 on Wednesday 20th June at around 11.30pm. A car had broken down on the hard shoulder. A young girl attempted to flag down a passing motorist but was run over. The other vehicle left the scene without stopping. The girl is now in a critical condition in hospital.

The police are looking for any witnesses and anyone that owns a small blue Volkswagen Golf partial registration number E634.

Please contact the police directly on their local number 0845 239754, or speak to staff at the college if you have information.

If anyone has been upset by this incident, or knows the girl involved, counselling will be available at the college on Monday morning.

Thank you all for your help. We hope that the young girl makes a quick and full recovery.

Principal Terstyen

Grant reads and re-reads the email but each read through just makes him feel worse. If only he could go back and do things differently.

He lies down on his bed and cries. He feels so guilty; guilty that someone was hurt and may die, guilty that he didn't stop, and guilty that he still hasn't reported what he knows. Most of all, he feels guilty that he is relieved that the partial registration is wrong...

He hears a noise downstairs.

"Anyone home?" Dean calls.

Grant is glad that he's not by himself any more. Should he tell his dad everything? He can't believe he's even considering it, but he's pretty desperate and needs to unburden himself. Perhaps, his dad will resume being a parent instead of acting like his buddy and will know exactly what he should do for the best.

Grant heads downstairs cautiously.

"Wassaaaapp," Dean grabs his son in an awkward bear hug and jumps around as if he's 18 again before realising Grant has been crying.

"Oh, what's wrong?" Now, he's embarrassed. Dean never cries in front of anyone and expects the same level of resilience in his son.

Grant can't hold back and bursts into floods of tears.

"Oh, who died?" Dean is really worried now as he's never seen his son lose it like this.

"Dad, we were driving the other night and we hit a girl. She's in the hospital. We didn't stop. I don't know what to do." The story comes flooding out of Grant and just telling it removes a great weight from his shoulders.

"Oh no." Dean's shoulders slump and he sits down heavily on the sofa next to his son. "Were you driving?" he asks after thirty seconds of silence.

"No, it was Pete," Grant responds.

"Who was with you?" Dean asks.

"Daniel, Alex and Scott," Grant relays.

"So, they all know? What's Pete got to say about it?" Dean is thinking fast.

"I don't think the other three know anything. They were in the back high on weed. I saw it all in the mirror. Pete got out to look at the damage then jumped back in when he saw we'd hit someone and drove off." Grant blames Pete, after all it is mainly his fault.

"Did anyone else see you? Did you tell anyone else?" Dean fires questions at his son.

"No. I don't think so. I think Darren knows. I'm pretty sure he fixed Pete's car up for him and then got rid of it although Pete claims we hit a deer." Grant tells his father everything and it feels good.

"Good, good. So the car is gone? Is there any way they can connect it back to any of you?" Dean heads for the light at the end of the tunnel.

"Well, no, I don't think so but…." Grant starts.

Dean interrupts, "Was there anyone with the person that was hit, anyone who saw you?"

"Yeah, someone else was there and they must've given part of the registration to the police, but they got it wrong." Grant isn't totally comfortable with the way his father is responding to his confession. He hasn't even asked how the girl is. He seems more interested in making sure the vehicle can't be traced and effectively assisting with the cover up.

"How do you know all this?" Dean asks.

"The police came to the college and an email went round." A tear runs down Grant's cheek as he remembers the details in the email. "Dad, what if she dies?"

"Woah, let's not go there. We just need to think of the best way to handle this," Dean answers reassuringly.

"I tried going to the police but….." Grant offers.

"Wait, what? What did you do that for? Did you tell them anything?" Dean snaps.

"No, I mean I tried, but….." Grant falters.

"Good lad. No sense in getting them involved. You haven't really done anything wrong if you think about it. It's all on Pete," Dean speaks confidently, as if it's the only way to read the situation.

"That's not exactly…."

Dean interrupts him again, "I knew you'd be smart kiddo. It sounds like Pete and Darren have already sorted the car which would've been a problem. We just need to make sure you were somewhere else when it happened if anyone comes knocking."

Grant is shocked and speechless. His dad has been different since his mum died, but he never, not in a million years, would have expected him to be encouraging him to lie to the police, to make up an alibi and to forget the girl lying injured in the hospital to save his own skin.

"I'm going to go and lie down," Grant manages.

"You'll feel better in a bit," Dean swivels back towards the TV and picks up the remote. Job done, as far as he's concerned. He turns on the local news.

"We are still trying to trace a blue Volkswagen Golf that left the scene of the incident…."

Grant freezes on the stairs. "What was that?" he calls.

"Nothing," Dean throws a quick glance towards his son as he quickly changes the channel.

A middle aged police station desk clerk is at home with his wife watching the local news when an item catches his attention: A hit and run on the B265 on Wednesday the 20th of June. A girl is in hospital with life changing injuries. Why is this ringing a bell? He searches his memory…

The next day at work, he heads up to the CCTV room. He speaks to the camera operator and obtains footage of the young male that had come into his station asking about a crash on the B265 on Wednesday the 20th of June. He enhances the image of the male and takes it to the Collision Unit.

The Collision Unit supervisor examines the image, then after consultation with her line manager, agrees to release it to the press. After all, a girl is in hospital and they have no other leads. They need to identify this male who obviously knows something about the crash.

Pete, Darren, Grant and Dean spend the next few weeks independently scanning local news reports. There are a few articles but nothing that might reveal their identity. The girl is now stable but still in a coma and expected to have life changing injuries. Her family have made a number of emotional pleas for the driver and passengers of the other vehicle to come forward.

The person who was with the girl on the night of the incident is 20 year old Dawn Perkins. She has been interviewed several times and is remembering more and more detail about the vehicle that she saw speeding away from the scene.

Chapter 7

A few days later

Grant runs and runs and runs. He feels as if his legs might fall off. He dribbles the ball and heads towards the opposition goal. He shoots. He scores. The crowd goes wild. He is pummelled to the ground by his team. His goal has won them the match. He feels exhilarated….then he remembers.

He has spent the last few days alternately listening to his father and Pete tell him to put it all behind him, and starting his journey towards the police station to make a full confession. His conscience is killing him.

Discreetly, he's even been to see the girl in the hospital. He managed to slip in and out unnoticed, just staying for a few seconds. On being discovered in the corridor, he pretended he was visiting another person on the ward and made a quick exit. He still doesn't know why he did it, maybe to reassure himself that she was still alive. Gazing at her still figure didn't help, though, and he noticed she had a severe injury to her leg which was in bandages.

Grant has been praying every chance he gets. He's still not convinced that God can do anything, or that he even believes in God any more. It's more of a desperate plea just in case God is there and hears him. He doesn't think God will be likely to respond positively to *his* prayers as he abandoned his faith soon after making a decision to follow Jesus. Grant feels like a fraud in all areas of his life.

He looks up from celebrating his goal and sees his dad in the crowd cheering. He looks older than Grant remembers. Perhaps, the stress of the cover up is taking its toll. Shaking his head, he casts off the negative thoughts as he heads for the changing rooms. It's time to celebrate the win!

However, he is stopped in his tracks when he sees two men standing near the entrance talking to his principal. They aren't dressed in uniform, but he knows who they are; they just have that official look about them. It's too late to change direction and he is heading straight towards them.

"Grant, can you come here for a minute please." The principal, who looks worried, calls him over.

Grant wanders over as slowly as he can, thinking of possible excuses on the way.

As he arrives, his father also appears on the scene, breathless.

"You can only talk to my son if he has a lawyer present," he puffs, before Grant can say anything.

"Now, why would you assume he needs a lawyer?" The principal looks genuinely bewildered but the detective's eyes light up.

"It's okay Dad, I'm ready to talk to them." Grant hangs his head.

"That's right lad, we know you know something," the taller of the two men states matter of factly.

Grant then sees the giant CCTV picture of his face in the smaller detective's hand and puts the pieces together. He wishes he hadn't allowed guilt to walk him to the station that day. He wonders who identified him and how far the image has been circulated. How embarrassing.

Dean also catches sight of the image and looks confused for a few seconds before retaking control of the situation. "Like I said, my lawyer will be present for any discussions you have with my son."

Grant's football friends have gathered as their curiosity gets the better of them.

"What's going on?"

"Who are these guys?"

"Is Grant getting arrested?"

"What for?"

The taller detective says calmly, "No, he isn't being arrested, we just need to ask him some questions. Let's go son."

Grant trails after them, relieved they haven't arrested him in front of his friends. As he gets into the car with the two men, he looks around for Pete, but he is nowhere to be seen.

Chapter 8

The girl wakes up, she can't see properly and doesn't know where she is. There is something in her mouth, she can't breathe and she wants it out. Her body aches all over. She looks around. Is she dead? No, she's in a hospital. She can see nurses. She bangs her arm wildly and a nurse comes running over.

"She's waking up!"

"It's okay, dear. You've been in an accident. Do you know what happened?" A kind nurse asks gently.

She can't speak so she shakes her head. *What is that in her mouth?* She points to the tube.

"Yes, we can take that out in a minute, it's been helping you breathe."

"Darling, oh darling. Are you awake?"

"She's awake at last. Thank God!"

Having been just outside on a 24 hour vigil, her family now rush to her bedside. The girl recognises her mum and brother amongst the throng and points at them.

"Do you know who we are?" her mum asks anxiously.

She nods. She can't smile due to the tube. She wants to communicate and find out what happened as frustratingly, she can't remember anything.

There is a strange tingling near her foot. She wants to scratch it but she can't move yet. She points to the area. The smiles freeze on the faces of her relatives and she realises that something is wrong, very wrong, but she is just so exhausted and she feels her eyelids closing as she drifts back to sleep.

The girl's mum approaches a nurse. "What should we do when she wakes up? Should we tell her?"

"She needs to know soon otherwise she'll see for herself and it will be a bigger shock," advises the nurse.

"It's so awful, I don't know how to tell her, or how she'll react. Why was she pointing down there anyway?" the girl's mum asks.

"Sometimes, amputees can still feel the nerves because it

takes a while for the body to realise that the limb is really gone," the nurse says quietly. "We are more resilient than we realise, though. She'll get through it."

The girl's mum and brother watch her sleeping peacefully and then automatically glance towards the leg that has been amputated below the knee.

The girl's mum bursts into tears. "If only she'd got to the hospital sooner, they may have been able to save her leg. I can't bear to think of her lying out there on that road in agony with no way to call for help. It's horrible."

"Try not to think about it, Mum. It won't do any good. We need to be positive for her sake. She's going to need a lot of help to adjust to a new way of life. It could've been far, far worse. At least she's come out of the coma without brain damage."

The girl's brother is optimistic by nature but even he is struggling with this one. *What kind of person knocks down a defenceless young girl and then leaves her for dead in the middle of the road??*

Chapter 9

Grant waits in an interview room. Technically, he's not under arrest but the detectives made it clear that if he tried to up and leave, they would be forced to arrest him.

Dean followed them to the station and started creating havoc as soon as he arrived. He called a solicitor on the way.

Grant sits silently. He still feels guilty, more so on learning of the partial amputation of the poor girl's leg. However, the more time that goes by the more confident he feels and the more inclined to stand up for himself. *How would the police ever be able to prove that they knew they had hit a person anyway?* Perhaps, his father's attitude is rubbing off on him, as he is irritated that so far he is the only one in trouble. Surely, Pete will come forward when he finds out that his buddy is in the firing line?

The solicitor arrives and, after a quick chat with the officers, she ushers Grant and his father into a side room away from the eyes and ears of the police detectives.

"Are you sure they aren't monitoring this?" Dean asks anxiously.

"That would be illegal," the smartly dressed Mrs Toldy answers in a brusque tone. "Look Grant, you haven't been arrested so you don't actually have to even stay for an interview if you don't want."

"I'd rather get it over with and they said they would arrest me if I tried to leave," Grant points out.

"Not very ethical," Mrs Toldy raises her eyebrows. "It means they do have some evidence but probably not much. I understand that you came into the station asking about an accident the day after it happened? The police couldn't trace anything but they've now discovered that there was a computer glitch that night so the officers had all been using paper records. Apparently, this information wasn't passed on to the day shift during handover from the night-shift."

"Oh!" Grant exclaims. He's glad the desk clerk hadn't found the accident because, in his emotional state, he probably would have blurted everything out, as he had done later to his father.

"So, what did you actually witness?" Mrs Toldy stares at him and waits for an answer.

"Wait, so if he tells you, you don't have to tell the police, do you?" Dean asks suspiciously.

"No, of course not. Grant is my client so I'm acting in his interests and will advise him whether or not he should tell his story to the police. I do need him to tell *me* what actually happened though," Mrs Toldy clarifies. She has immediately realised she is dealing with amateurs which won't be a bad thing when trying to negotiate with the police later down the line.

Dean nods at Grant giving silent permission for him to speak.

"Well, we were driving from a football party to go and have a few drinks somewhere else," Grant begins.

"Wait, who was driving? You, or someone else?" Mrs Toldy interrupts.

"My mate Pete was driving," Grant continues.

"And whose car was it?" Mrs Toldy intervenes again as she scribbles on a notepad.

"Pete's." Grant waits for her next question.

"So, you weren't even driving and it wasn't your car? I don't know why the police have even got you here in that case," Mrs Toldy comments.

"Do you mean they have no case?" Dean asks.

"Well, there's no crime if he was just a passenger," Mrs Toldy says. "Perhaps you'd better finish your story."

"I was in the front with Pete and three other mates were in the back smoking weed. Pete was going too fast and the music was super loud. I think he accidentally hit the volume button on the steering wheel. He went to try and turn it down again but we hit something hard. Pete did stop to see if there was any damage and I started to get out and see what we had hit but then Pete jumped back in and sped away," Grant misses out a few details to minimise his culpability.

"So, you didn't even see a person, or know that you'd hit anyone?" Mrs Toldy looks incredulous.

"Well, maybe Pete did as he went around the back of the car, but I didn't even get out," Grant confirms.

"Okay, but why did you go to the police station?" Mrs Toldy

looks like she is genuinely confused.

"Curiosity I guess." Grant hopes he will get away with what he knows is an insufficient explanation.

Mrs Toldy is satisfied. "Well, it's sad about this girl being injured, but I really don't think the police have a case against you. They need to talk to Pete."

"Well, there's no way to tie him to any of this as he didn't go to the police station, and his vehicle hasn't been identified," Grant adds.

"Well, they'll probably get to the vehicle in the end. These things are always on CCTV somewhere, or there may be a witness," Mrs Toldy cautions. "You just tell them what you've told me and they'll let you go."

"I can't tell them about Pete, I just can't. He'll kill me, or his brother will. They've already got rid of the vehicle." Grant feels ashamed even as he says this knowing it definitely makes them all look guilty.

"Right, let's deal with one thing at a time," Mrs Toldy says. "If you aren't willing to identify Pete, I suggest you answer "no comment" to all the police's questions. If you answer some questions and not others, they'll end up tricking you into giving conflicting information, or they'll figure out who you were with anyway. I still don't think they could prove any of you knew you'd hit someone, but if Pete got rid of his vehicle immediately, that would ring definite alarm bells for any detective worth their salt."

"And what about the girl?" Grant asks.

"What about her?" Dean says dismissively.

"Shouldn't I do something to try and help?" Even as he says it, Grant knows his suggestion is stupid as there can't be any links between him and the girl for obvious reasons.

"Best thing you can do is to stay as far away from her and your friends who were in that car until this thing blows over," Dean says confidently.

"Your father is right, now let's get this interview over and done with," Mrs Toldy says firmly.

The interview is conducted. The police ask their questions and Grant manages to answer "no comment" throughout. It feels awkward and unnatural; like he's doing something wrong but Mrs

Toldy had made it clear that the police would most likely be expecting it as most suspects don't say anything in a first interview.

After the interview, Grant is released and the police advise his solicitor that they will be in touch if they need to speak to him again.

They all troop out of the station. On the way home, Dean is overly cheerful and talks incessantly about football and holidays. As far as he's concerned that's the end of the matter and it's time to move on now. Grant remains silent.

Once home, Grant goes straight upstairs and lies on his bed. Now that he's dodged a bullet by omitting certain details, his conscience is on fire and he can't stop picturing the girl lying in the hospital bed. He feels more guilty than ever.

Chapter 10

A few months later...

Louise, is out of hospital and back at home. She has fallen to pieces and picked herself up again a hundred times since waking up and learning of the amputation. Everything feels quite intrusive as she's been repeatedly poked and prodded, but she's learning to adjust to her new reality.

Having had time to think, she is determined to make the best of her situation. She is grateful to be alive but has suffered a major setback because of her injuries.

Louise is a swimmer; a good one. She has captained the women's college team and won several medals. Reluctantly, she is now developing new interests like reading and writing, although she hasn't had much time to herself due to being inundated with visits from family, friends and neighbours. She has received more cards and flowers than she thought it was possible to fit in the house!

She started rehab a few weeks ago, but her leg is still in bandages. The doctors have said it will be a while before she can be fitted for a prosthetic, and even longer before she should go back in the water because of the chemicals.

In the end, Louise can't face returning to her old college because of the association with her former life; seeing the swim team heading off without her would just be too difficult, and the plaques on the wall reminding her of her former brilliance.

Today, she is starting at her new college with a brand new course; English literature. She fancies herself as a journalist if her Olympic swimming dream is no longer possible, although she hasn't quite given up yet as there's always the Paralympics.

Manoeuvring through the corridors on her crutches ahead of the other students, she arrives and makes herself comfortable in her new classroom.

Almost immediately, a loud group of lads come into the room

and gawk openly at her cast. Then, the rest of the students begin to arrive in ones and twos. She scans their faces for familiarity, or friendliness but most are wearing neutral, blank looks.

One guy does look vaguely familiar but she can't place him and he doesn't acknowledge her. He goes straight to a desk in the corner and sits by himself. When the test begins, the boy writes frantically filling page after page with his tiny handwriting. The minute the bell rings, he is up and having handed in his paper, he quickly makes for the exit with his head down.

Louise is intrigued. Even before the accident, she's always had something of a "saviour complex," although she doesn't see it as a bad thing. She enjoys helping and befriending the underdogs and lame ducks and has become much more interested in people since her schedule has been abruptly and dramatically changed. She feels like an outsider herself as a newbie at the college. This guy doesn't seem to have any friends and is obviously something of a loner. She decides to find out more about the elusive, hard worker who sits by himself in the corner.

Chapter 11

Grant works hard, very hard in the hope that if he focuses his mind on his college course, he might be able to put past events behind him.

He has tried talking to Pete many times starting with persuasion, then coercion and then out and out threats. Nothing worked. Pete would not even consider handing himself in and he is now supported not only by his brother, but also by the other guys who were in the vehicle. Eventually, they had put two and two together and realised it was Pete's car that had hit the girl. They held an urgent meeting and easily agreed to a pact of silence. Grant hadn't been invited, but his intention to turn them in had been angrily discussed and he had been labelled a traitor with no possibility of defending himself.

Despite his threats, Grant can't bring himself to actually tell the police knowing Pete would likely go to prison for the cover up, if not the hit and run itself. He has deliberately distanced himself from their friendship group as seeing them just reminds him of their horrible shared secret.

Learning that the girl is now out of hospital hasn't helped Grant move forward as the police are still actively investigating the accident. Every day, he wakes up fearing that he will be exposed and everyone will know the truth; that he left a poor girl to die on a roadside without offering help.

Then, one day, it happens. The police fiddle around with the part registration given by the witness and find Pete's vehicle on their ANPR cameras. The grainy images even show the driver and front passenger on the day of the accident. They research the previous registered keeper details and the knock comes on Pete's door.

Darren answers and tries to fob them off but they won't be deterred. The house is searched and Pete is arrested.

Pete is interviewed and follows the advice of his newly appointed, trainee solicitor to answer "no comment" to all the questions. He pays no attention to the caution and doesn't realise that, in this instance, his silence will definitely be used against him in court.

Pete is charged with failing to report an accident, failing to stop at an accident, causing serious injury by dangerous driving and attempting to pervert the course of justice by disposing of evidence. Pete is bailed to appear at the Magistrates Court in a week.

The police track down and seize Pete's vehicle from the new owner. Wrongly assuming the police wouldn't bother searching for it, Darren hadn't seen fit to change the number plates.

The new owner is not especially forthright, being annoyed at the inconvenience of having his vehicle seized, but he does confirm the date of transfer and that the vehicle had recently been repaired when he purchased it. The date of transfer was 21st of June, a day after the accident.

The car is forensically examined and, despite the time delay, microscopic traces of blood are still present on the front bumper which has not been replaced. The blood is sent off to the lab where DNA is extracted.

The detectives visit Louise at her home address to update her on their significant progress in the case. They ask for a sample of her DNA for comparison. She willingly provides a mouth swab as her parents look on.

As the officers leave, the family collectively hold their breath. They hope someone will at last be held accountable for the terrible injury caused to their loved one.

Chapter 12

Louise hobbles towards Grant in the college canteen where he is sitting alone, apparently studying.

"Excuse me, is this seat taken?" she asks casually.

"Not by me," Grant replies, barely glancing up from his textbook.

"I was wondering if you could help me. I'm new in school and I've missed a couple of the English classes. Any chance I could photocopy your notes? You always seem to write lots," Louise says it quickly.

Grant looks up and focuses on her. "Oh right, you're in my English class. Louise, isn't it? Yeah sure, I'll give you the notes next class. What happened to you?" He indicates her leg and crutches but, even as he does so, his brain registers with horror that he has seen this girl before.

He recalls the pale, helpless figure lying in a hospital bed with her leg in bandages and the smile freezes on his face. He knows exactly who this is and exactly what happened to her.

He glances at his watch hoping she hasn't noticed his sudden change of demeanour.

"I'm late for class," he manages. He scoops up all his books and shoves them hastily into his bag. Then, he quickly makes his exit bashing into tables and nearly knocking other students flying in the process. He doesn't look back as he concentrates on getting as far away from Louise and the vivid reminder of his terrible actions as quickly as he can.

Louise is astonished. She watches Grant leave and sees him almost crashing into things in his apparent desperation to get away from her. What on earth had she said? She has no idea.

Bemused, but concluding he probably has issues that are nothing to do with her, she returns to her lunch.

Grant rushes across the campus and straight for his car, the rest of his classes forgotten. Now, his only goal is to get alone somewhere so he can think but, even as he drives, the questions come thick and fast to his mind. *How has this happened? How has this girl come to my college? What are the chances? It can't be a coincidence, can it?*

He gets home. Dean is in the kitchen and starts talking immediately on his son's entrance, "Hey, guess what? Big win on the horses today, let's celebrate."

"Dad, the girl...the girl...she's in my class at college," Grant's face is white and he looks exhausted. He feels like he's awoken from a terrible nightmare that has become a reality.

"What, what girl? What are you talking about?" Dean is genuinely baffled. "An old girlfriend do you mean? Don't let it bug you. I see my old flames around all the time....."

"No, no, the girl from the accident, she's in my class and today she asked me for help to catch up on lessons she's missed," Grant explains in a panic.

Dean can't believe it. "What? That's impossible. She lives across town, doesn't she? How do you even know it's her? Aren't you just imagining things? Come on son, that's not really likely now is it?"

"It's definitely her. I saw her in the hospital and she's on crutches due to her leg injury..." Grant trails off as he knows his father will be furious about his visit to the hospital.

"Why on earth did you go to the hospital? What's wrong with you? Do you want to be sent down with Pete?" Dean can't understand why his son seems intent on incriminating himself. He sits down heavily and puts his head in his hands.

"I'm sorry, Dad, I just had to see if she was alive. What am I going to do now?" Grant asks. He has no idea.

"We'll have to move you to another college. It's the only way to stop all this blowing up, especially with Pete's arrest." Dean automatically looks for the escape route.

"What, Pete was arrested?? When? What happened?" Grant reels at this new revelation.

"I assumed you would know. It was in the paper and people are talking." Dean says. "He's due in court next week."

"Oh no, they charged him," Grant realises the implications. "But they haven't come to speak to me, perhaps he didn't say anything to them."

"I think he probably said nothing," Dean agrees.

"That's a relief, but I can't just move colleges. I have my football team and I'm doing really well since I started working harder," Grant is adamant and pulls himself together. "Maybe it wasn't her. You're right that it would be impossible. I think I'm just seeing things."

"Wait, though. You were so sure. It does seem unlikely, though?" Dean looks at his son through the laced fingers across his face.

"I'm going up to study. I'll see you a bit later." Grant manages a slight smile and heads upstairs.

He goes into his room and heads for his bed. He lies down and begins to formulate a plan. His roaming gaze falls on his dusty Bible on a shelf. He gets up and walks over to it. He feels slightly afraid of the book that he knows is God's Word. He sends up a quick arrow prayer to God. He asks for help to know what to do and then with his eyes closed, he flips open the large book. He puts his finger on the page and cautiously opens his eyes. The text reads:

"Be sure your sin will find you out."

He jumps backward hitting his head on a lamp. The Bible falls closed again and remains on the shelf.

Grant sighs and collapses back onto his bed. Even God can't help him with this. He'll have to sort it out himself.

Chapter 13

Pete appears in the Magistrates Court. Again, on the advice of his solicitor, he pleads not guilty. The case is set for trial in six months. He doesn't return to college. In fact, no one has seen him around and there are rumours that he's dropped out.

Grant heads for college keen to start work on a new and much more important project. In his English class, he approaches Louise and asks if he can sit with her.

"Yeah, sure," she says uncertainly. *Isn't this the same guy who ran away from me in the canteen?*

"Hey, I'm sorry about the other day, I suddenly remembered I needed to get somewhere," Grant offers a vague explanation. "Here are all my notes from the term so far." He produces a brightly coloured folder with everything copied and neatly arranged. He's even gone to the effort of tagging everything so it's easier to find.

"Wow, thanks so much, I didn't realise you were going to go to this much trouble. I really appreciate it," Louise smiles brightly.

"It was no trouble. Actually, I wanted to offer to tutor you. Some of the stuff we've covered is a little difficult to understand from the notes and it might be helpful. I have some time," Grant offers enthusiastically.

"Um, well. Can I think about it?" Louise can't understand what has effected the transformation from quiet, solitary loner to helpful, smiley, super-student in a matter of days.

"Sure, but I'd really love to help you," Grant pauses. "I heard what happened to you and I think you deserve some good luck after all that trauma." He holds his breath as he knows he is pushing *his* luck by mentioning the accident.

"Yeah, well. I'm doing okay. The driver is going to court in a couple of months so maybe I'll get something out of it, although I'd rather have my leg back." Louise avoids eye contact as she is forced to recall the accident.

Grant wishes he hadn't mentioned it but, seeing her reaction renews his determination to help her in any way he can, and to try and atone for his part in it all.

The bell rings. Daniel, Alex and Scott bump past Grant and Louise as they leave. They haven't made the connection but think Grant is even more of a loser for befriending the cripple that's just joined their class. They had thought he was becoming a bit nerdy, always studying, but now it's evident that he must've gone religious again.

Grant ignores them as he helps Louise up and hands her the crutches.

"Weird thing happened at college today," Louise says to her mum.

"Really, what's that, hun?" she answers absent mindedly as she prepares the evening meal.

"A guy in my English class who seemed really moody has given me all his notes and wants to tutor me," Louise tells her.

"Perhaps, there is some goodness in the world after all?" her mum smiles.

"It's just a bit odd."

"Perhaps, he's interested in you, love?" her Mum asks gently.

"I don't think so, I don't get that vibe from him. It's more of a do-gooder, or pay-it forward vibe. You know when someone does something nice for someone hoping that they will receive something good back, kind-of like karma," Louise laughs.

"I sounds like you're thinking too deeply about it. Perhaps he's just a nice guy. You certainly need the help," her mum encourages.

"He did mention that he had heard what had happened to me," Louise remembers.

"There you go then. He probably feels sorry for you. I'd let him help. It can't do any harm," her mum says, oblivious.

Chapter 14

3 months later….

Louise sits in the stands watching Grant play football. She has had her prosthetic fitted but still can't go in the water yet. She no longer needs her crutches and if you hadn't known her before, you would have no idea that she has an artificial leg.

She and Grant have become good friends, although it's definitely a one sided friendship in terms of effort. Grant has been doing all the running and nothing is too much trouble. She has come to rely on him a lot. The tutoring is going well and she feels confident that she will pass her exams.

The rumour mill is rife at the college, but Louise still doesn't get a romantic vibe from Grant. Although not religious herself, she almost feels like he's some sort of angel looking after her. Her family have met him a couple of times; they appreciate his friendship with their daughter and everything he has done to help her.

There have been a few hairy moments for Grant when he thought she might be on the verge of finding out, usually because of something careless he has said. However, his secret remains intact and he is becoming more confident that it will remain so. He still feels he hasn't yet atoned for his part in the accident. Having a focus and helping someone else makes him feel good. Everything seems to be going in the right direction and for now he's put a dampener on his conscience that had been threatening to overwhelm him with guilt.

No one at the college has connected the email they received about the accident to Louise. Why would they when her injuries weren't made public and are now no longer visible?

Everyone, apart from the principal has forgotten the visit of the detectives to interview Grant. The principal has concluded that it must've been a mistake as nothing further came of it.

Pete has formally dropped out of college and is rumoured to be working full time for his brother. No one has seen him. His trial approaches.

Chapter 15

The trial….

The day of the trial finally arrives. Pete appears fidgety and nervous in the Crown Court dock.

Louise and her family are in the court room waiting anxiously for things to begin.

Grant has finally given in to his father's nagging. They are in Costa on a last minute holiday. His decision was made the second Louise had asked him if he could come to the trial and support her. It was the only reasonable excuse he could think of. None the wiser, his father was thrilled and booked the tickets immediately. They are sunning it up on a beach drinking cocktails. Dean is loving it. Grant feels lost, ill and guilty and checks the news constantly on his phone.

The prosecution opens their case with a summary of the facts as they see them, the defence then give their side of the story. The jury still look fresh and interested as the witnesses are called.

Louise testifies that she can't remember anything about the accident but is asked about her injuries and the effect on her daily life. She tries to keep it together as she is questioned. Everyone feels sorry for the poor girl who fell victim to a reckless driver who had left her for dead.

Dawn Perkins is next. She describes her shock on seeing her friend being hit, run over and then lying in the road. Then her panic as the only source of help drove off at speed. Next, her gradual remembering of bits of the registration number. Finally, her relief when a motorist stopped and she was able to call for help.

The paramedics detail the injuries and the mess her leg was in. No one can really say if the delay led to the amputation, but it definitely didn't help.

The hospital staff document various aspects of her care and

rehab staff her recovery.

Her family describe parts of their ordeal but this is limited to the facts of the case.

The police document their investigation which makes them sound like heroes, but consists of the witness remembering the partial reg, their fiddling around and finding the correct vehicle on ANPR and the forensic testing that matched the victim's DNA to the vehicle. Hardly rocket science. They briefly cover the suspect's disposal of the vehicle and attempts to cover up his crime, his arrest and "no comment" interview. On hearing this, the jury look irritated and glance at Pete for any evidence of remorse, but he keeps his head bowed.

The new vehicle owner has refused to testify as he can't be bothered to come to court, so the police can't prove the transfer date, or Darren's involvement. They also don't mention either of Grant's visits to the police station. As required, this material has been disclosed to the defence.

The prosecution rests after two days.

Grant refreshes his phone obsessively. The crime reporter at the court keeps the updates flowing.

Dean has no idea that the court case is happening right now, or that this is the reason his son was suddenly keen to join him abroad after resisting for months. He does notice that his son is glued to his phone but assumes he is in love. Perhaps, with the girl he's been hanging around with in recent months.

The defence begin their case. They have only one witness; Pete takes the stand. Their legal strategy has been agreed. The "deer defence" is the only option. It doesn't explain the disposal of the vehicle, but as Pete has access to plenty of vehicles via his brother's business, they will say it's just a coincidence.

"Can you please tell the jury what happened on the night of Wednesday 20th June?" Pete's barrister asks him.

Pete, who now looks frightened, speaks almost in a whisper and is asked by the Judge to speak up.

"I was with some mates. We were going to a party after a football game. I let my friend drive my car for a bit but..." Pete is interrupted by both the prosecution and defence barristers and the

Judge. There is a gasp from the packed court room. Louise looks as if she might faint. Her mum grabs her hand and squeezes it.

"Counsel, please approach the bench," orders the Judge as he looks at Pete warily over the top of his glasses.

Both barristers have been caught off guard. They look to the solicitors sitting behind them who shake their heads and shrug their shoulders. They don't know what to make of this either.

The Judge speaks in a low volume before asking for the Jury to be removed so he can establish exactly what is going on.

Turning to the defence barrister he says, "Your client has just suggested that someone else was driving his vehicle at the material time. Were you aware that this was to be his defence?"

"Of course not, Your Honour. I mean, sorry Judge, no I wasn't. I'm just as surprised as everyone else." The barrister is genuinely puzzled.

"This creates all sorts of problems for us as well, Your Honour," says the prosecution barrister not wanting to be left out.

"I realise that but it's too late in the day for defences like this to be thrown up. I'm minded to let it continue and just to make sure that the Jury knows that this hasn't been mentioned before," the Judge suggests. "Do either of you have an issue with this?

"Well no, unless he is planning on naming the driver as then we would need to interview him," says the prosecution barrister.

"I'll talk to my client," offers the defence barrister.

Grant stares at his phone in horror. He keeps refreshing but there are no further updates. He is desperate to know what happened after Pete suggested someone else had been driving.

Was he named in court? Surely not? Pete wouldn't do that to him, would he? He can't hate him that much….

What if he has been named? What about Louise and her family? Oh no…everything is unravelling. What should he do?

Grant prays. He prays silently but desperately. Dean sits next to him still recovering from the hangover of their previous night's drinking session and completely and utterly oblivious to the turmoil in his son's life.

After an hour, the Court reconvenes. Pete *has* named the person he says was driving at the time of the accident. The prosecution have discovered that he has already been interviewed and answered "no comment" to all questions.

The Judge thinks it unlikely that the Jury will believe Pete's story this late in the day, but he's decide to allow his testimony to continue for now. The Jury returns.

"So, you were telling us how your friend was driving your vehicle. What happened next?"

"He hit something, a deer. He was going far too fast. Then, after stopping for a second and checking for damage, he jumped back in and we left. He'd had a few pints so I think he was worried about being done for drink driving." Pete sounds bitter as he relays his made-up version of events. He knows exactly what he is doing. He's furious with Grant, believing that he had turned him in to the police and the stuff about the ANPR was just used to cover up some sort of deal. Pete has been patiently waiting for his revenge.

"Can you name the friend for the court, please?" the defence barrister asks the agreed question.

"Yes, Grant Yale," his voice rings out around the court room.

Louise lets out a yelp. She can't help it. *How can Grant be involved in all this? The man who has befriended and helped her so much and that she has come to rely on. It can't be true, can it?*

Her dad has gone an alarming shade of grey and is frantically rubbing his forehead. Her mum looks like she has just been shot and is frozen in her seat. Louise gets up and starts sobbing as she leaves the court room followed closely by the rest of her family.

Pete fixes an innocent expression on his face. He knew that Grant had befriended Louise. Revenge is sweet.

Chapter 16

The court case resumes the following morning. Louise and her family have returned after their terrible shock the day before.

Overnight, the police have been busy. Their hasty and overdue enquiries now reveal that witnesses at the football match recall Pete, Grant, Daniel, Alex and Scott heading off in Pete's vehicle after the football drinks.

Grant is on a flight back from Costa so is currently unavailable.

Of the three additional lads, Daniel and Alex, on the advice of their parents, refuse to talk to the police. They fear the wrath of Pete and his brother.

However, Scott is persuaded to tell the truth.

He reluctantly takes the stand and puts Pete firmly in the driving seat for the duration. His testimony is undermined slightly by a past caution for dishonesty but it's obvious that the Jury believe him.

To top it off, the prosecution then recall Dawn Perkins to the stand. They ask her whether she can identify the driver of the vehicle on the night in question; the person that sped away leaving her alone to deal with her dying friend. She confidently points at Pete.

The police detectives look embarrassed, they hadn't even asked the question of this witness and had had no idea she could recognise the driver. Dock identifications are a last resort but can be surprisingly effective.

Pete's ridiculous defence has drastically failed. He doesn't care. He thought it would. He just wanted to hurt Grant and try and take someone down with him.

The Jury retire. They return with guilty verdicts on all counts just two hours later.

Pete is sentenced to two year's imprisonment. He is taken down in handcuffs.

The whole sorry debacle is over. Compensation will be agreed at a later stage. The police have a detected crime on their books. The

barristers and solicitors will all get paid. Louise and her family know who was responsible. Pete has been sent to prison....
But, what about Grant?

Chapter 17

Grant arrives back in the country and quickly hears the news which doesn't really come as a surprise. Luckily, the police aren't interested in pursuing him as they already have their man.

Grant has had time to prepare himself for what he knows he must do. He hasn't told Dean. He doesn't want his father to try and get him out of another mess. He needs to take responsibility for himself.

He makes his way to Louise's house. Her father answers the door. For a second, he thinks he might be on the receiving end of a well deserved punch. However, Louise's father, seething with anger, steps aside and keeps his clenched fists by his sides.

Louise comes downstairs on hearing the door. Grant asks to speak with her in private. They go outside into the garden. She has been crying and looks like she might start again but she holds it together and says, "Well?"

Grant begins his speech, "I know I can't say anything that will make up for what I did. I was in the car that night, though I wasn't driving. I knew we'd hit someone. I should've forced Pete to stop. I didn't and afterwards, my instinct was to cover things up.

Then, I couldn't believe it when you arrived at my college, and in my class! It was almost as if God had sent you there to give me an opportunity to make up for what I'd done. I know I haven't spoken to you about this before, but I used to be a Christian. I was going to church and had made a commitment to follow Jesus when my mum died suddenly two years ago but I let myself drift from God. It started off as needing time to grieve by myself. Then, it turned to annoyance at the people at church. Then, I became too involved with football and the party lifestyle. When I received money from my mum's will, Pete and his crowd appeared and I just wanted to fit in but I've become someone I don't recognise and can't stand to look at in the mirror.

I want you to know that I'm going to try and sort it out. I can't do it myself and I don't know if God will forgive me, but I hope

He will as I've done some bad things. I don't want to say any more as I know that you'll need time to think about it." A tear slowly trickles down Grant's face.

Louise doesn't say anything for a long while. They just sit in silence. Eventually, she says, "I really don't know what to make of this. Even though your motives were completely selfish and you lied, you have really helped me in my recovery. I think I would have liked you as you were before your mum died as I'm sure I've seen glimpses of that Grant since we met. Look, I'll deal with my parents. They'll be fine as long as I am."

Grant knows it's time to leave and give Louise time to think about things. She has given him hope for their future friendship though which he knows is much more than he deserves.

Grant has one more stop to make. He's tired of going it alone and he always makes such a mess of things. Even with Louise's kind words, the guilt is still unbearable.

He heads for the home of the pastor from his former church. He knocks on the door and is invited in. The pastor looks sombre and Grant realises that parts of the story must have already done the rounds.

They sit down with a cup of tea and Grant pours out his sorry tale once again, not sparing any details, as he wants to be completely honest this time around. The pastor listens and looks thoughtful.

Reaching the end, Grant takes a breath and although he dreads the answer, he asks his tentative question: "Do you think God can forgive me for all of this, Pastor?"

The pastor, with tears in his eyes, reaches for his well-worn Bible. He opens it to Luke chapter 15 and starts reading at verse 11:

"There was a man who had two sons. The younger one said to his father, 'Father, give me my share of the estate.' So he divided his property between them. Not long after that, the younger son got together all he had, set off for a distant country and there squandered his wealth in wild living.

After he had spent everything, there was a severe famine in that whole country, and he began to be in need. So he went and hired himself out to a citizen of that country, who sent him to his fields to feed pigs. He longed to fill his stomach with the pods that the pigs were eating, but no one gave him anything.

"When he came to his senses, he said, 'How many of my father's hired servants have food to spare, and here I am starving to death! I will set out and go back to my father and say to him: Father, I have sinned against heaven and against you. I am no longer worthy to be called your son; make me like one of your hired servants.' So he got up and went to his father.

But while he was still a long way off, his father saw him and was filled with compassion for him; he ran to his son, threw his arms around him and kissed him.

The son said to him, 'Father, I have sinned against heaven and against you. I am no longer worthy to be called your son.'

But the father said to his servants, 'Quick! Bring the best robe and put it on him. Put a ring on his finger and sandals on his feet. Bring the fattened calf and kill it. Let's have a feast and celebrate. For this son of mine was dead and is alive again; he was lost and is found.' So they began to celebrate.

Meanwhile, the older son was in the field. When he came near the house, he heard music and dancing. So he called one of the servants and asked him what was going on. 'Your brother has come,' he replied, 'and your father has killed the fattened calf because he has him back safe and sound.'

The older brother became angry and refused to go in. So his father went out and pleaded with him. But he answered his father, 'Look! All these years I've been slaving for you and never disobeyed your orders. Yet you never gave me even a young goat so I could celebrate with my friends. But when this son of yours who has squandered your property with prostitutes comes home, you kill the fattened calf for him!'

'My son,' the father said, 'you are always with me, and everything I have is yours. But we had to celebrate and be glad, because this brother of yours was dead and is alive again; he was lost and is found.'"

Note to Reader

Grant's story can be taken as a warning for all of us who profess to be Christians. We can find ourselves drifting from God without even knowing it.

Grant made a series of bad choices which took him further and further from his newly discovered faith. After the death of his mother, when really he needed them most, he withdrew from his church family. He became isolated and lost interest in their shared activities. He stopped reading his Bible. He only prayed when he wanted something from God and then only flippantly, and about the football.

Abandoning his church friends, he started to hang around with a group of lads who were a bad influence on him. Encouraged by his wayward father, he became more and more involved in their way of life, exchanging church services for football matches and alcohol.

By the time of the accident, Grant had already drifted well away from God. Instead of doing the right thing, he gave into the temptation to sin. He allowed himself to be swept along in a tide of deception and a shocking cover up. At any point, he could have come clean about his involvement but he chose to remain silent, assisted at times by his father who was determined to protect his son, whatever the cost.

Despite God's warning to Grant that his sin would find him out in the end, he chose to try and go it alone. He continued the deception and made it much worse by trying to atone for his sin via a web of lies.

In the end, as it always does, the house of cards came crashing down. His sin found him out and he was left a nervous wreck with only himself to blame.

The good news is that Grant did come to his senses. He stopped relying on others to cover up his mess. He took responsibility by apologising and seeking to make amends with Louise, who'd been the most hurt by his deception.

Then, in real repentance and faith, he sought the advice of his former pastor and asked if God would forgive him.

The wise pastor used the parable of the prodigal son to show Grant that forgiveness is always possible for those who are repentant.

The love of God for sinful humanity is demonstrated in the father who runs to meet his rebellious son, who has come to his senses, and throws his arms around him. The son is restored to a right relationship with his father.

This restoration is made possible by the death of Jesus on the cross for sinners. Jesus bridges the gap between us and God caused by our sin. We can approach God through His Son, Jesus.

I encourage you to get right with God today, don't leave it until you are in a terrible mess like Grant, or until you are so destitute you are wanting to eat pig food like the prodigal son. You can pray any time and ask for forgiveness of your sin and, believing Jesus died for you and trusting Him, you can be sure of a home in Heaven.

NATALIE VELLACOTT

A PILLAR OF THE COMMUNITY

A Short Story of Self Delusion and Pride

Chapter 1

Gary and Janet Yale are sitting in Starbucks drinking coffee. As anticipated, the funeral of their 46 year old daughter in law Annie, had been tough but there had also been an unexpected and disturbing twist. Now, away from the chaos and confusion, they are reflective as they discuss the day's events.

"What did Grant say to you when I went after Dean, you both looked upset?" Janet prompts her husband of 40 years.

"Oh, nothing much. I confronted him about making such a spectacle of himself and asked if it was really the time and place for all that stuff." Gary isn't willing to admit that he had been moved at the funeral so the lie slips easily off his tongue, but he still avoids eye contact with the lady who knows him best.

"That's a bit harsh. I'm sure he was speaking from his heart. He's just become a bit fanatical recently and Annie's funeral gave him a platform. I'm sure he'll regret it when he's had time to grieve properly." Janet assesses her grandson favourably.

"Hmm, maybe. I'm more worried about Dean. Now, what are we going to do about him?" Gary swiftly changes the subject.

"Not much we can do, is there. I mean, he's a grown man. It sounds terrible to say it out loud but I'm not sure that Annie's death will be the worst thing in the world for him. You know they were struggling," Janet voices the concerns they have both had for a while about their son and daughter in law's shaky marriage.

"I don't think that's fair. He wouldn't have wanted her dead," Gary pretends to be shocked by Janet's unusual forthrightness.

"I think he was more wound up by Grant's behaviour. That'll be the difficult issue especially if Grant carries on with his zealous attempts to convert everyone to Christianity. I think you should try and see Dean, or at least give him a call and make sure he's okay later?" Janet waits for her husband to agree to her suggestion.

"Okay, dear," Gary replies dutifully but really he is thinking that Dean just needs to get drunk and then sleep off the hangover.

Later at home,

"Right, I need to go to the church, they don't have anyone to play tonight," Gary says as he heads out of their front door.

"What, couldn't they have given you the night off in light of the funeral?" Janet says, surprised.

"They offered, but I said I didn't mind. You know they rely on me and I like to keep up my skills," Gary grins as he slips out and makes his way to their garage.

He waves at their neighbour but one who is cleaning his car in the driveway.

"Hi, Gary, thought I'd get on and do the car as you've got a lot on at the moment. So sorry to hear about your daughter in law."

"Thanks Albert, but I'm happy to do it. Tell you what, I'll do your lawn tomorrow if you like?" Gary offers.

"Really?" Albert's face lights up. "That'd be great as I've been dreading having to face it, it's these knees that are killing me."

"Of course, no bother," Gary calls back loudly as he opens the garage. Before getting into his car, he takes a quick glance around to see if anyone overhead his generous offer to his elderly neighbour.

He heads for the small parish church just around the corner from their house. It's their mid-week drop in for the homeless. Gary always plays the piano and helps serve the food to the regulars that traipse in and out.

He originally got involved when he gave a few pence to a street beggar who mentioned the church activity. When he had first turned up to offer help, they had suggested he could arrange chairs and tables and do some cleaning. Gary had reluctantly agreed to these mundane tasks although feeling that they were somewhat beneath him as an increasingly important figure in the community, because it meant he could avoid the short God talk that accompanied the men's meal.

However, in time and much to Gary's delight, the church decided to drop the talk completely, believing that their attendees would rather eat in peace. The volunteers could always chat with them one to one if they wanted and get to know them this way rather than preaching at them. The church had since found their numbers sky-rocketing. They had been forced to hire paid staff and to secure regular food donations from local supermarkets. Although some of the "customers" complained about being served the same meals week in and week out and pointed out that their utensils weren't always spotlessly clean, Gary and the church members have been thrilled by the uptake.

Tonight, the church have managed to secure an official photographer from the local paper to give them some publicity in the hope of generating some income. Gary ensures he is visible in the main photo and that he is holding some dirty dishes, demonstrating his willingness to get stuck in.

As soon as the photos have been taken, Gary makes his excuses and leaves the others to deal with the mess. They don't mind as they know he is involved in a lot of local projects and is very busy, they are just grateful that he still spares the time to come and see them each week, even if his visits are getting shorter every time.

Arriving home, Gary parks in his garage then, instead of using the internal door into his kitchen, he heads back around the front in full view of his curtain twitching neighbours. He begins a countdown in his head, "10, 9, 8, 7, 6...."

"Nice evening Mr Yale, where have you been?" Mrs Harma calls as she approaches from across the street.

"Just at the church helping the homeless as usual," Gary smiles smugly.

"Wonderful. If only there were more people like you out there who really cared." Mrs Harma gazes in admiration at her hero neighbour who often cuts her hedge and mows her lawn, only at the front mind you.

"Well, I do my best," Gary flushes slightly despite himself. "I'll do that hedge and lawn for you this week." He ensures he points towards the front.

"Thank you so much, I say, is there any chance you could do the back some time as well?" Mrs Harma asks.

Gary's been dreading this moment as Mrs Harma has a huge lawn and multiple shrubs and hedges at the back. It would take him weeks to make a dent in it, especially as it's so overgrown.

"I think you'll find that it's better for the wildlife if you leave it as it is," he convincingly replies. "If you cut it all back, they'll stop coming and I know how much you like your daily visitors."

"Oh, do you really think so? I do love to watch them digging and ferreting about, especially the muntjacs and the squirrels. Maybe I should leave it then."

"I'll do the front for you, no problem," Gary hastens back towards his house before she can make any further requests of him. He notices that several of his neighbours are out walking their dogs. He opens his front door and is greeted by his wife.

"How was the meeting?" she smiles. "Cup of tea?"

"Yes, lovely. I just saw Mrs Harma across the street, she was trying to get me to do her back lawns and hedges again. I've reminded her of the wildlife. If you see her, perhaps you can mention how amazing it all is to back me up?"

"You're terrible," Mrs Yale laughs at her husband's deviousness. "Why don't you just tell her you don't have the energy?"

"Because then I'll feel guilty every time she sees me doing work at someone else's house!" Gary says. "Have you thought any more about taking in one of those Ukrainian refugees? Did you see the news earlier? The government are paying £350 for each one now and Bob and Sarah have already signed up. I think we should do it," Gary seeks to persuade his reluctant wife who knows she'll end up looking after the poor soul as her husband is out most of the time.

"Well, you know that Bob and Sarah don't really have other commitments and they have the time and money to spare...." she trails off as she can't think of another excuse.

"Come on love. Let's do our bit. We can just offer to take a single woman if you'd rather. That would be easier for you." Gary knows he will win in the end as his wife is a soft touch. He does love her for it but he's noticed that she is getting tired earlier these days.

"Ok, then. I'll do the application tomorrow whilst you're at the golf." Janet secretly wonders whether her husband would be so keen on this grand gesture if Bob and Sarah weren't already signed up, but she's gotten used to Gary's determination to keep up with the Jones's and has convinced herself that his heart's in the right place…most of the time.

Chapter 2

Gary takes a swing on the golf course. He's getting good at this. Of course, he's only here because his dear friend Richard has recently had surgery and this is part of his recuperation.

"Great shot, mate," Richard says enthusiastically. *He's* only here because he's just had surgery and wants to be as far away from his nagging wife as possible.

"Yeah, really good hit but I'll better it," Jack says. He's taking part because his wife has gone to the Canaries for a week with her girlfriends and he's by himself.

The three men make their way around the course slowly. None of them are particularly good at the sport but they all slap each other on the back, cheer each other on and try to outmanoeuvre each other in equal measure. It's easy to support an underdog, but when one of them starts to win, well, everything changes.

The men finish the course. Jack wins, but only just. Gary thinks its because Jack was using a more expensive club. Richard thinks he just got lucky. All three are sure their individual skills are superior but they keep quiet, apart from Jack who revels in his victory.

They make their way to the bar in the club house and settle in for the rest of the afternoon. Gary briefly thinks of Janet at home probably juggling the housework with the elderly neighbour he had invited round for coffee and now the application to host a Ukrainian. Well, they're a tag team and he's doing his bit by helping out Richard.

"What about the war in Ukraine?" Jack comments as they sip their beer.

"Funny you should mention it. I've just decided to take in some of those refugees," Gary is pleased about this early opportunity to let his friends know of his plans.

Richard looks worried, "But, didn't your daughter in law just die suddenly? Don't your own family need your attention at the moment?"

Gary flushes and hesitates, "Well she did, but we've had the funeral and there's not much I can do for them right now. Dean just needs to be out and about with his buddies, Grant's joined the Jesus people and Sophie seems like she might be going that way as well. I'll be there for them when they're ready, but for now, there's others that need help. You've got a big place. Aren't you going to sign up?"

Now, it's Jack's turn to look awkward. "Well, we've thought

about it yeah. Maybe we'll do it soon." He doesn't want to commit to anything as his wife is very much in control and she will be furious if, when she gets back from holiday, he's signed them up for something like this. His wife and Ukrainian refugees, somehow he can't see it.

"Wait, so Grant and Sophie have both got serious about God, they're haven't joined those "born agains" have they??" Richard offers a subject change. "How on earth did that happen?"

"I don't really know what's happened. I mean, I'm a Christian of course, but Grant seemed pretty crazy at the funeral talking about Hell and judgement and practically begging people to listen. I think Sophie was upset by what he said. I'm hoping it's just a phase, or perhaps a way of dealing with the sadness of losing their mum."

Gary tries to sound appropriately accommodating but inwardly he's pretty annoyed by the change in his grandchildren, particularly Grant. He had had a weak moment at the funeral himself, but that was all it was, a weak moment. Now, he's fully in control of his emotional faculties and doesn't want his family to be known as religious nutcases. Church at Christmas, Easter and Remembrance Day is enough for now.

"Yeah, that's probably all it is. Kids need to believe their dead parents are somewhere even if they're not, it's harmless enough," Jack comments vaguely.

The others just look at him lost in their own thoughts.

Chapter 3

Janet rushes around preparing tea and answering the phone which rings constantly with people wanting to speak to Gary. She is just in the middle of another phone call with an elderly man whose wife has been rushed into hospital, when the doorbell rings. She stretches the phone cord as far as it will reach and opens the door.

"Oh hi Mrs Yale. Oh, you're on the phone. I'll just come in and wait, shall I?" Mrs Dranty smiles sweetly and heads in through the open door before Janet can reply.

"Yes, sorry, I'm still here Mr Fordy. I was just answering the door. I'll ask Gary to call you when he gets in, he's out at the moment." Janet tries to reassure the distressed old man and then hangs up to attend to her visitor.

She leans against the kitchen wall and sighs, willing herself to summon the energy for a few hours of nonsensical chatter with the lonely Mrs Dranty who has started popping round regularly in recent weeks. She's sure her husband must have encouraged the visitation but he says he only mentioned it once in passing and wasn't expecting her to take him up on it.

"Tea or coffee?" Janet calls through to Mrs Dranty who has already made herself comfortable in their lounge and is busily flicking through a magazine on the coffee table.

"What's that dear? Tea and some cake if you've got it. That would be lovely," Mrs Dranty replies.

"Sure, coming right up." Janet puts the kettle on then searches frantically for anything resembling cake and finds a plastic tub with the remnants of a fruit cake in the pantry. She sniffs it and looks at it. It'll have to do. She cuts a crumbling slice and puts it on a plate. She makes the tea.

"Here we are," Janet puts the tray on the coffee table and sits down for what she knows will be a long chat.

"Gary not here? That's a shame, I really needed to see him about my lawn and some other bits…but I know he's busy."

"He's with a friend that's just had surgery, I'm afraid," Janet dutifully omits the fact that they are playing golf as she knows her husband prefers for people not to think of him frittering away his precious time.

"Always helping everyone. You're very lucky to have such a husband. I saw him the other day driving a mini bus with a load of scruffy looking kids in the back," Mrs Dranty says this as if looking for an explanation for Gary's association with these ragged children.

"Yes, he drives for Kids Club, it's a special needs charity, twice a week, as a volunteer," Janet ensures she includes the fact it's unpaid.

"Oh, that makes sense," Mrs Dranty relaxes and smiles. "I'll bet they'll be rolling out the red carpet when he finally reaches the Pearly Gates."

"What? Well, he's only 65!!" Janet exclaims. She resists the urge to tell Mrs Dranty what it's really like living with a husband who is always helping other people and who frequently expects her to do the same.

Mrs Dranty sips her tea and eats her cake carefully. "Well, my late husband was exactly the same, always helping people, nothing was too much trouble, he always….."

Janet's eyes have glazed over and she has tuned out. She is exhausted. She snaps abruptly back to the conversation a few minutes later and finds she is being asked a question.

"So, do you think it's possible?"

"Yes?" Janet replies with no idea what she is agreeing to. She can hardly tell the older woman that she had bored her into zombie mode and that she had fallen asleep with her eyes open.

"Great. I'll expect him tomorrow morning." Mrs Dranty rises and hands her empty cup and plate to Janet who thinks she catches a gleeful glint in the older woman's eye, as she makes for the front door. Her plan has worked perfectly and it only took her 30 minutes.

"Should he bring any tools?" Janet guesses she's just roped her husband into some sort of garden work because Mrs Dranty had earlier mentioned the lawn.

"Just for measuring the space initially. You know, to make sure the new bathroom will fit." Mrs Dranty calls as she closes the front door behind her.

Janet collapses back onto the sofa. Gary will be furious. He has told her repeatedly not to make arrangements on his behalf as he wants to cherry pick his jobs.

In their own house, things have remained broken for a long time and she has been forced to accept that her husband is too busy to address them. It's a small price to pay for being married to someone so well thought of in their local community though. At least this is what she tells herself whenever she feels overwhelmed and lonely.

Janet rehearses her speech in her head. "I think she's getting dementia, as I didn't agree to that." Even as she thinks of it, she knows Mrs Dranty is far too switched on for her to get away with this. In fact, it wouldn't surprise Janet to have learned that Mrs Dranty may have had a recording device to capture their agreement in evidence.

Janet feels weary as she stares at the wall before longingly looking at her neglected knitting in a basket in the corner. She suddenly remembers the application for the Ukrainian refugee that she'd agreed to do. She fires up their ancient computer. She really hates doing stuff online, but it seems to be the way everything operates now. Just as she has found the website and begun reading the pages of instructions for completing the form, the phone rings, as she goes to answer it, the doorbell sounds again……

Chapter 4

"Did you get to see Dean in the end?" Janet asks Gary.

They are having a rare coffee together at home before Gary needs to address the promise his wife had inadvertently made to Mrs Dranty yesterday afternoon. Janet had explained what had happened and Gary had taken it well. Together they'd decided that the most straight forward course of action was for Gary to measure for the new bathroom, then for them both to order it with Mrs Dranty's credit card. Then, Gary would explain that he didn't have insurance to do the fitting, so she would need to get builders in. In fact, he had already contacted a friend of his who charged a fair price and would do a good job.

"I've tried calling him a few times and I actually went round there earlier. He doesn't answer the phone and Sophie was the only one at home when I arrived," Gary tells her.

"Did she say anything about how Dean is? Was she okay?" Janet is anxious about her son's family as they haven't really spoken since the upset at the funeral. They've all just returned to their lives before the tragedy as if nothing has happened.

"Actually, she looked really tired and her eyes were red and puffy. I think she'd been crying. She said her dad hasn't been around much and she's worried about his drinking," Gary relays.

"You know what, I really think it would be good for us to have her here for a while. What do you think, love?" Janet asks.

"I thought you weren't sure if you could manage a Ukrainian but now you want to add someone else to our household?!" Gary says, astonished.

"It's hardly the same and she's our granddaughter. I just don't think she's going to get any support from Dean for a while and Grant will be off with his church friends. I know Sophie was interested in the church stuff but I'm not sure if it will stick and she's probably pretty lonely. Being 14 is difficult enough without suddenly losing your mother," Janet reasons.

"Well, if you think you can take her on, sure. It'll make the tutoring easier as well. She can help with the Ukrainians when they arrive, take her mind off the trauma. It'll also be good for Dean not to have to worry about parenting as he recovers from what's happened," Gary agrees with her suggestion. He and Janet are both retired teachers and he has been tutoring Sophie in the classes she struggles with,

Science and Maths, for a while now.

"Great, I'll text her and see what she says," Janet reaches for her phone and sends a quick message to Sophie asking her to give her a call when she can. Her grand children find it hilarious that she does this; texts someone asking them to call her, rather than just passing on the message in the text. It's a generational thing and Janet prefers talking to texting.

Gary heads off to Mrs Dranty's house.

"Let me know how it goes. Fingers crossed," Janet calls after him. She feels guilty for getting him into this, but feels sure he can get out of it without Mrs Dranty thinking any less of him. After all, everyone knows you need appropriate insurance to do a big job like fitting a bathroom.

Janet hears the noise of her phone ringing. It's Sophie.

"Hi sweetie, are you okay?" she asks her grand daughter.

"I'm okay Gran," Sophie's voice is quiet on the other end of the line. She doesn't sound okay.

"Granddad said when he came round that he thought you might have been crying," Janet gently prompts.

Sophie bursts into tears.

"Oh Gran, it's been awful. I'm really worried about my dad and I don't know what to do," Sophie sobs.

"You shouldn't have to worry about him darling. You're grieving yourself. How's your brother?"

"He seems okay, he's got his church mates although he's been staying in his room a lot and he's also worried about Dad," Sophie tells her Gran.

"Well, me and Granddad have talked it over and we'd like you to come and stay with us for a bit, if you'd like? It'll give your dad a chance to sort himself out and Grant will be okay."

"Really, I'd love that!" Sophie perks up and brightens just at the thought of somewhere new and different rather than the depressing house which seems empty without her mother.

"Just so you know, we're also applying to host a Ukrainian, so you might have to share some space but you'll have your own room," Janet encourages her.

"That's fine. I think it's great that you're doing that. They really need help," Sophie observes.

Janet heart goes out to her granddaughter who is so kind hearted that she is thinking of others despite having just lost her mum.

"Well, look, get some things together and we'll come and pick you up a bit later. Don't worry if you forget things as we can always drop by and grab them, it's only 10 minutes in the car," Janet says.

"Are you sure? Wait, what about Dad?"

"I'll talk to him, but I'm pretty sure he'll be glad that you are being taken care of as I don't think he's up to it, sweetie."

"You're probably right." Sophie recalls her drunken father crawling in from another night with his mates. "See you later then."

Chapter 5

Gary sighs as he leaves Mrs Dranty's house. The hasty plan he and his wife had conducted had gone almost perfectly, but he still feels bad. He had seen the brief look of sadness and disappointment in their elderly neighbour's eyes as she had reassured him that of course she understood that he couldn't do the job himself without the correct insurance.

He feels guilty for lying and senses that Mrs Dranty knew that if he had really wanted to do it, he could have; where there's a will there's a way.

But, where would it end? If he fitted Mrs Dranty's bathroom, Gary feels sure that all of his neighbours would expect the same consideration, so unless he's planning on getting a job as a full time plumber, he's justified in refusing.

Gary arrives home, he's tired just from the visit and the lengthy explanations he'd given to Mrs Dranty. Janet is on the phone.

"Oh, yes. I'm so sorry Mr Fordy. Gary hasn't forgotten. We just had a family emergency to deal with. I'll get him to call you very soon." Janet turns as she hears the front door opening and shrugs at her husband as he comes in. She hangs up.

"I know you've only just got in, but I told Mr Fordy you'd call him yesterday, Bertha was rushed into hospital and I don't think he can get there by himself," Janet tells him.

"I just need a few minutes to sit down," Gary collapses into the nearest chair and within minutes is fast asleep.

3 hours later the phone rings again.

"Oh no," Janet mutters as she answers it. "I'll just get him, Mr Fordy, yes, he's just got in. I think I can hear him in the garage actually, give me a few seconds."

"Wake up Gary. It's Mr Fordy," she whispers urgently as she shakes her husband awake.

"What, hmmm. Five more minutes," Gary mumbles.

"No, it's Mr Fordy, you HAVE to talk to him now," Janet insists.

Gary rubs his eyes and tries to focus. "What? Okay, hand me the phone."

Janet obliges.

"Hello, Mr Fordy. I'm so sorry I didn't call you back earlier, you see I was...."

The old man is crying on the other end of the line.

"Mr Fordy?" Gary says.

Through choked sobs, Mr Fordy simply says, "Bertha died."

Gary is deflated and for once in his life, speechless. He has no idea how to comfort the grieving Mr Fordy. He has no bright ideas, no platitudes that wouldn't sound empty and no hope to offer. He wishes he had called Mr Fordy back earlier and offered him a lift to see his dying wife. Guilt threatens to overwhelm him whilst his own mind is trying to alleviate his conscience by listing all the other things he had had to do.

"Mr Fordy, I'll come round straight away." Gary manages the only thing he can think of. Perhaps, he can help arrange the funeral, or get the man some groceries or something. He knows it won't be enough.

Several hours later, Gary arrives home.

"How was poor Mr Fordy?" Janet asks sympathetically. She hadn't gone with her husband fearing the two of them might be too much for him at this difficult time.

"Oh, it was awful," Gary says. His wife notices that he is pale and his face looks drawn like a man in shock. "I had no idea Bertha was at risk of dying. Did you realise how serious it was?"

"Not really, I mean he did say she had been rushed into hospital but he wasn't specific and I assumed he would have made it sound more urgent...I guess he didn't want to bother us?" Janet feels teary at the thought of Mr Fordy not getting the chance to say goodbye to his wife because they hadn't responded to his pleas in time.

"All I could do was sit with him as he told me how he met Bertha and all about their lives together but he kept crying so it was difficult to hear him. It was worse because he didn't even mention the fact he hadn't got to the hospital. He was just very grateful that I'd come round and kept saying he knew I was a busy man." Gary shakes his head. "Then, he was rambling about Bertha being in a better place and asking me if I was sure that she was in Heaven. Obviously, I reassured the man best I could but I felt completely and totally useless. This must never happen again."

"You can't do everything for everyone, dear. I'm sure you did your best," Janet says soothingly.

The phone rings and Janet answers it.

"Gran, I've been waiting for hours. You did mean today, didn't you?" Sophie asks.

"Oh! Hang on, love. Yes, I did mean today. One of our neighbours just lost his wife and we've been dealing with that. Your granddad will come and get you now," Janet looks to Gary who sighs and nods wearily.

"It's just, I told Dad about it and he didn't believe that's where I was going," Sophie says.

"I was planning to talk to him beforehand, but I can do it when I get there," Gary says.

Janet relays the information to Sophie and hangs up.

"Another person we forgot and this time it's our own flesh and blood," Gary looks downcast as he gets to his feet and heads for the door.

"Sophie won't mind, but you will need to pacify Dean now. He'll probably make a fuss that we went behind his back and made the offer to her before discussing it with him. He's a bit like that these days," Janet comments.

"Oh, joy. I'm not sure I've got the energy for this," Gary responds.

"Perhaps, if you use a bit of reverse psychology on him. I'm sure he could do with a break and not having to worry about Sophie but try and make it seem like it's his idea rather than a cunning scheme that he's been left out of," Janet suggests.

"I'll do my best."

Dean answers the door to his dad. He looks a little annoyed but not furious.

Gary heads inside and is nearly knocked out by the strong smell of bleach in the kitchen.

"What is that smell?"

"Oh, I had to clean as a curry fell on the floor and it really stank," Dean says innocently.

Something doesn't seem to add up, but Gary hasn't time to figure it out and he needs to sort out Sophie.

"Hey, so you know a while ago, you suggested that Sophie stayed with us for a few days a week so she could get more done when I'm tutoring her?" Gary begins.

"Yeah, that was ages ago, though," Dean scratches his head.

Gary notices the dark circles under his son's eyes and that he seems to be struggling for words.

"We thought we'd do it now. I tried to come by and talk to you the other day but you weren't here." Gary hopes Dean doesn't ask for specifics as he doesn't have any.

Dean appears to be focusing on something else. His eyes are looking around as if he is concerned that his father might see something that he would rather remained hidden.

"Oh, okay. Yeah, sounds good. She's upstairs." Dean indicates the staircase.

Gary hears the slur in Dean's speech and realises that he's trying to limit his words. He moves a step closer and Dean nearly falls over backwards as he seeks to maintain the distance between them. Gary smells the alcohol and suddenly the picture, including the bleach smell, is clear.

"You really need...", Gary starts but doesn't finish his sentence. He's there to get Sophie. Getting into a confrontation with his son about his drinking will not help. He changes tack, "to call Sophie. Does she know I'm here?" Gary says. Somehow, the fact that his son doesn't seem to notice his change of direction, or that he's seen the alcohol, makes him feel sad.

Sophie appears on the stairs with a large bag over her shoulder.

Dean looks relieved as he says goodbye to his daughter. He doesn't ask how long she will be going for.

"Where's Grant?" Gary asks as an afterthought.

"You taking him as well?" Dean asks with a trace of irritation.

"He's out with church friends," Sophie replies quickly, sensing an argument brewing.

"No, of course not, I just haven't seen him for a while," Gary clarifies.

They head outside to the car. As they are loading Sophie's stuff, she looks back to the house and sees her dad standing in the kitchen staring blankly out of the window.

"How long has he been like that?" Gary asks once they are in the car.

"Pretty much since Mum died with the odd break. That's not bad actually. He's just hung over," Sophie says quietly.

"I smelt alcohol, so he's had a drink today," Gary says. "And what's with the bleach?"

"He came in drunk last night with some mates I think. The whole place was covered in bottles and cans this morning and absolutely reeked of booze and cigarettes," Sophie almost whispers the explanation. Even though she's speaking to her granddad, she feels humiliated and embarrassed by her father's recent behaviour.

"I'm sorry you've been dealing with that, love. You won't catch me or your grandma behaving like that, I assure you." Gary winks but his joke falls flat.

Sophie isn't really listening anyway. She is conscious that with every mile they travel they get further away from her family home. She sighs with relief as she feels the weight of responsibility for her father lifting.

Chapter 6

"I was on the phone to Gordon earlier and he's running for his town council." Gary, who is in the lounge, calls to Janet in the kitchen. "I'm thinking maybe I should apply for ours."

Janet stays silent and pulls a face.

"What do you think?" Gary repeats the implied question.

Janet inwardly groans. She's been waiting for something like this to happen. Her husband is already trying to do far too much and she knows the amount of work that would be involved in running for the council. This, not mentioning that they would be even more in the spotlight, which she hates, and expected to live as perfect citizens, always in the public eye.

"Well, isn't there an upper age limit?" Janet asks hopefully.

"Of course not, well not unless you're over 75. It's mostly retired people like us who have the time," Gary replies confidently. He's already been researching the role.

Janet's hopes that the suggestion was just a throw away idea are fading fast as she realises her husband is serious, and set on the idea.

"Okay, well if that's what you want to do. What are the requirements?" Janet asks hesitantly still hoping Gary won't qualify.

"Well, I need to be involved in the community, a known figure. I already help the neighbours, do the church stuff and drive the mini bus so that's a good start. I need to be involved in local projects and charities. Hopefully the Ukrainian will get here soon now that we've applied." Gary is checking things off a list in an article in front of him.

"Hmm. What else?" Janet says absent-mindedly. She's not bothered about the things Gary already does, it's the big changes that she's worried about.

"Well, I'll probably need to go to more meetings about local issues and maybe try and get in the papers a bit more. I might even be able to get a column or something," Gary says vaguely.

"What would you write about?" Janet asks. Her husband may be helpful and productive, but he's not known for his journalistic skills. Indeed, she's never known him to express any type of interest in anything of the sort before. He reads *The Daily Mail* each day and that's the extent of it.

"Oh, I don't know. Local events. How hard can it be?"

"Very, if you don't have a clear plan or vision for what you want to communicate," Janet says firmly. She being the retired English teacher with Gary's expertise mainly in Science and Maths, can already see where this is leading.

"Oh. This one could be more difficult. Respect for diversity, including the various faiths. The person who wrote this article suggests attending services for all of the major faiths at least once a month and making sure they are the largest and most visible representations in the community," Gary says.

"Hmm, won't your work at the drop in cover that?" Janet asks.

"I don't think so as it's not really a religious service and the church is tiny. I'd probably need to find another one. Which other religions do you think I'd need to think about?"

Sophie joins their conversation having entered the room. "Islam, obviously and probably Hinduism and Buddhism. You're listing the major religions, right?"

"Well, yes, but only the ones that have a good number in the UK and that hold services that I can attend," Gary says to his granddaughter. "I'm thinking of running for the town council."

"Well, you could come to church with me, but I'm not sure you'd like it." Sophie laughs as she imagines her grandparents standing amongst the strobe lights in the darkened room as the worship band creates the atmosphere.

Janet laughs nervously.

"Wait, I've had a great idea!" Gary exclaims. "Why don't we go to the Parish church where they had the funeral?"

"We, you mean I'd have to go as well?" Janet says. "But, Sunday is my rest day, I love being able to chill out with a late start and a good book."

"Darling, if I run for the council, it'll need to be a joint effort. How many councillors appear without their devoted partners by their side?"

"I guess you're right," Janet agrees reluctantly. "Are you sure it's worth it though. You already do a lot for people."

Gary isn't listening. He's already planning his take over of the council. He's looking up the attendance statistics at the Parish church to make sure it's central and has the largest congregation.

"Don't you need a nomination for that type of thing?" Sophie is fiddling with her phone but casually listening to her grandparents conversation. "It says here that to become a councillor you'll need at least 10 nominations from people that aren't related to you. It doesn't really make sense as how many people wake up and think, 'I'll nominate this person for town council today'?"

"I think you have to canvass and try to persuade people to nominate you, honey," Janet points out.

"Oh, how awkward. I'd hate that," Sophie flushes.

"Well, your granddad has plenty of locals who'd be happy to support him, I'm sure, but yes it does feel a little uncomfortable." Janet looks uncertain about the whole idea.

Gary had been quiet as he made his plans but he's tuned back into the conversation. "I'll ask some of the neighbours and folks at the drop in, then there's the mini bus staff. I hope I don't have to ask Mr Fordy, but if necessary…."

"Oh no!" Janet gasps. "You can't possibly do that. The poor man."

"You're probably right," Gary concedes "But if needs must."

Janet busies herself preparing food. She is horrified that her husband would even consider prevailing upon the widowed Mr Fordy especially as they had totally failed to help him in his hour of need. She had hoped never to have to cross paths with the man again fearing the pained expressions and broken hearted retelling of stories about his wife that Gary had described. Gary might be able to deal with it but she knows she cannot.

Gary is determined and once he sets his mind to something he always achieves it. He feels like he deserves some recognition for his hard work since his retirement. Sitting on the town council would be a badge of honour to add to his many achievements. He can't wait to get there and see his name amongst the others on the boards at City Hall. It might even lead to an MBE later down the line.

Gary allows his mind to drift to a fantasy world where he is King, adored and love by everyone.

Chapter 7

Gary walks out of the blood bank. Things had gone perfectly. He knew that if he timed it right, several acquaintances would be in the queue. After a short chat, he had easily secured two more nominations. That makes nine.

He gets in his car and heads home whistling cheerfully. He slows as he nears the house of Mr Fordy. Only one more nomination and Mr Fordy had been so very grateful on his last visit. The words of his wife pop into his head. He feels a touch of guilt but time has already healed the bulk of it and he's forgotten how terrible he had felt after his last visit. He shakes the remnants off as he pulls his car over and gets out. He heads towards the front door. He rings the bell.

Mr Fordy takes a while to answer the door.

"Oh it's you, Mr Yale. Come in, come in," Mr Fordy smiles with his mouth but there is pain behind his eyes.

Gary notices that his neighbour has aged significantly and that he is wearing a stained shirt. He follows Mr Fordy inside his house and observes the state of the kitchen before Mr Fordy quickly closes the door on it. Bowls and plates with half eaten food are strewn around and a smell emanating. Gary decides it's none of his business unless Mr Fordy asks for help. It would be rude to point it out when Mr Fordy had clearly not wanted him to see it. Besides, it would be an ongoing job which Gary really doesn't have time for. He'll talk to Janet later about tactfully suggesting a cleaner.

They head into the lounge.

"Tea or coffee?" Mr Fordy asks.

"I'm actually okay, I've just had one," Gary lies. A white lie as he wants to spare the old man the embarrassment of dirty cups, or a poorly made beverage. "I just came to check that you were doing okay?" Another lie but he can hardly make his request without some polite chit chat.

"Well, Bertha and I would usually be having coffee about now and it's difficult to face things without her. I remember….."

Gary tunes out as Mr Fordy starts reminiscing once again. He needs to find a subtle way to bring this discussion back to his reason for being here. He remembers some advice he's recently read in a self help book; try to relate the thing you want to talk about to something that is important to the person you're talking to. Mr Fordy is obviously only interested in his late wife Bertha. That is the point of connection.

Suddenly, Gary has a brain wave.

"So, Bertha's funeral is next week, you said?" Gary abruptly cuts into Mr Fordy's stream of consciousness.

The old man's face lights up at the mention of his wife but quickly darkens at the reference to her funeral. "Yes, next Tuesday."

"Is everything planned already? I mean, do you need any help organising any of the speakers or anything?" Gary asks.

"Well our children have done most of it but it has been difficult as they live so far away," Mr Fordy tells him. "I say, would you like to say anything?"

Gary flushes. "Really? I'd be honoured. I could talk about her love of the garden and how we all used to sit outside with a coffee after I'd mowed the lawn."

"Well she did love the garden, but her main passion was reading, she loved poetry. Maybe I can find one of her favourites for you to read," Mr Fordy replies.

"That's very personal, might be better coming from a family member," Gary quickly suggests. "I just remember that she loved the smell of the cut grass and the way the birds twittered in the hedgerow after it had been pruned."

"That's true and she definitely appreciated all the work you did for us. We both recognise that you are a busy man," Mr Fordy says.

Gary takes a breath then goes for it.

"She once said to me that I should run for town council," Gary cringes despite himself. Bertha hadn't quite said this. She'd actually said that she knew someone like Gary who was always helping people who had become a Neighbourhood Watch coordinator. Still, it's not a big leap.

"Oh. She didn't say that to me but it might not be a bad idea. Is it something you've been thinking about then?" Mr Fordy says. He's interested in any of his late wife's wishes, however obscure and irrelevant they may appear.

"Maybe. I think I'd need to be nominated though," Gary says as if he's not really thought it through.

"Well, I know that Bertha was always worried about the speed the cars around here travelled, especially on the stretch of road just outside our house. Would you be able to do something about that if you became a councillor," Mr Fordy asks.

Gary smiles. It wasn't too difficult after all. "Yes, of course. We could also place a bench on the green across the road in her memory if you think she would have liked that?"

Mr Fordy's eyes fill with tears.

Gary feels awkward. He doesn't mention that he plans to use the laying of the bench as a way of drawing attention to his campaign for the council. He knows it will be easy enough to get his own name on the plaque next to Bertha's as the funder and facilitator as he's seen them before.

"So, I'll pop a nomination form in the post for you. I can fill it in for you if you'd like and then you can just sign it?" Gary says. He's already standing up to leave.

Mr Fordy looks confused, "Wait, oh, okay. Yes, that's fine. So, are you going to say anything at the funeral next week?"

"I think it would be better if your family did that. I'll definitely be there though," Gary offers. He's thought better of speaking at the funeral fearing that one of Mr Fordy's children might be suspicious of his motivations; swooping in out of nowhere and giving a form of eulogy when they've never even met him. Besides, he's got what he came for and doesn't want to go overboard. He says goodbye and heads home.

Now for dealing with his wife who he knows will be furious or maybe, he won't tell her. What she doesn't know can't hurt her and she won't care when he gets elected and becomes Councillor Yale.

Chapter 8

Nominations received. Gary is in the running. Janet is even starting to catch the vision and is busying herself with the campaign. Only Sophie seems bemused by the whole idea. She had been even more so when, for the first time in living memory, her grandparents had gotten up early on Sunday and headed to the Parish church.

Afterwards, they had discussed the fantastic building and huge number of prominent people in attendance. Gary had used the opportunity to network and let people know about his campaign.

The vicar, who they had recognised from Annie's funeral, had even been persuaded to allow them to place a flier on the church bulletin board. Gary had pointed out that it wasn't really about politics, but doing good things in the community and helping people. The vicar was very much in favour of these things. In fact, his short sermon had been on that very subject which had definitely helped Gary in his endeavour.

The vicar had flushed slightly when Gary had initially introduced himself and he had made the connection to the recent funeral that he had led. He recalled the urgent young man who had invaded his platform with a grim message of judgement and damnation before he had managed to restore order by moving to the next hymn as quickly as possible.

However, Gary had apologised for his grandson, Grant's "inappropriate outburst" blaming it on overwhelming grief over his mother and assuring the vicar that Grant had since calmed down and reflected on his behaviour. He promised that he would arrange for Grant to apologise himself at some point in the not too distant future knowing that this wouldn't be necessary as it would all be forgotten by then. Just as well, as Grant definitely wouldn't be up for apologising as he still seemed as fanatical as ever.

Still, the situation had been smoothed over with Gary ensuring he made a large public contribution to the collection plate that was passed around. He had achieved his goal and become buddies with another important community figure. He'd even arranged a round of golf, not on Sunday of course, but for later in the week.

Helpfully, through his multi-faith connections, the vicar had also pointed Gary in the right direction for services and gatherings of the Muslims, Buddhists and Hindus. The latter meeting in an upper room in the church each week. In fact, some of the vicar's congregation attended these meetings to learn more about other faiths. The vicar was keen to point out that he intended to get to one in due course and that they had discussed having joint meetings occasionally on a Sunday. But, this had been narrowly voted down by the congregation and someone had sent an anonymous message to the Bishop who had made it clear that such collaborations wouldn't be tolerated under the current C of E regulations.

Gary is pleased that he can kill two birds with one stone by getting involved in this Parish church and congratulates himself on his bright idea of attending in the first place.

Chapter 9

"Did you know you were in the news?" Sophie calls.

"Really, which paper?" Gary asks.

"No, I mean online, the local news on Google," Sophie answers as if it's obvious.

"Oh. What does it say?"

"Just that you've been nominated for town council but it describes you as a prominent figure in the local community as well as a church goer and supporter of other faiths." Sophie laughs. "Yeah, for all of five minutes. And it says here that you've taken in a Ukrainian family. Who are the sources I wonder?"

"Actually, I was asked to write it myself," Gary admits shamefacedly. "But they must've edited it. I said we had applied to host a Ukrainian but I didn't mention a family and didn't say they had arrived, obviously."

"I hope they don't dig into your background and find out you've only just started some of these things. That would be really embarrassing," Sophie says.

"I doubt they'll bother, hon, it's only the local council. Not the office of Prime Minister!" Gary laughs now.

"It's a bit like an MP though isn't it?" asks Janet as she joins their discussion.

"A bit, but on a much lower level and more about the community than politics," Gary says. He really doesn't know the difference but his family don't need to know that.

"I hope you don't have any skeletons in your closet Granddad as I'd hate for all that to be out in public," Sophie worries. "You know, there was an important woman last year who had been speeding but she said she wasn't driving. The police proved she had been and she ended up getting sent to prison!"

"Woah, slow down Soph. I would never do anything like that and it was because she lied and said her husband had been driving, so she was convicted of attempting to pervert the course of justice. She wasn't sent to prison just for speeding," Gary explains. Even as he does so, he remembers including his wife on his car insurance even though she never drives his car as it brought the premium down significantly, and occasionally bringing printer paper home from work when they had run out. These things are not the same though and Gary pushes them out of his mind.

"What about all the drama when you were suspended after that boy said you'd grabbed his arm?" Janet recalls.

"It wasn't proven and the allegation was dropped, you know that, sweetheart," Gary responds.

"I know, but his parents did move him to another school and I think they're still local. You don't think they'll bring it up again when your name's in circulation?" Janet looks anxious.

Gary thinks back to the incident where he had lost his temper with the trouble maker and grabbed his arm leaving a red mark. "Of course not, it was ages ago. If they do, I'll just do what I did then, deny it which is the truth anyway." Gary has become so used to his version of events that it almost feels like he is telling the truth, at least that's what he's convinced himself. His conscience occasionally rears its head but he shoves it back in its box where it belongs.

The phone rings and Janet reaches to answer it.

"Oh hello Mrs Dranty. Oh, they've arrived have they? That's good. Yes, you saw his name in the paper. Thankyou for the nomination, he really appreciates it. No, I'm afraid he's not available at the moment. Yes, okay, no problem." Janet hangs up and turns to Gary who had signalled that he didn't want to speak to their neighbour.

"What did she want?" Gary asks.

"The builders have arrived and she saw your name on the list in the paper. I think she just wanted to let you know that she's going away for a few days as the water will be disconnected. You really should talk to her when she calls next time or go and see her when she's back," Janet encourages. "You need her on side."

"I will, but I don't want to get roped into the building work, or asked to collect supplies or something. You know she'll have me doing little jobs if I go near the place before the work is finished," Gary points out. "She's probably left me a 'to do' list on the fridge!"

"Fair enough, but she's away for now so when the job's done you should get round there. You know what she's like. You don't want her to go off you and start babbling that she nominated you but you've shown no interest in her ever since!" Janet replies.

"Yes dear," Gary says absent mindedly.

Chapter 10

Gary and Sophie head for the front door.

"Where are you going love?" Janet asks.

"I'm going to drive the bus, they changed the day this week because of the bank holiday," Gary answers.

"No, I know about you. I meant Sophie?" Janet says.

"I'm just going to see a friend," Sophie replies vaguely.

"Okay, make sure you're home by ten please sweet," Janet instructs. They barely see their granddaughter these days. It's been several months since she moved in and she's no bother but she isn't around a lot and Janet doesn't really know what she's up to. They've just been so busy getting the campaign up and running.

"Sure, see you later," Sophie says. Moving in with her grandparents has given her freedoms she didn't even know existed and she's enjoying being independent.

Sophie walks to the bus stop and Gary gets the car out of the garage. He's not quick enough though and Mrs Harma calls his name from across the road. Gary has stopped deliberately lingering outside his house in order to be visibly helpful to his neighbours as he has been inundated with requests recently.

"Hi Mrs Harma, I'm just going out, driving the bus for those kids." Gary calls as he tries to head off the conversation but Mrs Harma comes bustling over. She looks worried.

"It's just, you know you said to leave the back garden for the wildlife?"

"Yes, it's lovely isn't it. We enjoy ours," Gary gushes.

"Well, yes, but Roy and Joan are complaining about one of the plants encroaching on their garden. They want me to cut it down as they say it's illegal or something…Could you take a look?" Mrs Harma pleads.

"Let me look later, but I'm sure it's nothing serious," Gary reassures her.

"They used a name big hogweed, I think it was?" Mrs Harma says.

Gary spins around to face her, "Giant hogweed?? Are you sure? Oh dear. Now don't touch it okay?"

"Well I tried pulling it out earlier, but couldn't manage it," Mrs Harma confesses. "What will happen?"

"Did you wear gloves?" Gary asks urgently.

"Of course," Mrs Harma says "But I've been feeling a bit itchy and my hands and arms are all red now." She shows her sore arms to Gary.

"Go and have a bath or shower and change your clothes. You really need to get any bits of the plant off you. It's really quite dangerous," Gary advises. He knows all about this plant and the damage it can cause.

Mrs Harma looks petrified.

"What will it do. You're frightening me."

"I'll go and get Janet. I really have to go," Gary says.

He knocks on his own front door, explains things to his wife and reminds her that Mrs Harma has nominated him, then leaves her to deal with the situation as he heads off to drive the bus.

"Oh, if only I'd known that this plant was dangerous. I would have got rid of it or got it sorted out before it got so big," Mrs Harma moans to Janet.

"Tell you what, you really need to go and have a shower and change as Gary said. I'll have a look in your garden whilst you're doing that and we'll see what we can do. How's that?"Janet asks.

"Okay, my arms are itching so maybe a shower will help."

Janet wanders around to their neighbour's back garden as Mrs Harma heads indoors for a shower.

Janet gasps when she sees the totally overgrown and unmanageable state of the forest that has sprung up across the road. How had they not realised and why had Gary allowed it to get to this impossible position? She had thought her husband's tricks to get out of dealing with Mrs Harma's lawn were amusing but now, she feels desperately sorry for the old lady, as well as wondering how on earth it can be rectified without costing the earth.

Walking around, she sees a small quantity of the infamous giant hogweed recognisable for its cow parsley like appearance. Then, she sees something even more alarming, a plant she identifies as Japanese knotweed is growing in abundance all across the garden. It has invaded all the other plants and is up against Roy and Joan's fence. No doubt, the roots have already travelled.

Mrs Harma appears beside her, fresh and clean from her shower, although her arms still look swollen.

"Can you see it? Is it that?" She points to the giant hogweed.

"Well, yes, that's a problem. But I'm afraid you've also got Japanese knotweed everywhere," Janet says slowly trying to keep her tone even so as not to alarm her neighbour further.

"Is that bad?" Mrs Harma has no idea.

"It will need removing. Both plants will need to be destroyed as they are invasive and get out of control very quickly," Janet tells her. "You won't be able to do it yourself. It will need specialists with their equipment and chemical sprays."

"Oh no, but what about my wildlife?" Mrs Harma is crestfallen "Will it be expensive?" she asks as an afterthought.

"I'm sorry but your wildlife will probably be taken out with the weeds and yes it will be very expensive." Janet puts her arm around the lady as she delivers the double blow.

"Oh no," Mrs Harma sits down heavily on a garden chair.

"Shall I call an expert and try and get a quote? I can ask whether there's any way to preserve some of your garden," Janet suggests. She already knows what the expert will say; that the garden is way too overgrown and out of control for anything but total obliteration but she wants to give some hope to the old lady whose life is wrapped up in her garden. She hopes she can convince the expert not to hint that if the garden had been taken care of properly in the first place, this may not have been necessary.

"Yes, please do," Mrs Harma says gratefully.

Janet heads back across the road to make the call leaving Mrs Harma to grieve the loss of her pride and joy.

Chapter 11

"BOOM!" The sound is so loud that Gary and Janet, who had been sipping coffee in their back garden, jump to their feet and automatically look to the sky.

A plume of smoke is rising from a house a few doors down on their side of the street. They rush down their garden path to the front of their house and, joining other residents similarly concerned, run towards the source of the noise.

"WHAT?" Gary exclaims.

Everyone has stopped short of the site. There is a collective disbelief as the residents of Gorse Close stare at the pile of rubble that had been Mrs Dranty's detached house. The smoke and dust linger in the air and there are no recognisable items on display.

Looking around in dismay, Gary sees the builders leaning against a small white van a short distance from the explosion. They had been drinking tea, but their cups are smashed on the ground. They also appear to be in shock and have made no effort to move towards the collapsed building. There is a deathly silence.

"WAS ANYONE IN THERE?" A shout from a neighbour.

"No, the old lady went away for a few days," one of the builder's finds his voice as he continues to stare at the devastation.

"What happened?"

"Is anyone hurt?"

"Has someone called the police?"

"What about the gas board? It must be a gas explosion."

The voices begin to clamour as people demand answers. No explanations are offered. In the confusion, the builders regain their faculties and quietly enter the small white van, then slip almost unnoticed from the scene.

"Wait, don't let them leave."

"Did someone get the registration?"

"Who are they?"

"Who do they work for?"

"Who hired them?"

Gary watches the white van as it reaches the end of the street, then he grabs Janet by the arm and pulls her back along the pavement to their house.

Once inside, he breathes a sigh of relief. "She must've used different builders as they weren't the ones I recommended."

Janet stares at him.

"Really? Is that what you're thinking about right now? What about the danger of the explosion? What about the fact that Mrs Dranty's entire life has just been destroyed in five seconds flat? Sometimes, I don't think I know who you are!"

"Well of course I'm thinking about those things but we know Mrs Dranty is away, the builders were having a tea break by the look of it and no one was injured. I'd say that's pretty lucky," Gary says, slightly less confidently after being rebuked by his wife.

"So, I guess now it's time to make sure Gary Yale's campaign hasn't been damaged," Janet says in a tone that he hasn't heard before.

"Yes, exactly. Reputation is everything at the moment and things like this could be disastrous if they go the wrong way." Gary hasn't sensed the exasperation in her tone and is oblivious to her feelings on the subject.

"More disastrous than your house exploding resulting in homelessness and possible bankruptcy, not to mention if anyone decides to sue for shock, stress or potential injury? I hope someone has the right insurance…" Janet's voice is rising as she lists the consequences.

Gary is unknowingly treading on thin ice. "Well, no, of course not. I wonder why she didn't use the builders I recommended."

"ENOUGH. Enough about the stupid builders and your worthless campaign. I'm going to go and find out if Mrs Dranty has been told what's happened and make sure the news is broken gently. You can stay here thinking about yourself if you want but I've had enough!" Janet angrily pushes past Gary who is left with his mouth hanging open. He hadn't realised that his wife was angry, make that furious. He's never seen her like this and it scares him.

"Wait! Make sure you tell her that it wasn't the builders I recommended," Gary calls after her. Apparently, he can't help himself.

Janet turns and gives him a look that suggests *she* is about to explode before heading out of the front door.

His wife out of the way, Gary sets about minimising the damage. He calls his builders to find out why they hadn't taken the job.

"Hey Adam, you know that job I offered you, yeah the bathroom at the little old lady's house?" Gary says.

"Oh hi, Gary. Yeah sorry I wasn't there today, I had an appointment. Hope it's all going well, though?"

Gary feels his stomach drop and the bile rising in his throat.

"Wait. So it was your team at the house today?" he manages.

"Well, who else did you think it would be? You gave us the job!" Adam laughs.

"Oh no no no no," Gary moans.

"What's the matter?" Adam says. "Did they arrive late, or spill coffee on someone's carpet?" he laughs again.

"You really don't know?" Gary says. "They blew up the house!!"

There is silence.

"What? What on earth? I hope this is a joke. It's not really funny though mate!" Adam says.

"I'm deadly serious. The whole house exploded then collapsed. Maybe a gas leak. You'd best get on to your insurance asap," Gary advises.

"Wait, was anyone hurt? The boys? Or the lady? Anyone? No, wait, the lady went away didn't she?" Adam starts to panic.

"No one was hurt as far as we could tell. Your lads were on a tea break near their van but it's total destruction city there mate," Gary informs him. "Expensive mistake. How long have those guys been working for you?"

"They're new," Adam admits. "I thought it'd be okay as it was a simple job and I was only gone for a day."

"It gets worse. I don't think they hung around afterwards. They shot off without waiting for the police, or anyone," Gary says.

"Oh man. They probably didn't know what to do and panicked. I'll come over there right now," Adam says.

"Listen mate, I know this probably isn't the right time but is there any way you could keep our association quiet, you know I'm running for the council," Gary asks desperately.

"Seems a little unimportant right now, but sure. I'll pretend I don't know you." Adam shakes his head in disgust as he hangs up.

Janet reaches Mrs Dranty and helps her make arrangements to stay in alternative accommodation. Initially, she had offered for her to stay with them, but Mrs Dranty was reluctant to impose herself. She also seems to have forgotten that it was Gary who had recommended the builders in the first place, at least she doesn't mention it to Janet.

Adam Daily arrives at the scene and assesses the damage. He does have insurance that will cover his worker's incompetence but he is appalled at the mess and shocked by the scale of the destruction. He is relieved that no one was hurt but also realises that it was a close call and he will be forced to dismiss some, or all of his workers. In fact, the insurance claim puts him out of business.

As requested, he doesn't mention his connection with Gary Yale, no matter how tempting it might be to put a permanent spanner in the works of his acquaintance's campaign.

Chapter 12

Over the next few months, the settlement is agreed, the house is rebuilt and Mrs Dranty moves in to a new-build with all the mod cons that she had been lacking before. She seems pleased with the arrangement, the insurance even having footed the hotel bill as she had nowhere else to stay. She doesn't like the colour of her front door but that's a small price to pay in the big scheme of things.

Meanwhile, Mrs Harma, with Janet's help, has had the council round to do extensive work in her garden. Due to her low income it has all been done for free. The giant hogweed and Japanese knotweed have been destroyed (for now) and there is some wildlife left. They have planted some new species and she is eagerly awaiting their growth in the Spring.

Ron and Joan, next door, are satisfied that she didn't intentionally allow her weeds to overrun her garden and are happy that the situation has now been resolved. They are all on good terms once again.

Mr Fordy is pleased when the promised bench in memory of his late wife Bertha appears on the green opposite his house. He notes that the name of Gary Yale looms large beside it, but he's sure this was probably a legal requirement documenting the funding source. He often sits on the bench reminiscing about his late wife. Nothing has been done about the speeding in his road, but he assumes this will happen if, and when Gary becomes Councillor Yale.

None of them have seen or heard from Gary since he secured their nominations. He seems to have disappeared completely. None of them really blame him for the various calamities that have befallen them, but they do sometimes wonder whether he is really the trustworthy individual he makes himself out to be.

They also wonder whether they should have been so quick to nominate him for the local council. They all follow the local news and are aware that the election will be held very soon. Having previously been rooting for Gary, they now feel indifferent about the result.

Chapter 13

Gary sits at home. He is nervously awaiting the election result.

He decides to check their joint email account once again. There are no new messages but he does notice something in the draft folder that hadn't been there before. He opens it. It's an application to host a Ukrainian. Gary is confused. Why is this in his draft folder, it was sent months ago. Wasn't it?

"Janet, can you come here for a second?" Gary calls.

Janet has long since calmed down after her furious exit to clear up her husband's mess and properly deal with Mrs Dranty several months ago.

She appears.

"Why is this in our draft folder?" Gary points to the application.

Janet puts on her glasses and squints at the tiny writing.

"Oh, yes. I remember that. It's the application for a Ukrainian refugee. I was wondering the other day why we haven't heard anything yet," Janet says.

"I know what it is! I mean, why is it here, in our drafts folder? That means it was never sent," Gary says, trying to remain calm.

"Oh, you know me and technology. But I definitely sent it," Janet breezes.

"You definitely didn't!" Gary exclaims. "Have you any idea what this is going to do to me if I'm elected??"

"What do you mean? Oh, because you've told them all that you're going to be receiving Ukrainians?" Janet suddenly twigs.

"Not only that, but some of the papers think we've already got some. I didn't bother to correct them as at least we'd applied. But now we haven't even done that. What a disaster!" Gary is dismayed.

"Why don't we just apply now?" Janet says, trying to helpful.

"That's not the point. It'll look as if I lied. I've already had to hide away for months to avoid our neighbours. Now, it'll be even worse."

Gary feels the weight of the world on his shoulders. He's also been attacked for attending services for all the different faiths. They're *all* offended as they say he isn't really committed to any of them and his attendance is a shallow gesture. The person who wrote the original article suggesting that aspiring councillors should attend multi faith meetings hadn't mentioned that this might be the outcome so Gary feels aggrieved. He was just trying to respect diversity.

The small church that hosts the drop in are also annoyed that Gary isn't attending *their* services. They saw in the media that he is now attending the much larger Parish church around the corner and don't understand why he doesn't join them on Sundays as he's already involved in their work.

Gary's campaign website is up and running but keeps getting hacked and he's had to close the message board due to spam and vicious messages being frequently posted including several that have threatened to kill him.

Gary is still rushing around helping with community projects but he's now attending far more meetings than anything else. He often finds that he has no idea how to even begin solving some of the problems that arise. Not finding a solution seems to anger people. The anger is often directed at him as the one who has failed to come up with a workable solution.

Gary is also living in fear that his son Dean's alcoholism and wild behaviour will taint him by association. To date, Dean hasn't done anything criminal, as far as he's aware, but his son has definitely reverted to teenage behaviour, is often drunk and is spending lavishly.

Grant too, now with no suitable role model, has moved beyond his religious phase and is venturing down a dubious path. Although, Gary feels this might be better for his grandson, at least more in keeping with his age, than the Christian fanaticism he had been displaying before, he is concerned about negative publicity.

Although he won't admit it to anyone, Gary sometimes wishes he had never started the election campaign. He had been happier when he was just pootling around and helping his neighbours every so often. The campaign has taken on a life of its own and has taken over everything. Gary feels the pressure of other people's expectations. He knows it is also negatively affecting Janet who is often rushing around on his behalf.

Nevertheless, he can't bring himself to pull out when he is so close to victory. He still relishes the thought of the power that will come with the role. He longs to be well thought of and for people to see that he really is a good person. If he can just distance himself from those who've seen him mess up and know he's fallible, and if people would give him a chance, he will be a great councillor and everything will be all right in the end.

Chapter 14

The election result is in! Gary will become Councillor Yale. It seems his lack of transparency regarding the hosting of a Ukrainian family hasn't affected his chances, nor his involvement in the various disasters of his neighbours, not his suspension on suspicion of assaulting a pupil all those years ago, and not even the wild behaviour of his relatives. Either people don't know, or they just don't care. The verdict is in and Gary is basically a good guy.

They celebrate with lobster and champagne at Gary's favourite restaurant. Gary decides not to dwell on the narrowness of his victory. A victory is a victory and he deserves some good fortune after all he has suffered.

They are just tucking in to their hearty meal when Janet points across the restaurant to a small table with a lone figure.

"It's Mr Fordy," she mouths.

Gary sighs. "Has he seen us?" he asks. "I forgot to talk to you about arranging a cleaner. His place was a real mess when I went there last time."

"Oh? When was that?" Janet asks, surprised. "I thought the last time you saw him was when Bertha had just died. I didn't think you'd even been to Bertha's funeral, did you?"

"No, I couldn't make it as something else came up," Gary lies and suddenly remembers that he hasn't told Janet that, going explicitly against her wishes, he had secured his final nomination from the *very* recently bereaved Mr Fordy. "I went round there another time to see how he was."

"He looks okay," Janet observes. "Oh, look. He's coming over."

"Congratulations Councillor Yale," Mr Fordy says as he arrives at their table. "And thankyou for the bench, it's a nice memorial. Remember you promised to do something about the speeding as well. Nice seeing you both." He hobbles out of the restaurant.

"Bench? Speeding thing? Memorial?" Janet says. She looks totally baffled.

"Yes. Just a few things he asked for if I became councillor," Gary waits for his wife to figure it out knowing she will. He braces himself for the tongue lashing.

Janet face changes to thunder. "I don't believe it. You actually asked for his nomination when he'd just lost Bertha. What is wrong with you?"

"It worked out okay and I will do something about the speeding when I get a chance," Gary says. "Look, it wasn't my fault Bertha died and Mr Fordy's never blamed me for not taking him to the hospital. I don't really think I did anything wrong."

"You never do," Janet mumbles and looks away. She's been forced on many occasions to intervene to protect her husband's reputation and she's fed up of him justifying himself.

Gary knows what she's thinking.

"I just try to help people and sometimes things go wrong, or people don't like the result, or they want more than I can give. Should I just not get involved and leave them to their own devices?"

"I don't know, dear. I just feel that I spend a lot of time defending you and trying to make sure people understand that your motivations are good. But watching the way you went about winning this campaign sometimes makes me wonder whether I know the real you at all," Janet says wearily.

"What do you mean?" Gary asks, he is on edge.

"Well, things like using our kindness to Sophie to show that you are a family man when really any grandparents would have done the same thing, and pretending that we hadn't been selected to host a refugee when we actually hadn't submitted the application, and a hundred and one other things like that. Is it really all worth it, all the pretence and using people, just to get to the top?" Janet feels that for herself it hasn't been worth it and she'd rather they could revert back to how they were before.

"I can explain all of those things and I did them for the right reasons. You'll see that none of them were really my fault and at least I'm not a criminal. You saw some of the things that came out above some of the other candidates. At least I try to do the right thing and I'm sure I've helped more people than not," Gary finishes.

Janet stares at her husband and they finish their meal in silence.

Chapter 15

Councillor Yale sits on a park bench. He's feeling slightly woozy having just given blood but is proudly wearing the badge that announces that he is a "Super Donor". He feels good about his morning's work and is heading to a Council meeting in an hour or so. The sun is shining and the birds are twittering away. It's quite pleasant.

Now, he is rudely interrupted. He opens his eyes to find someone standing directly in front of him, blocking the sunlight that he had been enjoying. A youngish girl holding a piece of paper is hovering awkwardly.

"Hi, I'm sorry to disturb you. Would you like a Christian leaflet?" The girl asks cheerfully with a smile.

Gary remembers his new title and responds politely, as a councillor should,

"Well, I think perhaps you'd better give that to someone else. I'm a Christian already. Thankyou, though."

"Oh, okay. Can I ask how long you've been a Christian for?" The girl looks genuinely interested and doesn't seem at all put out by his refusal of the leaflet.

Gary wasn't expecting the question, he hesitates,

"Well, all my life. This is a Christian country after all," he says.

"I became a Christian when I was 23," the girl responds.

"What were you before that?" Gary asks confused.

"A non-Christian or someone who didn't believe," the girl replies. "Can I ask you what you think the Christian faith is all about? I mean, what is the key message?"

Gary is starting to feel flustered by the questions and this over confident girl who seems to think he is deficient in some way. It's making him a little uncomfortable.

"Well, it's about loving your neighbour, going to church, praying and doing good to everyone. I'm a councillor, I go to church every week....and I was christened." Gary adds the last feeling that it won't hurt his case. He feels sure this girl will leave him alone now that he's proven himself, but she is staring down at him with what looks like pity!?

"It sounds like you do a lot of good. Do you think you will get to Heaven?" the girl asks.

"That's a bit deep isn't it? If there is such a place, yes I've done my bit," Gary answers confidently.

"But are you sure? I mean, how good do you have to be? How do you think God decides who He lets in?" the girl persists.

Gary is feeling irritated. Who is this girl to judge him, a well respected councillor, at least twice her age. "Yes, I'm sure, are *you* sure?"

"Yes, I'm sure," the girl matches Gary's confidence but he no longer feels confident. The girl is unsettling him.

"What have you done? I've helped people all my life, given to charity, driven mini buses for special needs kids, helped at a drop in and soup kitchen, wanted to host a Ukrainian refugee (he can't quite bring himself to lie to this girl), supported my family, and I'm a Super Donor." He points to his badge but even as he does this he feels a bit pathetic knowing he doesn't have to prove anything to this stranger in the park, but feeling inexplicably compelled to do so.

"It's not a competition. I was trying to show you that being a good person isn't what it's all about. God doesn't judge us based on whether we are good or not. If He did then we all fail and none of us would get to Heaven," the girl has sat on the bench and seems determined to continue this conversation.

At least she's out of his sun now. Gary looks at his watch. He doesn't need to be anywhere just yet. He might as well finish this. He feels sure he can beat this young girl at her own game.

"Didn't Jesus say that we should love God and love our neighbour. Those are the greatest commandments, right?" Gary asks.

"Well, yes, but we can't love God or our neighbour perfectly all of the time. That's the point. We aren't perfect and God's standard is perfection. He gave us the law to show us that we can't live up to it," the girl explains.

"Nonsense. What's the point in having rules if they can't be followed. That's not right, besides I follow the rules and compared to everyone else, I'm a good person. I'm sure of it. That's why I was elected to be a councillor because I'm a pillar of the community," Gary says proudly. As he says this, he is reminded of his underhand tactics in securing some of his nominations and of the various issues that have arisen due to his selfish motivations. He pushes this out of his mind. This girl doesn't know anything about him.

"Compared to God, none of us are good. The Bible says that if we say we haven't sinned we are saying that God is a liar and the truth isn't in us," the girl says softly. She looks at Gary intently.

"I'm not saying that I never do anything wrong, just that compared to others I'm pretty good and I'm sure the Man Upstairs, if he exists, will let me into Heaven, if there's such a place," Gary says, "In fact, I reckon they'll be over the moon to see me on that day!"

The girl winces and her expression changes. She stands up.

"I have to warn you that you're on the wrong path. I don't mean to be disrespectful as you clearly have more life experience than me. There are two types of people in Heaven, perfect which none of us are and forgiven. I've been forgiven by trusting that Jesus died for me on the cross and….."

Gary cuts across her, "I've heard this nonsense before. I don't care to hear it again and certainly not from the likes of a young girl like you. I don't know who you think you are. I'm a respected councillor! How dare you tell me that I'm on the wrong path."

"I'm sorry for upsetting you, Sir. I hope that one day you'll understand why I tried to tell you the truth. I don't usually give this booklet to people as it contains a tough message, but I believe it is what God wants to say to you today." The girl places a small blue booklet next to him on the bench. She quickly walks away.

Gary huffs to himself about the audacity of the girl. He glances at the booklet realising that now that she's left it next to him he'll either have to take it with him, or find a bin. He can't just leave it there, or do what he really wants to do and tear it up and throw it back at the girl as someone will report him for littering. Besides, she's nowhere to be seen.

He's also curious about her last statement that the booklet contains a tough message. Gary is brave enough for anything and feels sure that nothing contained within a small booklet written by a religious zealot will phase him.

He picks the booklet up and reads the front cover.

"The Parable of the Pharisee and the Tax Collector (Luke 18 vs 9-14)"

Gary has never heard this story before so, intrigued, he turns the page and reads the following:

"To some who were confident of their own righteousness and looked down on everyone else, Jesus told this parable:'Two men went up to the temple to pray, one a Pharisee and the other a tax collector. The Pharisee stood by himself and prayed:'God, I thank you that I am not like other people— robbers, evildoers, adulterers— or even like this tax collector. I fast twice a week and give a tenth of all I get.' But the tax collector stood at a distance. He would not even look up to heaven, but beat his breast and said, 'God, have mercy on me, a sinner.' I tell you that this man, rather than the other, went home

justified before God. For all those who exalt themselves will be humbled, and those who humble themselves will be exalted."

Note to Reader

Gary Yale appears to be an upstanding citizen. Since his retirement, he has been tirelessly helping others. However, he often acts without consideration for his wife and most of the time his motivations are selfish.

Gary wants to be popular, well-thought of and a pillar in the local community. He's happy to use people that cross his path in order to succeed. Over time, his conscience is dulled and he feels less and less guilty about his actions.

When Gary's corner cutting and lies catch up with him, he distances himself from the mess and blames others. He is self satisfied, looking down on and judging others, and thinking of himself as basically a good guy.

At the end of the story, Gary is confronted by a Christian who, not knowing anything about him, expresses some truths that he finds uncomfortable and therefore refuses to hear.

Many of us are just like Gary, we may not do things in the same way, or to the same extent, but we often have mixed, or wrong motivations for our good deeds. We may go through religious rituals, or claim to be obeying God, but who are we really serving?

The Bible tells us the truth; we cannot restore our broken relationship with God, or find peace with Him by doing good deeds. No matter how much good we do, it will never make up for the wrong we have done. Our goodness is always tainted by sin.

Gary refused to hear the answer to his sin problem. He didn't even accept that he had a problem preferring to justify himself. We aren't told whether Gary recognised himself in the parable at the end, but unless he is willing to humble himself and ask God for forgiveness, he will face an angry God on Judgement Day.

The parable of the *Pharisee and the Tax Collector* is an illustration Jesus used to highlight the offence of self righteousness to God. The Pharisee, rather than praying, is essentially talking to himself about how good he thinks he is, whilst the tax collector recognises his sin and humbles himself before a Holy God, pleading for mercy. God justifies and forgives the tax collector but not the Pharisee.

Those who are forgiven will go to Heaven, not on the basis of their good works, but because they have believed that Jesus died on the cross for them and have received his perfect life as a free gift. It is on this basis only that we can be made right with God and have a home in Heaven.

Will you humble yourself like the tax collector or stand on your pride and self righteousness like Gary and the Pharisee?

DARE TO BE DIFFERENT

A Short Story of Choices and Consequences

NATALIE VELLACOTT

Chapter 1

Sophie feels the waves of the music wash over her as she sways to the soft, repetitive rhythm. Her eyes are closed, she is emptying her mind of everything but the sound.

"*Jesus, Jesus, Jesus, Jesus.....*" Others in the room are losing themselves as well as they chant the name of the one they are worshipping.

"Don't worry, just let go and let God," a male voice whispers in Sophie's ear.

She feels the lightest touch on her forehead and disorientated, she starts falling backwards. Her eyes flick open in panic but someone catches her in the nick of time and gently lowers her to the ground. From her new position, lying on the comfortable carpet, she looks around, at least half of the youth at the meeting are now on the floor.

The music continues, interspersed with hysterical laughter that appears to be coming from a boy Sophie knows as Damien, he is in her class at school. Several adults approach him and lay their hands on his head as he writhes on the floor. Their heads are bowed and Sophie isn't sure what they are doing. After a few seconds, one of the adults collapses and starts rolling around next to Damien. She too is laughing hysterically.

The rest of the room is oblivious as they are all caught up in their own mystical experiences.

After an hour or so, the music winds down, people start to awaken from their trances, shaking their heads as they get to their feet. Most of those who haven't ended up on the floor look bewildered and anxious, like they have missed out on something amazing.

A good looking man, in his early twenties, heads up on the stage and takes the microphone. "Right guys, that's it for this week. It's incredible what the spirit can do when we ask him, isn't it? If anyone didn't feel it tonight, make sure to chat to one of us about what you can do to speed up the process. Sometimes, we are putting up barriers we aren't even aware of and it might even be that you have a spirit of bondage or oppression that you need to be freed from. Make sure to join us again next week and we'll see you at worship on Sunday."

Sophie gazes at her youth leader, Most of the girls have a crush on him and, despite being married, he seems to enjoy the attention. She floats towards the door, still in something of a daze.

Finally, after weeks of praying and hoping, it has happened. She has been "slain in the spirit". She had felt the power coursing through her veins, it was unstoppable and a little uncomfortable. She didn't like the feeling of being so out of control, but her friends had already reassured her that this was normal and that she would get used to it.

"Wow, so it happened at last!" Amanda rushes over to Sophie and grabs her arm.

Sophie jumps, the loud noise of her friend awaking her from her reverie.

"Yeah, it was awesome," Sophie gushes, knowing this is what Amanda is expecting.

"I told you, it's the best, and now that it's happened, you've opened the way for even better experiences," Amanda grins as they head out of the church.

Sophie doesn't say anything else. She is thinking though and questions have started to arise. Questions that she doesn't know the answers to; if the power was from God, why wasn't everyone affected in the same way? Is this really what God wants from them? What did the youth leader mean when he spoke about bondage and oppression? It sounded scary. More significantly, had she really been "slain in the spirit" or had she been pushed, lost her balance and fallen over?

Chapter 2

"Hey love, hurry, you'll be late for school," Janet calls to her granddaughter.

"It's okay Gran, I'm ready," Sophie responds a little testily. She's been living with her grandparents for nearly a year since the death of her mother, her father having reverted to a teenage partying lifestyle and seemingly unable, or unwilling to care for her.

"Just try and come straight home from school today, remember that your granddad is having the photos taken for his election campaign and he wants us both to be included," Janet reminds her. She feels a little guilty that Sophie is being dragged into Gary's attempts to become a town councillor, but it was inevitable after he told the media that they had generously taken in their granddaughter.

"Sure, no problem," Sophie replies absent-mindedly as she heads out of the door.

Rather than being annoyed by the possibility that her grandparents, more specifically her grandfather, is using her, Sophie finds it all quite amusing. She couldn't care less about politics, but she is interested in human rights and climate change. Gary has assured her that his campaign will address these issues and has said repeatedly that he really wants to make a difference in the ordinary lives of local people.

Sophie arrives at the bus stop just as the bus is pulling up. She shows her student ID to the driver and gets on, taking a seat next to her friend Jamie.

"Hiya, what's new?" Jamie greets her.

"Not much although you missed an awesome meeting last night," Sophie enthuses.

Jamie pauses, she looks a little uncomfortable, "Oh. I had stuff to do. I'll be there next week. What happened then?"

"Same as usual for worship night, but I was finally 'slain in the spirit', you know like you were that time."

"Actually, to be honest, that's why I couldn't make it. When I told my mum about that, she said it sounded like a cult and told me I can't go anymore." Jamie looks down.

"What!? That's crazy! A cult? Cults are like where people make vows and sacrifices and stuff and then threaten all sorts of bad things when you want to leave. Aren't they?" Sophie is genuinely confused, she has never considered how their church group activities might appear to someone looking in from outside.

"I guess it is kind of odd and the more I think about it, the more weird the whole "slaying in the spirit" thing seems. I just can't see the benefit of it for anyone," Jamie says hesitantly.

"It's not just about that, though. It's worshipping God with freedom and its exciting to see where He leads," Sophie defends her youth group.

"I also feel weird about John. He's married, right?" Jamie asks although she knows the answer.

"Yes, just for two years, though and they don't have any kids," Sophie isn't sure why the extra information is relevant but she adds it anyway.

"He always stares at me intently when he's speaking, you know the look. It feels wrong, somehow and I've seen him doing it to other girls. I think he likes the attention he gets and he never wears his wedding ring to youth group," Jamie points out.

"I think it just gets in the way when we're playing games and things, but yeah I do know what you mean. I wonder if he would be like that with his wife around," Sophie ponders.

"Why doesn't she come?" Jamie asks.

"I don't know. I've not even seen her in church for quite a while actually. Someone said she had gone to see her family for a while," Sophie feels guilty as she thinks of the admiration she has for John, along with half the group, mind you. She changes the subject, "You're still coming on Sundays, though?"

"I don't know. My family are already irritated because they want us to go out together at the weekends, you know BBQ's and beaches in the hot weather. I think I'll just have to cool it for now. God understands though, right?"

"Of course. We're not under law, but under grace. Jesus came to set us free from all the old rules, that's the good news and technically you don't have to go to church to be a Christian." Sophie says this with growing confidence as she recalls her pastor's sermon the previous week.

Chapter 3

Sophie, Jamie and Amanda, along with most of their class, sit around a large table in the school canteen at lunch.

"Hey guys, did you see the fliers for the beach and BBQ party on Sunday? It's for Jo's 16th and everyone's invited if you bring your own food and booze," Amanda says enthusiastically.

"I did. I was thinking we could go after church as Jo and her clan will probably be at the meeting first anyway," Sophie suggests.

She can't help but think that God has done something incredible amongst her classmates over the past year or so. It had started with just a few of them attending the large and vibrant, Church of the Living Water, but the services have now become so popular that it can be difficult to get a seat.

The leadership had discussed removing the seats completely to accommodate the growing numbers of young people, but the suggestion was swiftly vetoed by a few faithful stick in the muds who make no secret of the fact that they are dismayed at what is happening to their church. Nevertheless, they refuse to move on, as they were there first.

The challenge of the sudden influx of young people has instead been dealt with by adding a mid week worship night, as well as other more social activities. On Sundays, whilst sticking with a broadly traditional schedule, the guest preachers have become younger and more trendy, the sermons are shorter and more topic based to ensure relevancy, and to allow time for the worship band to work up an atmosphere as they perform.

Sophie loves it; the constant activities and being always surrounded by like-minded people, she never feels lonely and there's always things to do. She wishes she'd got involved in church earlier, but it had only been at her mum's funeral that she had seriously thought about it for the first time.

At first, she had been bullied for her new-found interest in religion. She had nearly abandoned church completely as it had all seemed too difficult. But that was before her classmates became interested in the fun activities that the church was hosting. Now, at least one of the bullies actually attends the youth group as well and has apologised to Sophie for her previous behaviour.

"Let's all go. We can be there by 12 if we go to the early service. Then, we won't miss any of the fun," Tommy, a slightly older boy who is being forced to repeat his final year, chimes in.

"Wait, who's going to get the alcohol?" Jamie asks.

"I thought your parents wanted you to do stuff with them at the weekends?" Sophie whispers to her friend.

"They'll be okay as a one off," Jamie replies sheepishly.

Sophie realises that the "family day" excuse was just that, an excuse to get their daughter out of the suspected cult. She feels embarrassed but it's not worth making a meal out of it. Besides, she has something more important to talk to her friend about:

"Do you think Jordan will be there?" she whispers trying to keep her tone casual as she refers to Jamie's older brother.

"Probably, he and his college mates always hang out down there at the weekends. They're a sad bunch, though. Why do you ask?" Jamie isn't suspicious as she sees her older brother as a nerd and hasn't even considered that he might be an object of desire to anyone of the opposite sex.

"Just wondered, I wanted to give him back the game he lent me a month or so ago," Sophie tries not to let her voice betray her as she offers an innocent explanation.

"Oh, whatever. Just leave it at the house next time you're round. It's not important," Jamie says dismissively. "We need to get to class, I'll see you later."

Sophie heads to history but spends the rest of the afternoon daydreaming about Jordan and counting down the hours until she'll see him on Sunday.

Chapter 4

"What's the matter?" Sophie asks as she picks up the call from her brother, Grant. She knows something must be wrong as he rarely calls since she moved out to live with their grandparents.

"I just need to see you, that's all. Can we meet?" Grant says urgently.

"I guess. I'm pretty busy though with everything. You're the driver, why don't you pick me up after school and we can chat. Maybe at KFC?" Sophie says hopefully, taking advantage of her brother's apparent desperation to see her.

"Yeah, that's fine, I don't have lectures this afternoon. I'll be at the gates at 3.30. Don't be late, it's important," Grant says mysteriously and hangs up.

Sophie is slightly worried but more than that she is curious. She's sure it can't be anything too bad as he surely would have told her on the phone. But, she hasn't seen or heard from him for months and she's occasionally overheard her grandparents talking about his increasingly wild behaviour.

She had been shocked at first as the last time they had spoken, he had seemed to be on the straight and narrow and encouraging her to go to church.

However, her own life had taken over and she didn't have time to waste worrying about her older brother especially now that they were living under different roofs. It was more a case of out of sight, out of mind rather than deliberate disinterest.

Now, though, she wonders what it could possibly be about. She glances at the wall clock as she arrives at her English lesson. It's already 2.30, only an hour to wait and it's Friday….she tunes out and starts daydreaming about her friend's older brother again.

"Right, let's go to KFC if that's what you want to do?" Grant says as he collects her from school.

"Awesome, thanks," Sophie says. She had enjoyed the attention that being picked up from the school gates by someone other than a parent had created, even if it was only her brother and he was driving a Fiesta.

"What's the problem, then?" Sophie can't wait any longer to at least establish the topic of concern. She notices a nasty smell emanating from the back of his car and wrinkles her nose.

"We'll talk when we've got some food but it's Dad," Grant says, his mouth fixed in a firm line.

Sophie notices the dark circles under her brother's eyes and his dishevelled appearance. She glances around for the source of the smell and sees bedding, clothes and bits of old food in the back of the car.

Sophie nods and falls silent. She really hopes her brother hasn't been sleeping in his car, but the evidence suggests otherwise.

They arrive at KFC and Grant orders their food. They sit in a booth.

"How bad is he?" Sophie asks as they wait.

"Pretty. He's drunk most of the time and I think he's addicted to gambling too. It's the will that's done it; such a lot of money with no conditions and all in one go," Grant sighs heavily.

"Why have you been sleeping in your car?" Sophie asks bluntly.

"Oh, that's not me. It's Dad. I got fed up of him coming home wasted in the middle of the night and trashing things. He lost his key so I told him I'd leave my car unlocked and he could crash there. I didn't expect him to take me up on it, but he's done it a lot and he always leaves the takeaway remnants behind, hence the smell, sorry…." Grant explains.

"It's like he's a tramp," Sophie tries not to respond with disgust as she listens to her father's latest embarrassing behaviour. "I don't understand why he can't sort himself out. It's been a year and their marriage wasn't great anyway. It can't be grief, is it?"

"I don't know. I think he under estimated how much Mum did for him and, despite their problems, I think he loved her in his own way. Now, the novelty of being single and rich has worn off and he's struggling," Grant says.

"Well, what do you want me to do about it?" Sophie can't really understand why her brother has dragged her into this, she's just a school girl and would rather have remained in ignorance.

"I wanted your advice about getting Gran and Granddad to try and help him?" Grant says.

Sophie realises the situation must be serious as there's no way that Grant would be suggesting this unless it's a last resort.

"No, that definitely won't be a good idea. You know that Granddad is trying to get elected to the council. There's no way he'll risk tainting himself by getting involved at the moment. He'd only do it if it could all be anonymous and kept secret but that's not likely as he's courting publicity for his campaign," Sophie fills her brother in.

"Oh man. I completely forgot about all that. No, that definitely won't work. I just don't know what else to do," Grant looks dejected.

Their food arrives and Sophie thinks for a few seconds:

"What about your church? Your pastor was always helpful, wasn't he?" Even as she says it, she knows that Grant won't be receptive to this idea.

"Well, I'm not really involved in the church any more so I can't ask the pastor," Grant admits.

"What happened, you were so keen?" Sophie pretends that she hadn't suspected that he had drifted away based on things she had heard from their grandparents.

"I don't really want to talk about it because I'm not living the way I should be," Grant mumbles. He doesn't want an interrogation, just a resolution to his father's problems as they are increasingly encroaching on his life.

"I don't know what your church teaches, but my leaders say it's not about how you live, but about being forgiven. We all do things wrong everyday because we have a sinful heart. Being a Christian makes us free from all that because of grace. You should come to my church if you feel guilty!" Sophie laughs.

Grant doesn't looks amused. He begins to respond but thinks better of it. Who is he to tell his sister that, by the sound of it, she's in a liberal church that won't save or help her, when he's not even going to church or calling himself a Christian!?

"Never mind, I'll sort something out. Maybe he'll go to rehab, he's got the money for it," Grant says. He wishes he hadn't got his sister involved as she doesn't seem too bothered about their father.

"Sure, hey, on Sunday after church a load of us from school are going to the beach BBQ. I heard some of the college guys are going to be there too. Are you going?" Sophie asks.

"If that's the same thing the football lads are going to, then maybe," Grant replies.

"Perhaps, I'll see you there, then," Sophie says as they head back out to Grant's car.

Grant drops her back at their grandparents. He waves from the car as he sees his Grandfather but quickly drives off before he can approach him. He doesn't need another lecture.

Sophie heads inside. She puts her father's tragic life out of her mind and instead thinks about how useful it will be to have her brother, old enough to buy alcohol, at the party on Sunday.

Chapter 5

It's Saturday and it feels like rush hour at Dave's Tasty Snacks, an extremely popular restaurant in the town centre. Sophie rushes around waiting tables as her manager Donna barks orders at the, mostly inexperienced and definitely clueless, staff.

Sophie doesn't mind the busyness, it's still a novelty and she had been thrilled to land the job as there was a queue of applicants. She had beaten half of her classmates to be here and is determined to do a good job.

"Can I take your order?" Sophie asks a group of her peers as they huddle in a booth. She takes their order of milkshakes, burgers and fries and enters the information onto a computer that prints the order in the kitchen. She doesn't envy the kitchen staff who not only have to keep up with the customers coming through the door but also have to deal with people lounging at home and ordering on the app. Some even attend in person then order on the app but Sophie can't understand why anyone would do this as table service is free!

"Hey Ben, did you see that guy earlier left you a £20 tip!?" Sophie calls to her colleague.

Ben looks a little awkward before responding:

"Yeah, £5 extra each."

The policy is that tips are shared amongst the staff who are paid minimum wage.

"Sophie can I see you and Natasha for a minute please?" Donna calls from the door of her office.

The two girls quickly finish their task and head for their manager's office. Donna is a stickler for time keeping and has a sharp tongue at the best of times.

"Right, now I need you both to work tomorrow. I know it's short notice but Sandra has called in sick. I'll pay you time and a half."

Natasha and Sophie glance at each other. They are both members at Church of the Living Water.

"Sure, no problem. I could do with the cash actually," Natasha responds without hesitating.

"I really can't do tomorrow, I have a church thing," Sophie says feeling slightly guilty that she's more bothered about missing the BBQ party than church. She knows the latter will be more likely to get her out of working, though.

"Hmm, Natasha, please go back to work." Donna waits for her to leave. "Sophie, you need to show willing, I can't force you to work, but there are plenty of other people who would love this job, and flexibility was one of the things we were looking for when we hired you."

"I know, but I did say I couldn't work Sundays when I applied," Sophie reminds her boss. "And, there is an exemption to Sunday working if it's for religious reasons." She knows she's pushing her luck as her church leaders aren't bothered if she works on Sundays. In fact, for those who struggle to make ends meet, they even encourage it and tell members just to attend a mid-week meeting instead. It makes the most financial sense as a lot of businesses pay more for Sunday working. But her boss doesn't need to know this.

Donna's face darkens at the mention of the religious exemption. "Well, okay, but I'll need you for a few hours at the end of your shift today instead."

Sophie baulks. She has plans to go shopping for something to wear to the BBQ. Realising she has no choice, she nods and heads back to work.

She clears a table and notices Lewis clearing one nearby. She sees him pick up a £10 note and slide it into his pocket. She doesn't think anything of it as she's done this herself when it's busy and put it in the tip pot later.

"What did she say, are you working tomorrow?" Natasha whispers to her as they cross paths between serving customers.

"No, but she's told me I have to work extra today," Sophie hisses.

"Wait a minute, you're fifteen, aren't you? That's illegal. You can only work four hours. She must know that."

"I know, but I said I was sixteen on the application as I thought it would give me an edge over my classmates," Sophie admits. She drops her eyes, feeling ashamed of the lie. "Terry and Mark said that everyone does it and that the management here never question it."

"Oh," Natasha who is slightly older than Sophie, and knows Terry and Mark from church, looks surprised. "Well, I guess you'll have to just get on with it then."

"At least we have some tips, so it'll be worth it." Sophie brightens up as she realises that as well as the tips, she'll have more money to spend. Extra hours are usually paid on the day, out of the till, in cash.

The morning shift finally comes to an end. Sophie sighs as she watches Ben, Natasha and Lewis getting ready to leave. She heads for the tip pot. It's been busy and she is hopeful that they will have plenty to share. She counts out the coins and removes the £20 note. But, wait, where is the £10 that Lewis had collected?

"Hey, has everyone put their tips in here?" Sophie asks as the others return from their lockers.

"Of course."

"Yes."

"How, have we done?"

Sophie hesitates. She doesn't want to single Lewis out, maybe he will remember later and share the money with them. She gives the others their share and takes her own.

The next shift arrives to take over and Sophie puts the matter out of her mind as she smiles and heads over to a family waiting to be served.

Chapter 6

"Bye Gran, I'm off to church and then I'm seeing some church friends so I might be quite late," Sophie calls as she starts to leave the house.

"Wait, love. Your Grandad and I would be happy if you would come to our church at some point. We think you'd like it. The vicar is doing a series on loving our neighbour and this week it's respecting diversity."

"That's great Gran. I'm glad you've found somewhere you're comfortable. I'll tell you what, we'll do a swap some time. You come to my church and I'll go to yours?" Sophie keeps her expression neutral as she makes the suggestion. She can't think of anything worse than returning to the depressing place where her mother's funeral had been held but she knows that her grandparents will never attend her "lively rock concert style" service as they've had the discussion before.

Janet's eyes widen slightly but she responds in kind, "Well, okay dear. I'll discuss it with your grandfather."

"See you." Sophie stifles a laugh as she finally leaves. She doesn't mean to mock her grandparents but they are funny sometimes.

After an extended time of worship, during which several people stand up and speak in strange languages that Sophie can't understand, the pastor gets up to speak. He explains that the people had been speaking in tongues and are delivering messages straight from God. Sophie briefly wonders how God is expecting them to understand the messages if they are in a foreign language but it's not really her place to say anything. She makes a mental note of those who have spoken and resolves to sit nearer them in future. They obviously have a special blessing from God and she wants to be part of what is going on. Indeed, these special people now seem to have the attention of many in the church, especially the children.

The pastor's short talk focuses on unity and the importance of majoring on the things that keep people together rather than issues that divide. He mentions the LGBT community in particular and the terrible attitudes that some Christians have towards people born with these attractions that they can't do anything about. He opens his Bible and reads a verse from Acts 10: *"God has shown me that I should not call anyone impure or unclean."* The text, while taken out of context, appears to back up what he has been saying. The congregation murmur their approval.

Then, he encourages the mostly young people gathered to attend the services of other churches locally. The church is part of something called "Churches Together" which means that next week Father John Redet from the Roman Catholic church around the corner will be giving the talk. Additionally, the local parish church, also in their network will be hosting their first gay wedding next Saturday and they have extended an invitation for all to come along to show their support.

The congregation nod and smile. Love and tolerance are what it's all about. They are pleased that their church is moving in the right direction and doing what Jesus would have done. Other churches around them are dwindling in numbers and seem to be all about sin, judgement and death. So gloomy and depressing and not what people want to hear. No wonder they are failing.

Sophie loves her church, the talk was so inspiring and she feels more keen than ever to love everyone around her, even those who are irritating at times. She half thinks about attending the lesbian wedding before remembering that she will be working on Saturday.

"Wasn't that a great talk?"

"He's so clear, I just love his sermons."

"It's so refreshing that the church is finally moving into the 21st century."

Sophie thanks the pastor for his message as she walks past him.

"You're welcome. Any plans for the rest of the day?" the pastor asks.

"A big group of us are going to the beach for a BBQ," Sophie says.

"Wonderful. Enjoy the fine weather. I might even pop down myself with my family, make the most of the day. If you'd have mentioned it earlier, I could have suggested everyone here joins in!"

Sophie flushes a little at the thought of her pastor joining their gathering as she envisions having to hide the booze and any evidence of illicit substances. But the pastor has a slight glint in his eye which makes her think that he might know exactly what will be going on at the BBQ and that it wouldn't phase him one bit.

Moving on, she looks around for Jamie and instead sees a group of her class mates standing around John, the youth leader. He laughs and pushes one of them gently on the shoulder as another girl touches his arm playfully. Sophie doesn't join them. She searches the crowd for John's wife and again doesn't see her. His behaviour concerns her, but when she's spoken to her friends about it they just say it's harmless flirting. Sophie wonders whether his wife would see it like that if she were here.

Some of John's fan club eventually see Sophie standing awkwardly by herself and come over to join her.

"Are you ready to go?"

"We've invited John."

Sophie grimaces but forces a smile as she remembers the talk about love and unity. She should give him the benefit of the doubt.

Chapter 7

The party is in full swing when Sophie and her friends arrive at just after 1pm having taken a detour to stock up on goodies. The beach is rammed with people in the skimpiest attire that could be imagined. Loud music with a rhythmic beat is playing. There are bulging plastic bags scattered everywhere. Plenty of food and drink to go around. There is a big sign that reads "Happy Birthday, JO!"

The newly arrived group look around for somewhere to change and in the end resort to holding towels up to preserve each other's modesty.

As she changes, Sophie sees a small group wearing shirts and ties, the women in long dresses, walking along the prom. She squints and sees that they are carrying Bibles. They look out of place amongst the revelry as they pass through. A few of Sophie's group have seen them as well:

"Don't they realise it's Summer?"

"They must be from that strict church that my parents used to go to."

Then, a young lad asks Sophie, "Doesn't your brother go there, to that church I mean?"

"He used to but I don't think he goes any more," Sophie says, feeling embarrassed on behalf of her brother and on behalf of the strange group who have obviously failed to realise that they need to blend in if they want to be accepted in normal society.

Now that she has changed, Sophie turns her attention back to her friends and begins scanning the beach for people she knows. She sees Jamie making her way towards them and goes to meet her, thinking of a way to ask again about Jordan without giving herself away.

"Heyup. Look what I've got." Jamie holds out the plastic bag and opens it for Sophie to see inside. It's full of cans and bottles of alcohol.

"How on earth did you get that??" Sophie asks, astonished both at the audacity of her usually timid friend and at the quantity of alcohol which will last them all day.

"Jordan," Jamie answers.

"Oh, is he coming then?" Sophie grabs her opportunity.

"Later, he told me to go ahead. We need to keep some of this for him and his mates but they'll bring more," Jamie explains.

"Wow, awesome!" Sophie is thrilled that the object of her affection will be arriving and that he has provided them with alcohol, obviously intending that they have a good time. It doesn't occur to her that the older boy's motives may not be entirely honourable as she sees him through rose tinted spectacles and he can do no wrong.

They walk back towards the rest of the group who are similarly excited by the offering. Some of them produce their own small bottles and cans stolen from parent's fridges, but nothing on the scale of Jamie's collection.

They pop open drinks, then lie down on towels and allow the sun to do its work as the music creates the atmosphere. It could easily be a beach in Ibiza, although none of them have been, they've just seen pictures on-line.

Several hours later, Sophie wakes up. She feels pain and looks down. She is very red, lobster red in fact.

"Guys! Why didn't you wake me?" she cries.

There is no response. Her friends have deserted her but their belongings are still scattered all around so she knows they haven't gone far. Disorientated and hurting, Sophie scans the beach. The sun is still shining brightly. She's going to be in some serious pain tomorrow.

"Hey, Jamie. What happened? Where did you go?" Her friends begin to return. Jamie is soaking wet and giggles as she falls onto her towel. Amanda also laughs and sways as she flops down next to her. The others exhibit similar behaviour as they arrive and Sophie realises they are all drunk. The plastic bag that had been full is now empty and there are containers everywhere.

"Weeee sawww you waking uppp and thought weee ssshould tell you about the ssssun!" Jamie slurs.

"Yeah, thanks. Better late than never." Sophie isn't amused and also feels left out. She looks around for any remaining booze but it's all gone, she'd only had a few sips of her bottle before falling fast asleep.

"Hey, there you are!" a male voice calls.

Sophie freezes. She knows that voice. It's Jordan.

"Yeahhhh. Hhhhere am I," Jamie responds as Jordan appears with several of his college friends.

"Are you drunk?" Jordan asks. "Where's my booze?"

Jamie giggles and the other girls join in. Sophie is horrified.

"I think they drank it all," she offers.

"What?! But I gave her a whole bag. How?" Jordan looks genuinely baffled. "If they'd drunk all of it, they'd be comatosed."

"Maybe some of the others in the group took it, I don't know. I was asleep," Sophie says.

"I can see that. You are seriously burnt," Jordan states the obvious. "Al, can you get some more booze? I need to make sure my stupid sis is alright."

"Sure mate, but you owe me."

Jordan's friends leave together to carry out his instructions. He turns to Jamie but she is passed out on the towel. The other girls are all now asleep or unconscious. Sophie checks their breathing.

"They're alive," she laughs. "Ouch, I don't think I should move much."

"You need to cover up, or you'll end up in the hospital," Jordan says, concerned. "A shame to damage a pretty face."

Sophie blushes as she catches his mumbled compliment and is glad he can't see it because of the camouflage.

"So, you don't drink because you're religious? But I thought most of this group go to church?" Jordan asks her curiously.

"No, it's okay for Christians to drink. I just fell asleep. I feel like I missed out actually," Sophie says.

"Oh, so it's a party now, confess later kind of thing? Coz most of these girls are off their trolleys and I'm sure God doesn't permit that!" Jordan indicates the intoxicated girls including his younger sister.

Sophie wonders if he's mocking her but he looks serious enough.

"Well, our religion doesn't assume that we're perfect people, it actually expects that we're not," Sophie defends her friends.

"I see, a reason to go to church on Sundays...."Jordan smirks.

Sophie looks around and sees John in the distance surrounded by his usual crowd of adoring teenage girls hanging on his every word.

She hesitates before pointing him out, "That's my youth leader, I'm sure he wouldn't be here if it was wrong."

Jordan shakes his head. "*I* don't think it is wrong but I don't claim to be religious in any way, shape or form and you should steer well clear of that guy as he's not a nice man."

Sophie looks at Jordan and realises he's talking about John.

"What do you mean?"

"I won't say any more, but believe me, he's trouble," Jordan says this with conviction.

"He's married," Sophie says.

Jordan can barely disguise his shock which quickly turns to disgust. "Like I said, not a nice guy. If he's your youth leader, I'm glad our parents have stopped Jamie going. Boy, standards in the church are definitely slipping."

Hoping for a subject change Sophie digs in her bag.

"Here's the X-Box game you leant me ages ago. Sorry it's taken so long to give it back." She hands it to Jordan.

"Honestly, I'd forgotten who had it, it was so long ago. Thanks, I love this game." Jordan looks at *The Simpson's* game lovingly before placing it carefully in his pocket.

"So, what are you up to these days?" Sophie asks wanting to keep the conversation going.

"Not a lot. I help out with filming for a local company sometimes and take photos for magazines." Jordan is deliberately vague.

"Really? That sounds great, anything I will have heard of?" Sophie doesn't sense his tone.

"Um no….Oh look, the others are back," Jordan sounds relieved.

Sophie feels disappointed but she can't forget the comment Jordan had made about her "pretty face" now damaged by sunburn. She is frustrated. If only she hadn't fallen asleep. Mind you, then she probably would have been drunk when he arrived. She concludes that sober and sunburnt is slightly preferable.

Chapter 8

"Time to go," Sophie says.

The drunk girls have gradually awoken. At first they complained of headaches, but spirits mixed with water and juice, helpfully provided by Jordan's friends, seems to have cured them of this particular problem. Jamie is still asleep but every so often someone checks her breathing.

Sophie has downed a few drinks, trying desperately to catch up, and prove that she is one of the crowd, but she still lags a long way behind and is by far the most sober.

Jordan and his friends are regular drinkers so can handle a lot more than most of the younger people.

Sophie nudges Jamie, "Hey wake up, we're leaving now."

No response.

Sophie shoves her harder, "Seriously, Jamie, let's go!"

Nothing. Jordan gets up and moves towards his sister.

"Hey, sis! You okay?"

"Check her breathing…"

Everyone gathers round as the panic begins to grow.

"Someone call 999…."

"What's happened?"

"Did she take something?"

"How old is she?"

"JAMIE, WAKE UP!"

Jamie is breathing but she is unconscious.

"Oh no! She must've taken something. What did she take?"

Jordan shakes her.

Someone calls an ambulance.

A passing doctor strolling on the prom runs over and helps the group place Jamie in the recovery position. He monitors her breathing and checks her pulse as they wait for the ambulance.

"We need to know what she's taken. It'll help them treat her," the doctor says to the worried group.

"Don't look at me, I was asleep," Sophie says quietly. Surely, Jamie wouldn't have taken something, would she? She has been unpredictable lately and turning up with that huge bag of alcohol had already been out of character.

"Perhaps it's just the alcohol, she drank a lot," someone suggests.

"No, I don't think so. Unless..is she on medication?" the doctor asks.

"Just anxiety pills," Jordan says softly. He has gone white and looks terrified.

"Combined with certain drugs, that could be very serious," the doctor says, worried.

"Ecstasy...but she only took one pill," a voice from the crowd that has gathered.

Sophie looks up and sees Damien, the boy that had been writhing around on the floor at church at the worship night last week.

"WHAT? Who gave it to her? Where did she get it?" Jordan is furious. His fists are clenched.

Sophie puts her hand on his arm.

"Let's make sure she is okay first, we can deal with accusations later."

The paramedics arrive, check Jamie's vitals and, having been informed about her meds and the ecstasy tablet, they load her quickly into the ambulance and head off at speed, the blue lights and sirens shattering the celebrations and bringing everyone immediately out of their drunken stupors.

Sophie collapses onto her towel. She had seen the look the two paramedics had exchanged and she fears for her friend.

None of them had been allowed to accompany Jamie in the ambulance as there wasn't space. They have rung several taxis and are waiting impatiently.

Jordan has a face like thunder and looks like a ticking time bomb as he scans the beach for Damien who has sensibly taken the opportunity of the brief interlude to melt away into the crowd.

Sophie had observed him, though, running across to John, and saying something to him, prior to making his escape.

Fearing for poor Damien who she knows can't possibly be responsible for supplying drugs to her friend, Sophie decides to speak up:

"Jordan, I really don't think it will be anything to do with Damien. Perhaps, you should ask John if he knows anything about it," she suggests innocently. She's curious to see what will happen when John is confronted and she really doesn't like him in any event.

Jordan's eyes widen as he registers the new information. It makes sense. He stalks across the beach towards John who, seemingly unperturbed, is chatting with some young women.

Arriving, Jordan grabs John by his collar and, dragging him away from the others, he punches him straight in the face.

Sophie is shocked. She hadn't expected Jordan to be so wild and out of control but if John has given Jamie drugs then it's nothing less than he deserves.

The rest of her group begins walking towards the scene. Sophie follows, fascinated but a little fearful and not wanting to miss any taxis that arrive to take them to the hospital.

"You gave my sister drugs?! She's fifteen years old and might die. She's on medication," Jordan cries as he pummels his opponent.

John is in shock but as he recovers himself, he grabs the smaller man's arms and defends himself from the blows. Jordan has been drinking and is significantly weaker. John works out and appears to be relatively sober. He easily restrains Jordan.

"What are you talking about? There's no way. I'm her youth leader. Who told you that?"

"I know all about you," Jordan cries as he lies on the sand unable to free himself.

"I don't know what you mean? I don't even know who you are?" John says calmly, though he has paled significantly. He discreetly pushes Jordan's face further into the sand preventing him from saying anything else.

"Jordan, let's go, the taxis are here," Sophie calls him.

"We need to go to the hospital, but this isn't over," Jordan says fiercely although he's in no position to threaten anyone and he knows it.

"It isn't over, no. You've just assaulted me. I'll let you go and see your sister, but we will get to the bottom of this afterwards," John replies as he releases Jordan and steps back ensuring he doesn't receive a parting blow.

Jordan, Sophie and the others run off and jump into the waiting taxis. They head for the hospital.

John walks away from the crowd and having checked that he isn't badly injured, he gets straight on his phone.

"Get rid of the rest of them, someone got hurt," John instructs before quickly hanging up.

However, his haste has made him careless and his brief conversation is overheard by a small group of college friends who have recently arrived at the beach having been to a football party. One of them is Grant Yale, Sophie's older brother.

Chapter 9

Sophie dreams about Jordan as she wipes down a table and collects the tip. Looking around, she stuffs the £20 into her pocket. Why should she follow the rules and share the tips if the others aren't going to?

She has been working at Dave's Tasty Snacks for a month or two now and, after initially feeling aggrieved that people are only looking out for themselves, she decides to join them and works extra hard to satisfy her customers so she can make more money.

Jamie had spent three days in the hospital having her stomach pumped and is likely to make a full recovery. The doctors said that she had been extremely lucky as the combination of the drugs, alcohol and medication could easily have stopped her heart. She can't remember anything apart from drinking a lot. She definitely would not have taken any drugs.

Jamie's parents were devastated, spending day and night by her bedside until she could be released. Jordan too kept vigil.

The parents have heard that the drugs were supplied by a youth leader at the church Jamie had been attending. Although at first they found this hard to believe, in time, they willingly accepted the gossip as fact and congratulated themselves on having stopped Jamie from attending the awful place.

The police have spoken to John informally, but as there was no concrete evidence as to who supplied the drugs, or even that drugs had been consumed, the matter was quietly dropped.

Sophie too has distanced herself from the church for now in order to keep in with Jamie's family, more specifically with Jordan. She's planning to meet him after her shift today as he says he needs her help on one of his projects.

Sophie is snapped out of her auto-pilot cleaning routine by the shrill voice of her manager, Donna.

"Sophie, come and see me please."

Donna has had it in for her ever since their conversation about the Sunday working and Sophie has been waiting for the other shoe to drop.

Conscious of the money in her pocket, she heads for the office,

"Hi Donna, how can I help?" she asks sweetly.

"Well, it's come to my attention that you might not be the age you told us you were when you submitted your application," Donna says smugly.

Sophie gulps. She is completely blind sided.

"I take it from your silence that my source is accurate. Obviously, I could fire you on the spot, but you're a good worker and I can't be bothered to train someone else up for the sake of it. So, I'm going to offer you a deal," Donna has clearly planned what she is going to say.

Sophie nods dumbly.

"You will work Sundays for normal pay for the foreseeable," Donna instructs.

"What? Every week?" Sophie says, stunned.

"Yep, for now but you'll be paid on the day so at least you won't have to wait for your dosh," Donna smiles cruelly.

Sophie is trapped and annoyed. If she had agreed to work Sundays before, she would have been paid time and a half and not had to work every week. She can't complain though and she knows it. She goes back to work.

Finishing her shift, she heads to an address to meet Jordan. It's down a murky passageway and, on entering the communal doorway, up a few dingy flights of stairs. She feels uneasy, but this is Jamie's brother, she knows him and has met his parents. It must be okay.

She knocks on a door and waits for it to be answered. After a few seconds, Jordan appears and a girl, who looks a bit younger than Sophie, slips past her and rushes down the stairs clutching her bag. Sophie looks after her, confused, but Jordan ushers her in.

"Don't mind her, she came to visit my mate," Jordan explains and points to a dodgy looking guy lounging on a sofa fiddling with a laptop.

Sophie isn't sure whether she feels relieved that she isn't on her own with Jordan, or scared that she *is* now alone with *two* guys in a flat with nobody knowing her whereabouts.

"Can I get you a drink?" Jordan offers politely.

"Sure. What is all this stuff?" Sophie looks around at all the cameras, computers and wires everywhere. She also glances over the friend's shoulder at his laptop and sees photos of a young girl in various stages of undress. The friend, realising he is being observed, quickly shuts his laptop.

"This is our studio," Jordan replies. "We do photo shoots here and edit video footage taken elsewhere. All sorts of tech stuff really."

"When you said you took photos, I didn't realise you meant photos of people. Is that why that girl was here?" Sophie suddenly notices the well stocked rails with all different varieties and sizes of clothes hanging from them.

"Well, yeah. We do photo shoots for catalogues and things," Jordan continues as he makes Sophie a drink.

"Like, modelling? Was that girl a model?" Sophie's curiosity is aroused.

Jordan looks to his friend who answers for him:

"Yeah, she's a model," he says. "It's well paid work for someone willing to go the distance."

As they talk, Sophie becomes more and more uncomfortable. She has realised that the photos on the laptop were of the girl that she had seen leaving. So, these guys are not just taking photos, they are making adult content.

"Don't you have to be eighteen to be photographed like that?" Sophie asks.

Jordan glares at his friend who looks guiltily towards his laptop.

"Oh, sorry, those photos were for something else, they weren't taken here. We just do clothes modelling for catalogues, that's all," the friend mumbles unconvincingly.

Sophie keeps her mouth shut. There's no way the girl that she had seen leaving was eighteen and it was definitely her in the photos. Clearly, she's stumbled into some shady business venture but they probably do clothes modelling as well. She's keen to find out more. What teenage girl isn't interested in becoming a model?

"So, what did you need my help with?" Sophie asks.

"I would like you to pose for one of my shoots. It's a new customer and I think you'd be perfect for the clothing range," Jordan says hopefully.

"Okaaayyyy....what type of clothing and how much will I get paid?" Sophie asks hesitantly.

"All sorts of stuff," Jordan says vaguely. "And then afterwards, I thought we could have dinner?"

Sophie's heart skips a beat.

"Great, let's get started. Where are the clothes?"

Jordan smiles.

Chapter 10

Sophie gazes adoringly at Jordan as they eat together at her favourite restaurant. The awkwardness of the afternoon is eclipsed by her excitement at being on a date with her dream guy.

The photo shoot had started off okay; suits, shirts, skirts, tops, and always with due consideration to her modesty. She hadn't enjoyed the fact that Jordan's friend was the one taking the photos, or that two other men had appeared from a side room during the session. They had sat around tapping buttons on their phones and occasionally leering at her.

Then, the swim wear had been produced. She had wanted to refuse, but a voice in her head kept reminding her that these garments were worn in public, it wasn't like it was underwear. She shouldn't be such a prude.

Jordan had watched her as she went off to change and commented quietly to the three other guys:

"That's enough for today. We don't want to freak her out. She'll be ready in a few weeks."

Sophie had then shyly appeared in a skimpy bikini set for the final photos to be taken.

Jordan had said how great she looked and how well she had done, almost as if she was a pro. Then, after she'd changed, he'd whisked her away for their meal causing her to forget anything else she may have wanted to say, including any request for payment.

Now, they are together at last. Jordan isn't the best at making conversation, but Sophie happily chatters away. She notices when he gets out his phone a couple of times, but he always comments that it's work related and puts it back as soon as he has sent a quick text.

"So, which catalogue are the photos for?" Sophie eventually asks.

"Sweetie, let's not talk about work. I know it's exciting for you, but it's nice for me to get a break from it when I've finished for the day," Jordan says.

Sophie doesn't mention that he seems willing to tune back into work when he receives a text about it. She is just happy to be here with him.

"How is your sister? I haven't really seen her around school," Sophie says.

"She's fine. She had a few weeks off and our parents are keeping her on a tight leash. She's literally going to school and then having to come straight home with no detours at the moment," Jordan says. "I still haven't caught up with that hypocrite who nearly killed her."

Sophie notices that Jordan's eyes flash with anger as he speaks of John. "How can you be sure it was him?" she says, wanting to defuse the situation.

"There's no doubt. He'll get what's coming to him in the end."

Sophie feels frightened and for the first time is very aware that she doesn't really know anything about the man sitting across from her.

Jordan deliberately lightens his tone. "You were really great today. You know what would be really helpful?"

Sophie ignores the fact that, now that it suits him, he is talking about work again.

"What?"

"Well, I'd get more money for the photos if I can say that you're eighteen. We could also do more shoots if the catalogue like the ones we did today." Jordan makes the suggestion casually.

"But I'm not," Sophie blurts out.

"I know, but didn't you say you'd told your boss at work you were older? What's the difference?" Jordan asks.

"Not much, I guess," Sophie admits. "It feels wrong, though and it's already got me in trouble at work."

"Only because you were found out. It's not wrong, everyone does it. You know the girl you saw earlier, we helped her get a fake ID and now she's making a lot of money," Jordan encourages.

"Didn't your friend say that you hadn't been taking photos of her?" Sophie says, confused.

"Oh no, that's not what he meant," Jordan deflects. "I know a place that does them for a few quid. We could go there after we've eaten if you want?"

"Well, okay, sure. I guess it can't hurt and I don't have to use it," Sophie looks out of the window and avoids eye contact with Jordan as she resumes picking at her food.

The waiter brings the dessert menu. Sophie looks longingly at the ice-creams but Jordan gives her a disapproving look. "We'll just have the bill please," he says to the waiter. "Can't have you piling on the pounds now that you're about to be a star. If anything, you could do with losing a bit. Have you thought about getting a full makeover at the salon?"

Sophie blushes. She feels awful. "I haven't.... I mean....I don't know."

"It would be money well spent and you'd easily make it back from the modelling. Just your eyebrows and a few other things. It'd make you look much more sophisticated and they could do your make up and hair. If you do it just before a photo shoot, that'd be perfect," Jordan pushes her.

"I'm not sure I've got the money for all that," Sophie stammers.

"Didn't you say your boss was making you work weekends? It takes money to make money you know," Jordan smiles. "I'll show you a good salon that won't charge the earth if you like?"

"Well, okay then." Sophie grabs the coffee that's just arrived and holds it in front of her face to hide her humiliation.

Chapter 11

"Amanda, please?" the nurse calls.

Sophie and Amanda look up. Amanda passes the copy of Cosmopolitan that they had been sharing to Sophie as she heads towards the nurse.

They are at the weekly free clinic where school girls can obtain advice, medication and contraceptives without the knowledge of their parents.

Amanda's relationship with Steve, a boy at church, has been getting serious and they are ready to take it to the next level. Sophie had been surprised to hear of Amanda's plan as she had always thought that Christians didn't believe in sex before marriage. However, Amanda had been to see the pastor and he had said that it was more a case of being sure they were prepared, responsible and committed to each other. He had pointed out that it would be foolish for them to get too serious without being sure they were compatible in *every* way.

What Amanda had said did make sense and explained why most of their classmates were sleeping with their partners whether or not they professed to be Christians. Someone else had commented that they couldn't be expected to live as things were in biblical times. The Bible needed updating for a modern audience.

Sophie had briefly seen a Bible passage that had popped up on her daily readings on her phone which seemed to contradict all of this. But, Amanda had said that she needed to look at the bigger picture and reminded her that God understands our weaknesses.

Sophie had been quite pleased to hear all this and it reassured her that when the time came with Jordan, she wouldn't need to worry about offending God. However, they've only just started dating and he seems very focused on the modelling work for now especially since she'd done as he asked and obtained the ID stating she was eighteen. She had felt a little guilty about lying to the shop assistant and had nearly got her date of birth wrong, but Jordan had jumped in and corrected her in the nick of time as he mentioned her eighteenth birthday celebration and what they had planned. It had been a little disconcerting to see the way he had suddenly become all couply and had taken her hand in order to dupe the clerk. He was a good performer, but she chose to believe his momentary affection was genuine ignoring the sick feeling in the pit of her stomach.

Sophie puts the magazine down and glances at the clock. It's been thirty minutes and she wonders why Amanda is taking so long. She wanders down the hospital corridor looking for toilets.

As she spots them further along the hall, she sees a face she recognises but hasn't seen for a while. The woman is wearing a gown and hobbling along with a nurse at her side. Her face is streaked with tears.

Sophie ducks into the toilet corridor and listens as they pass:

"He didn't want it. I would have loved to have had this one but he always agrees and then changes his mind at the last minute. It's awful," the lady sobs as she explains things to the nurse.

"It's okay dear. Many women find themselves in this situation and it can be better to keep peace in your relationship than to try and keep a child one party doesn't want," the nurse says sympathetically.

Sophie covers her mouth with her hand to stop her gasp being overheard as she disappears quickly into the ladies toilet.

Re-emerging, she checks that the coast is clear and heads off to go and find Amanda, buzzing with the gossip she knows she must share before she explodes.

On her return, Amanda is waiting for her. "Where were you?" she asks indignantly.

"Oh, sorry, I went to the loo. You'll never guess who I saw?"

"Who?" Amanda's face lights up as she senses the importance of the question in her friend's demeanour.

"Elaine!" Sophie tells her.

"Who?" Amanda doesn't get it.

"John's wife. You know from church."

"Oh. I thought you were going to say someone really interesting, or even famous," Amanda says, disappointed.

"It's not who I saw that's important, but what she was doing here," Sophie continues. Even as she says it, she feels slightly bad about turning poor Elaine's tragedy into the latest soap opera instalment but she just can't help herself.

"Well, go on then," Amanda says impatiently as they head for the door.

"She was getting an abortion and by the sound of it, it's not the first time." Sophie's eyes gleam as she waits for her friend's reaction.

"Seriously? I'm not that surprised though. A lot of women have had abortions."

"I guess, but she also said that John had made her and that she wanted to keep the baby," Sophie hopes the additional information will renew Amanda's interest.

"She actually said this to you?" Amanda looks doubtful.

"Well, not exactly. I hid when I saw her and then overheard her conversation with a nurse," Sophie admits.

"What would the church think about that?" Amanda thinks aloud.

"I guess they won't know. I've never heard the vicar say that abortion is wrong. He seems more focused on individual freedoms. Perhaps it's okay if both parents agree?" Sophie responds.

"I think that's right. I'm sure God would be sad if an unwanted child was brought up by parents who didn't love him, or her, and giving it away would be worse as it would end up in care." Amanda comments.

"And that almost always ends in disaster," Sophie laughs as she thinks of the various children at their school who are in the care system.

"It's good to know that there's a last resort if things don't work out and I ever end up in that situation," Amanda says.

"Definitely," Sophie agrees as they link arms and head out of the hospital.

Chapter 12

The atmosphere is intense and those gathered are alive with anticipation. What will happen at worship night this week?

Jamie, Sophie and Amanda sit entranced as they wait for the meeting to begin. Jamie had managed to persuade her parents that she had been grounded for long enough and is staying the night at Amanda's. She seems less suspicious of the church since her recent escapade. Sophie can't understand why, unless her near death experience has made her feel safer in the church than outside of it.

John appears on stage as the music reaches a crescendo. Everyone claps wildly as the musicians temporarily rest their instruments.

"We are in for a treat tonight," John begins. His eyes dart around the building and shine with an unnatural sheen. "IT'S HEALING NIGHT!" He shouts "We know that God wants us to be healthy and happy and to live our best lives now. There are lots of people here with health issues. Tonight, we intend to take back control for these people who are under the devil's curse. They will be given new power to overcome their ailments so that they can fulfil their dreams.

"Wow, do you think they'll be able to do anything about my memory problems?" Jamie whispers hopefully to Sophie.

"Let's wait and see but it sounds possible," Sophie replies and squeezes her friend's hand.

Jamie hasn't recovered her short term memory since the drug taking incident. She still can't remember taking any drugs, or who may have given them to her. She is sure it can't have been John even though her brother is convinced it was.

"Right, what we're going to do as the band plays, is we're going to list problems on the big screen one by one," John explains. "Anyone suffering from anything that appears needs to walk to the front. Then, a gifted healer will assess whether the problem is being caused by a demon, a lack of faith, or something else. Then, it will be dealt with and you will be freed as God has promised."

"That's amazing. Can he really make that kind of promise?" Jamie asks.

"Well, Jesus never refused a healing and the disciples (that's us) were told they would do greater things than He did. So, I guess it's true," Sophie says. She briefly wonders why these gifted healers aren't spending all of their time freeing people from diseases in the hospital but feels sure there will be a satisfactory explanation at some point.

"Let's begin," John says as he presses a button and the big screen becomes the focal point.

The band starts softly playing and singing, *"It is well, with my soul"*. Sophie, knowing the tune, hums along before realising that the band are just playing that line repeatedly rather than moving on to any of the other lyrics.

The first phrase that appears is BI-POLAR DISORDER. The three girls look around the room. They are only aware of a couple of people with this illness in the church. They have invariably demonstrated bizarre behaviour on a number of occasions and it isn't openly discussed. Several times the church leaders have signed as guarantor for large payments made by a lady called Jane. It's common knowledge that none of the money has been repaid and that Jane had used some of it on an all inclusive holiday with her entire extended family.

"I guess they're hoping they'll recoup some of their money if they heal her," Amanda hisses. This causes a giggle from Sophie and Jamie before they quickly manage to suppress it.

"I don't know what they were thinking giving her the money in the first place. She's never been able to control her spending," Sophie says.

"It's not her fault, it's an illness," Jamie says.

"True, but it's like giving an alcoholic a drink," Amanda replies.

"I think they wanted to test her to see if she could do it," Sophie comments. She's never been able to understand the church leader's rationale for distribution of funds and no one else seems bothered enough to query any of the decisions.

"Look, it's her."

The three girls watch as Jane makes her way slowly to the front of the room and approaches the stage.

John walks quickly towards her, grabs her hand and, beaming, thrusts the microphone towards her.

"So, Jane, tell us how long you've been struggling with this illness," he says.

"Well, I was diagnosed ten years ago but I've had problems all my life. It started when…."

"Thankyou," John cuts her off. "George, a professional healer, is going to examine you now."

An intense looking, middle aged man appears from the shadows at the side of the stage.

There is a sharp intake of breath from the onlookers who hadn't known anyone was there. The whole thing reminds Sophie of a magic show.

The band are still playing their line, *"It is well, with my soul. It is well, with my soul. It is well, it is well with my soul."* The rhythm is becoming a mantra and the audience inadvertently find themselves chanting the lyric over and over again.

"That's right, feel the healing power in the words and know that it is well with your soul," George says as he takes the microphone from a bewildered looking Jane. He walks around her several times before stopping directly behind her.

"In the name of Jesus Christ, come out!" he commands before slapping Jane sharply across the face.

Jane reaches up and touches her smarting cheek, her eyes fill with tears,

"Oooohhh, this is horrible. That was really hard," Sophie says.

"I don't think I can watch," says Jamie. "If I go up there about my memory issues, is he going to slap me?"

"I guess it depends whether you've got a demon or not," Amanda chuckles.

"Shut up," Jamie snaps.

The crowd all watch the stage as Jane stands there sobbing and clutching her face.

"You've been healed, praise God!" George says. "Now, remember you've been healed, that means you no longer need to take any medication. If you do, it's a sign of a lack of faith and God may withdraw the blessing and reverse the miracle.

John moves towards the two of them on the stage:

"The church leaders want to demonstrate confidence in the power of God by giving you this cheque for £1000, Jane," John tells her. "We know that you previously suffered from uncontrollable spending as part off your illness."

The audience strain to see if the cheque is real.

"You must give us the cheque back, un-cashed in one week's time as evidence of your healing. Agreed?" John grins like a Cheshire cat as he offers the absurd condition.

Jane looks frightened, then determined:

"Yes. I will do it," she loudly states before she is ushered quickly behind a curtain on the stage.

"Wait, how will we know if she was healed or not?" Sophie whispers.

The audience is restless as they are wondering the same thing but the focus is now back on the big screen and the new word EAR-ACHE.

At least a dozen people head for the stage.

Chapter 13

Jordan grins at his mates as he tells them the good news:
"She's finally ready. I told you it would be worth the wait."
"Do you really think she'll go through with it, though?"
"Of course, she adores me. She'll do anything I ask. Just make sure you do the drink when she arrives so she'll be more relaxed, okay?" Jordan instructs. He glances at the packet of sedatives and pushes aside the last traces of his guilty conscience. They aren't going to harm her, the pictures will be great and they'll all be richer at the end of the day.

Sophie gets into Grant's car. He'd called her again and as it'd been a while since their difficult conversation about their father, she'd arranged to see him.
"It's not about Dad again, is it?" she asks anxiously.
"No, but you probably should know he checked into rehab a few weeks ago but only lasted a few days before he went out on another bender. I really don't know what we're going to do with him."
Sophie changes the subject, "Did you hear that Granddad got elected? I guess Dad's and your antics weren't enough to taint his campaign."
"Actually, I did. It's good for him although I'm not sure whether he'll be able to deal with the pressure. Didn't he recommend some builders who caused a gas explosion or something?" Grant asks curiously.
"I don't know about that, they don't really tell me much. I know that Grandma has been annoyed with him a lot recently and there was something about the neighbour over the road and their garden being condemned I think," Sophie mumbles. She hasn't really been at home that much and when she has she isn't that interested in the mundane activities of her aging grandparents. "So, what did you want to talk about?"
Grant takes a breath and steels himself. This isn't going to be easy.
"Look, I wanted to tell you that I've sorted myself out. I know I've not been a good example to you and actually that's not the half of it, but you don't need to know about that."
Sophie turns to face him as he drives. "What do you mean? You mean you've calmed down a bit? What?"
"I made a big mistake and someone got hurt. It's taken me a while

to sort things out. I'm back at church and have made things right with God," Grant explains.

"I don't get it. You were always a Christian, right?" Sophie asks.

They arrive at a park and leaving the car they walk towards a burger van.

"I believed, yes, but I messed up and drifted away from God, then made some terrible choices," Grant admits. "I'm ashamed of some of the things I've done and I'm worried about you."

Sophie looks at him in astonishment. "Why are you worried about me? What has your messing up got to do with me?"

"I feel like if I had stayed on track spiritually, I may have been able to give you advice. As it was, I couldn't say anything as I'd just be labelled a hypocrite and that would've been true," Grant says.

They buy burgers and sit on a bench over looking the park to eat them.

"My life's great. I've got a perfect boyfriend, a job, friends and an exciting church that I love. I know Dad's a bit messed up and our grandparents can be a bit annoying at times, but things are good, honestly," Sophie says, enthusiastically.

"This will be difficult, then," Grant says as he places his burger down and looks at her earnestly.

"What's wrong? You're scaring me." Sophie feels like Grant is about to tell her something that she would really rather not know. "Is it about Jordan?"

"Partly, yes, but not just him. Look. I've heard things. Most of the things that concern me seem to have their roots in your church to be honest," Grant says gently.

"Well, that can't be right as church is all about love, harmony, tolerance and unity. What could be wrong with that?" Sophie says. "Actually, you know what. I don't think I want to hear any of it. It sounds like you're just going to be negative and try and ruin things for me. I don't want that."

"I really need to tell you some things. I won't be able to forgive myself if I don't and then something happens. This is serious, sis," Grant persists. "You know the BBQ party when Jamie ended up in the hospital?"

"Of course I do. You think I would've forgotten that?"

"I overheard that youth leader at your church, straight after you all left for the hospital. He got on the phone and told someone to ditch the rest because someone had been hurt. I know he was talking about the drugs."

Grant's words hang in the air.

"Actually, he could've been talking about anything. He's a church leader, Grant." Even as she says it, Sophie's mind drifts to the tear stained face of Elaine at the hospital, having just carried out her husband's wishes.

"He's not a nice guy, Soph. I know other stuff as well," Grant continues.

"So? What am I meant to do about it? I don't have any authority in the church to question the leadership and the church is really great, so what if there's one leader who's got a few problems. We're all sinners, right?" Sophie says defensively.

"I'm worried about you." Grant realises that Sophie isn't in the mood to listen to him so he shelves the rest of what he needed to say to her for another day.

"You don't need to worry, I'm doing fine. Worry about Dad if you want to worry about someone." Sophie tries to lighten the mood. However, in the back of her mind she knows that she has shut her brother down and refused to hear him on the most important subject of her boyfriend, Jordan.

Chapter 14

Grant drops Sophie in town and she makes her way to the salon. She has an hour before she is due at Jordan's studio. She wants everything to be perfect for the big shoot he has promised that will make her into a big name. Obviously, not her own name as that wouldn't work. She has chosen Chantelle Selene as her pseudonym and using it makes her feel important.

Heavily made up and with her hair transformed, she almost doesn't recognise herself in the mirror that is placed in front of her by the stylist.

"Wow, that can't be me, can it?"

"Just be careful out there, love…" the stylist says, concerned.

"My boyfriend wanted me to look a certain way for a big modelling shoot he's doing," Sophie says proudly.

"I know, but just make sure you know what you're getting into. This guy's a bit older, right?" The stylist has teenage daughters of her own. She knows she's treading a thin line, but feels the naive young girl in front of her needs to at least be warned that things aren't always as they seem.

"It's fine. He's the brother of a school friend," Sophie tries to reassure her.

"Oh, well that definitely makes a difference. Does your friend know what you're doing?"

Sophie hesitates. "Of course. We're meeting up afterwards," she lies. "Now, how much do I owe you?"

"£100 please, love," the stylist says and hands her the bill.

Sophie gulps. This is costing several week's wages, she hopes it'll be worth it. She hands over the money, thanks the stylist and leaves the salon.

Feeling more than a little self conscious as she walks through the town, aware that she is attracting attention, she quickens her pace as she approaches the studio.

Her phone rings and she reaches in her bag to answer it.

"Hey Soph, guess what?" Amanda says.

"Um, I'm a little busy right now. What is it?" Sophie doesn't want to be hanging around in the town for longer than she needs to. She ducks into a doorway.

"You have to hear this," Amanda says, sounding excited. "It's about Jane."

"Why, what's happened," Sophie listens intently.

"I was out with my family earlier and we were walking along the cliffs at Brigate. There was a big crowd of people near the cliff edge watching something. We went over to see what it was and saw a police car nearby. There was a brightly coloured parachute, that looked like it would cost an arm and a leg, with a person attached to it. We moved nearer and saw that it was Jane. She was singing, *'Let's go fly a kite'*, you know, the song from Mary Poppins and then launching herself towards the cliff edge." Amanda stops to take a breath.

"Oh no, she didn't jump, did she?" Sophie gasps.

"That was the funny thing, she kept running backwards and forwards and around in circles. Everyone was shouting at her to stop, including the police. I think there was a negotiator there as they thought she might be suicidal but she just seemed to be off her trolley, like happy as anything and believing sincerely that she could fly!" Amanda pauses.

"So, what happened in the end?" Sophie asks, incredulous.

"Well, she spent so long faffing around and running back and forth singing that by the time she actually launched herself off the edge, the police had set up a safety net so she just landed on that. Goodness knows what would have happened if the net wasn't there though as she may have plummeted straight into the sea, or onto the rocks," Amanda continues.

"Oh! How awful," Sophie manages.

"Yeah, and her dog was running around after her yapping its head off. They just managed to stop it from jumping straight after her."

"So, are they both alright?" Sophie asks.

"Just about. Jane was obviously sectioned and the dog is being looked after by the RSPCA for now," Amanda finishes.

"Well, I wonder what George and John and the church will have to say when they hear about this," Sophie comments.

"Do you know, I reckon they'll just blame it on her lack of faith to be healed and say that God reversed the miracle," Amanda says.

"Yes, I bet you're right. They already paved the way for it, didn't they? Oh, I bet she used the cheque money to buy the parachute as she's never had much money," Sophie realises.

"What a disaster! I think we might need to rethink going to these worship nights. It's obviously a load of nonsense and in Jane's case, highly dangerous," Amanda concludes.

"Actually, my brother was trying to warn me about John earlier as well. He says that he heard him tell someone to dispose of the rest of the drugs when Jamie went to hospital that night," Sophie admits.

"Really? Well he doesn't really have any reason to make that up. He doesn't know John, does he?" Amanda asks.

"Not really. Look I really need to go as I'm in the middle of something but we'll catch up later, okay?" Sophie remembers that she's all made up and looks like she has nowhere to go.

She hangs up and walks the last few steps to the doorway that leads to Jordan's studio. Then she heads up the murky stairwell that still gives her the creeps and knocks on the door.

Chapter 15

"Wow," Jordan exclaims as he sees her. He takes a quick step back and admires her. "You look terrific!"

"Right, shall we get started then?" another male appears and two more look up from the couch where they are tapping away on their phones and laptops.

Sophie looks around. The studio looks darker today and she notices additional props. The camera equipment looks snazzier and in addition to the racks of clothes, there is another rack of what looks like underwear.

"Wait, what's going on?" she says. "I thought it was just going to be you and me for this shoot."

"Slight change of plan, baby, but nothing to worry about," Jordan says as he hands her the orange juice prepared by one of the others.

Thinking it will buy her some time, Sophie downs the drink in one. She feels weird but doesn't really know why as it's not that much different to her previous visit with the swim wear shoot. She feels a little woozy.

"I think I need to sit down, Jordan?"

Sophie reaches for him but he moves away and one of the other guys puts an arm around her and leads her to a chair placed in front of the camera.

"Wait, no, I'm not ready," Sophie protests.

"I think you'll be more comfortable if we take off some of these clothes," one of the guys says as he starts to remove her coat. Another guys busies himself with the camera. Jordan has turned away and is looking out of the window. He is trying to forget that this is one of Jamie's friends. He feels bad but he's in debt to these guys and is in no position to argue with their demands. Besides, they'll just do the nude shoot and move on, no real harm done.

Sophie panics as she realises what is happening and the predicament she is in. She tries to focus on the guy she thinks is Jordan but everything looks fuzzy. The guys are removing her clothes…..

A loud knock at the door.

"Police, open up or we'll put the door in. NOW!"

The guys jump. They grab the camera equipment and Sophie, and run into a room at the back. Jordan is frozen to the spot. Recovering himself, he switches on the normal lights and calls:

"Wait, I'm just coming." He walks to the door giving the guys enough time to leave by the back exit Fire Escape.

He opens the door.

Grant barges in. "Where's my sister? I'll do serious damage to you if you've hurt her!"

"What, where are the police? Who are you?" Jordan asks, totally bewildered but relieved that they're not all about to be carted off to jail for taking indecent photos of underage girls.

"I'm Sophie's brother. You should be ashamed of yourself, man. How did you get involved in this? You're Jamie's brother, aren't you?" Grant looks at him in disgust.

Jordan crumbles. "I'm sorry mate. I'm in serious trouble and these guys didn't give me much choice."

"Why, my sister, though?" Grant asks.

"She liked me and it was easy," Jordan admits. "They weren't going to hurt her though. It was just for the photos."

"Oh, well that's okay, then, even though she's only fifteen," Grant says sarcastically. "This isn't over. Where is she?"

"They went into that room," Jordan points. He doesn't bother to raise the issue of the fake ID as Grant knows he knows her real age.

Grant rushes towards the closed door and, finding it locked, kicks it down.

The guys have gone. Sophie is collapsed in a ball on the floor. Grant is relieved to see that she still has most of her clothes on although make up is smeared all over her face. He had thought he might have been too late. It had taken him ages to work out which flat they were in and even longer to talk himself into impersonating the police, knowing that this in itself was a crime.

Grant rushes to her, "Are you okay, Soph?" he asks softly.

"Where are we? What's happened?" Sophie asks sleepily. "I thought I heard the police...."

"Don't worry, everything will be okay. I just need you to get up and we need to get out of here," Grant tells her as he lifts her in his arms. Pushing past Jordan with a final scowl, he carries her down the stairs and outside to his car.

Chapter 16

Sophie wakes up. It's a familiar scene. She recognises her old room in her old house. She lies in bed and stares at the ceiling with the stars that glow in the dark, still there from when she was a child. Why is she here, though? She doesn't live here any more.

"Good, you're awake," Grant says, as he brings her a cup of tea.

"Yeah, but I've got a banging headache and I'm totally confused. Why am I here? What happened? Where's Dad?," Sophie asks.

"Okay, one thing at a time. Dad is out, probably at the pub. I've told Gran and Granddad that you're here so you don't need to worry. You've got a headache as I think the guys gave you a sedative. I saw a packet on the side when we left Jordan's place." Grant fills in some of the blanks.

Sophie's face turns white. "Did I....? Oh no, they were trying to take off my clothes....Did they drug me? Photograph me naked, what??"

"Relax, I got there in time. You still had most of your clothes on, apart from your coat and jumper. So, they didn't get what they were after," Grant reassures her.

"But, Jordan?" her expression is pained.

"I'm sorry, Soph. I think he was in debt to them and effectively sold the prospect of an adult photo shoot with you to clear the debt...." Grant is embarrassed and horrified by the whole situation.

Sophie bursts into tears. "I should've let you tell me about him the other day. Did you know what he was going to do?"

"Not exactly. I knew that he was involved with some bad people and that his motives probably weren't honourable. I followed you after you got all made up at the salon but then lost sight of you for a bit and only found the right flat just before I burst in. I don't understand why they hadn't got further with the photo shoot honestly," Grant says.

"Oh, I had a phone call from Amanda just as I was approaching the flat so I ducked into a doorway opposite to talk to her. It took a while," Sophie explains. "I thought the police came in though. I was panicking as I suddenly realised the terrible truth but then I heard someone shout 'POLICE'. The guys ran into another room and dropped me on the floor as they escaped."

"That was me," Grant says sheepishly. "I knew it was the only way to get them to open the door."

"Impersonating a police officer. I never thought you'd do that!"

Sophie laughs. Grant is pleased to see some colour coming back to her face.

"Look Soph, we really need to talk. I tried to talk to you the other day but you didn't want to listen. Now, I need you to listen. You can reject what I say if you want, but I feel responsible for what has been going on with you in some ways because my own life hasn't been straight-forward." Grant sends up an arrow prayer that this time his sister will listen.

"Okay, well I guess it's the least I can do as you rescued me from those sleazy guys and you were right about Jordan and John," Sophie reluctantly agrees. She feels embarrassed, but her brother has shown that he cares about her so she determines to listen.

"If you think back to Mum's funeral. Do you remember the conversation we had when you were upset?" Grant begins.

"Yes, I couldn't believe that becoming a Christian was as easy as you made it seem," Sophie recalls.

"I should have told you at the time that the decision to follow Jesus may be easy, but the Christian life is tough and you need to consider what will be involved so you can be prepared for problems," Grant explains.

"Well, it was tough; I was bullied at school for going to church. I decided to give it all up," Sophie explains.

"Okay, so why did you go back to the church?" Grant asks.

"The church seemed to change, probably to accommodate all the young people that started going. They got new leaders and suddenly everything got easier. Then, being a Christian helped me blend in with everyone else because they were all going to church too, including one of the bullies!" Sophie remembers.

"I'm not sure exactly what's been going on at your church," Grant says carefully, "but they aren't teaching you the truth according to the Bible. Christians can't just blend in with non-believers. A Christian is someone whose life has been completely and radically changed. They have been born again and are a new creation. Think of it as travelling in one direction beforehand doing whatever pleases you and then doing a complete one-eighty and going the other way following Jesus."

"I'm not sure I get it. Are you saying it's more complicated than just believing? Are you saying that the people at my church aren't Christians? What exactly are you trying to say?" Sophie feels frustrated that she isn't understanding her brother, sensing that what he is saying is important.

"I'm not very good at this. I think the best thing for me to do is explain it through a story, recorded in the Bible in Luke chapter 14 vs 25-34. Jesus told it when large crowds were following Him:

"If anyone comes to me and does not hate father and mother, wife and children, brothers and sisters—yes, even their own life—such a person cannot be my disciple. And whoever does not carry their cross and follow me cannot be my disciple.

Suppose one of you wants to build a tower. Won't you first sit down and estimate the cost to see if you have enough money to complete it? For if you lay the foundation and are not able to finish it, everyone who sees it will ridicule you, saying, 'This person began to build and wasn't able to finish.'

Or suppose a king is about to go to war against another king. Won't he first sit down and consider whether he is able with ten thousand men to oppose the one coming against him with twenty thousand? If he is not able, he will send a delegation while the other is still a long way off and will ask for terms of peace. In the same way, those of you who do not give up everything you have cannot be my disciples.

Salt is good, but if it loses its saltiness, how can it be made salty again? It is fit neither for the soil nor for the manure pile; it is thrown out.   Whoever has ears to hear, let them hear."

Note To Reader

I'm sure many reading this may feel sorry for Sophie. She made a profession of faith at her mother's funeral but, as in the Parable of the Sower, fell away when trouble came.

Then, she tries again, but finds herself in a liberal, worldly church which makes being a Christian seem like the easy option to blend in with everyone else.

Now, she is surrounded by friends, including many of her classmates, and the Church of the Living Water has turned into a social club where all the popular people go. It is all about love, unity and tolerance, not about God. It is no longer about counting the cost of following Jesus into a completely new way of life, but about being culturally relevant, on trend and having a good time. The spiritual is not to encroach on the rest of life so as to cause as little inconvenience as possible.

The leaders are worldly; encouraging and excusing sin, giving unbiblical advice and shallow, out of context teaching, failing to uphold standards of holiness, and refusing to exercise any form of church discipline. Charismatic extremes have infiltrated the church and are leading people down confusing and dangerous paths.

The main youth leader is flirting with youngsters, dealing drugs and putting pressure on his wife to abort their babies.

The church has become like the world and Sophie is building on a foundation of sand. Sometimes, her conscience rears its head and she vaguely remembers Bible verses that seem to correct her, but these are over-ridden by her peers who, confusingly, also call themselves Christians.

Sophie's lack of foundation means that she isn't prepared when temptation comes. She lies her way into a job, lies to her boss about her reasons for not wanting to work Sundays, then steals tip money because everyone else is. She goes to a beach party intending to get drunk and only fails because she falls asleep.

She fancies an older boy who finds her attachment to the church amusing because he knows she shouldn't be doing the things she's doing, including dating him as a non-believer. She obtains fake ID, seeks the wrong things and ends up in a dangerous predicament due to her poor choices and trusting the wrong people.

Meanwhile, her "Christian" friends are sleeping around, taking illicit substances, getting drunk and pursuing worldly ambitions.

What a mess!

Sadly, this is what a lot of our churches look like today, especially where young people are concerned. In conducting research for this book, I stumbled across on article written by a church leader in England that celebrated and upheld many of the clearly unbiblical things documented in this fictional narrative.

In the end, Sophie is confronted by her brother Grant, a real Christian attending a true church, who cares enough to tell her the truth. He uses the parable that Jesus told about the cost of discipleship to help her see the hypocrisy and danger of the unbiblical practices in her church and life. Sophie and her friends, and indeed most of the members of the Church of the Living Water, are living exactly as non-Christians would live. There is no visible difference between their lives and the lives of those around them who don't believe. They aren't even attempting to live by the Bible. They don't even read it and never pray, apart from shallow prayers for blessings at their signs and wonders meetings.

It might be that we are called to do the same for someone we know who is caught up in a church that has become like the world. The point of this story is **not** salvation by works. We are saved through faith in Jesus alone, but it's not an invitation to an easy life. The phrase "Easy Believism" or "Decisionism" has been used for those who make decisions for Jesus on an emotional whim at meetings, or crusades. They haven't counted the cost and aren't truly converted.

The parable tells us that before becoming Christians, we should seriously consider the cost, as it will involve giving up everything to put Jesus first. The story ends with the salt losing its saltiness which is exactly what happens when professing Christians and churches become like the world. We are meant to be salt and light to the world which means that our lives should be radically different to those around us. We are serving a higher Master and He should always come first.

We must seek churches and church leaders that are focused on the Bible as their source of authority. Churches where members encourage and challenge each other to greater standards of holiness. Churches that are reaching out to those outside with the saving message of hope in Jesus.

With a proper foundation, the true church will create disciples that confess Jesus not just as Saviour but also as Lord of their lives.

EAT, DRINK & BE MERRY

Natalie Vellacott

A Short Story of Addiction and Greed

Chapter 1

"My name is Janie and I'm an alcoholic."

"My name is Thomas and I'm an alcoholic."

"My name is Irene and I'm an alcoholic."

There is a pause and everyone in the circle turns to look at Dean.

Dean sits with his arms folded. A grim but determined look on his face.

"Okay, let's move on," the facilitator says nervously.

"My name is Paul and I'm an alcoholic."

Dean smirks. He looks around at the group, feeling nothing but contempt for every one of them. It's his third time in rehab and Alcoholic's Anonymous meetings are a mandatory part of the programme. Well, attendance is compulsory, but that doesn't mean he has to contribute.

As members of the group begin recanting details of their tragic lives, Dean switches off. He dreams of the £10,000 his father has promised him if he successful completes rehab. He can't wait to get back down to the pub with his mates and is sure he can double his money at the casino. He's on the verge of a winning streak and can feel it.

"Dean, do you want to share anything with the group today? Remember it's all confidential so nothing you say will leave this room," the facilitator asks hopefully, then, receiving no response, he chews the end of a biro.

Dean stares him down, not feeling the need to say anything. He's been doing this for weeks and is surprised they haven't given up by now and let him stay in his room.

"Shall we finish then?" the facilitator does give up.

The group stand and, holding hands — apart from Dean — they chant their prayer:

"God, give me the serenity to accept the things I cannot change; courage to change the things I can; and wisdom to know the difference. Amen."

Dean can't believe that seemingly intelligent people are falling for this nonsense. Most of them don't even believe in any god, certainly not a God who listens to the prayers of individuals. He knows from previous sessions that, according to the logic of the professionals, one of the things that can't be changed is alcoholism. He's been told over and over again that it's an illness and therefore, not something anyone can blame him for. This belief suits Dean very well because it means that he doesn't need to feel guilty when he manages to sneak contraband into the centre or when he shares it with others who can't bear the thought of going "cold turkey".

Dean only has a week to go and he can't wait to get out of this place, pick up his money and celebrate his freedom.

Gary and Janet sip champagne at an exclusive dinner for councillors and their families. Gary is enjoying his role and, aside from a few blips during his campaign, really feels that he is worthy of his title.

He glances at the champagne bottle which briefly reminds him of his son in rehab. He couldn't allow anything to tarnish his reputation and Dean's behaviour had been getting worse and worse. It was only a matter of time before he committed some kind of criminal act or killed someone whilst driving home drunk. Gary's grandson Grant had felt the need to inform his grandfather of the deterioration, and Gary, fearing headlines like: "Councillor's drunken criminal son incites riot", had reluctantly intervened.

Dean, having burned through the significant amount he had received from the will of his late wife Annie, had effectively blackmailed him demanding money in exchange for a three month stint in rehab. The situation was less than ideal for Gary, as having a son in rehab for the third time wasn't exactly meritorious, but if it did become public knowledge, the fact that he had paid for it out of love and concern for his son could be spun into a good story for everyone involved.

Plus, since becoming a councillor, Gary had quickly learned that throwing money at things was usually an easy way to make the problem go away.

Janet had wanted to visit Dean but the rehab didn't allow visits for people in their three month programme. She'd contented herself to talking to him on the phone once a week. She had thought his speech had sounded a little slurred during their last chat, but when she'd brought it up, he'd said that it was the medication they made them take to combat withdrawal. He'd seemed pretty upbeat and Janet was allowing herself to hope for real change this time.

Chapter 2

Dean is enduring yet another meeting but he doesn't care as he's getting out today!

The group are discussing the impact of their behaviour on the people around them. Dean nods along and can't believe he's managed to keep his mouth shut for his entire stay. He'd been quite vocal on previous visits but no one had paid any attention to anything he'd said, so he'd decided a quiet defiance might serve him better.

He tunes in as Janice is speaking, "I've two teenage children, a boy and a girl, they've basically had to grow up without me. I feel so guilty. My husband has been brilliant, though. I don't know what they would have done if he hadn't carried us all through this difficult time."

"Do you have any support from other people?" the facilitator says. It's a lady this time. Dean finds her annoying as she is sickly sweet and patronising.

"Well, my parents are around but they live far away and my husband's parents have died. Grandparents aren't the same as parents and I feel that my children are my responsibility."

Dean stares at his hands. These discussions usually bounce off him or go over his head, but this woman's guilt bothers him. He's not entirely sure why. After all, his situation is completely different, his parents live nearby and were more than happy to help by taking in Sophie. She seems happier with them, at least, he thinks she is. He hasn't been paying very close attention.

As for Grant, he's 20 now and an adult. He's doing really well, especially playing for his local football team. Also, their mother died and he couldn't cope with the burden, so it's completely different. And, he's an alcoholic so he can't help himself....

"Dean, you look like you might want to say something?" the facilitator says having noticed his contemplative mood.

Dean thinks quickly and decides no harm will be done by a final speech, "Just wanted to say that it's been great. I won't see you all again as I'm never coming back. Peace to you all." He doesn't add the word "suckers" to his farewell but has to swallow it as it arises unbidden to his lips.

The facilitator looks disappointed. Everyone else looks dismissive, they know he's just playing the game. Many of them have joined him in his late night rule-breaking as they've managed to smuggle in some drink, or assisted him in home-brewing an array of potentially lethal cocktails. They can't grass him up without getting in trouble themselves but they are annoyed that he is getting out and they are stuck. They are also annoyed with themselves for being weak and that, thanks to Dean, they are further away from their attempts at sobriety than ever before.

Dean gathers his belongings and waits for Gary to pick him up. He knows his father's motivations are entirely selfish, but he doesn't care.

His phone rings, he looks at the screen. It's a private number. He answers it tentatively wondering who it might be.

"Congratulations, Mr Yale. You have won this month's LottoMillions jackpot."

"Yeah, right. That'd be too good to be true as I wait for my pick-up from rehab," Dean says sarcastically.

"I can authenticate myself so you know it's a genuine call," the man on the phone says quickly. He's used to people not believing him. "I mean, you did enter the draw online, right?"

"What, I don't have time for this," Dean snaps. "I'm hanging up now."

"Don't you want to know how much you've won?" the man asks.

"Let me guess, more money than I could ever dream of?" Gary replies.

"Well, some would say it's life changing. In fact, most would agree it definitely is. 10 million pounds!" the man gets the figure in so that his jackpot winner will pay more attention.

"This has to be a joke. I've just spent three months in rehab to get ten grand off my old man and now you're saying I've won a hundred times that??" Dean is starting to take this call more seriously but still isn't quite buying it. "What do I need to do to get the money?"

"Great. So first, I need to check that you aren't in any sort of pool or group that you're contracted to for these winnings?"

Dean hesitates as he thinks of the rehab group who had begged him to place their £1's on the online draw as he was the only one with a laptop and internet connection. They had agreed to share any winnings, but now that he's gone, as long as he remains anonymous, they won't have any idea that their collective efforts have won the jackpot.

"Nope. It's just me." Dean replies. "Sorry my phone froze for a second there."

"That's quite, alright. So, secondly, I need to know if you want any publicity or whether you'd rather remain anonymous?"

"Anonymous. I don't want people knowing my business and, from what I've seen, people who go public end up in a right mess," Dean says confidently.

"Well, that can be true, but I've seen that happen to anonymous claims as well because they can't explain where their sudden wealth has come from and it causes jealously and suspicion in their relationships." The jackpot co-ordinator hopes he can convince this man to change his mind as the publicity is good for business.

"Anonymous," Dean says even more firmly.

"Sure. I'll need you to come to our office so we can verify your ID and go through some paperwork. When are you free?"

"I can come later today," Dean says as he makes a mental note of the address. *Perhaps this is real after all. It can't be a scam as I don't have anything for them to take, unless they've somehow found out about the £10k.*

Gary arrives and pulls up at the kerb as Dean hangs up.

Chapter 3

"Hi son, you look well," Gary says politely as Dean gets into his brand-new, immaculate Mercedes.

"A Merc, Dad?" Dean asks.

"Perk of the job. They didn't like what I was driving before," Gary explains. "Um...where do you want to go? I've got a cheque for you in my pocket..."

Dean momentarily thinks of telling his father not to bother about the money, but then he'll have to tell him about the jackpot which he's not certain is real yet.

"Great, Dad. Just drop me off in town and I'll take it straight to the bank," Dean says.

Gary feels awkward. There's an uncomfortable silence between them. They've been growing apart for years. Gary's now a local councillor and pillar of the community and Dean is his wayward, reckless, alcoholic son. Why couldn't he have produced a hard-working, diligent lawyer or doctor instead?

"Sure, I'll do that. What are you planning to do?" Gary feels he should ask.

"Don't worry, I won't embarrass you and the money will keep me going until I get a job," Dean reassures him.

"Any ideas what you want to do?" Gary asks.

"Bartender," Dean jokes.

Gary sets his mouth in a firm line. He wants his son to take things seriously.

"Don't worry, I'll not do that, but maybe they have another job for me at the pub," Dean says.

"Why the pub? Shouldn't you stay away from places like that now?" Gary asks. "And why do you smell of disinfectant."

He'd noticed the smell as soon as Dean had got in the car but thought it might be from outside. Now, he's realised it's emanating from his son, a really strong smell of bleach or some kind of cleaning spray.

"It's where my mates are and they know me there. Not many people want to employ someone who has a drink problem, Dad," Dean knows he sounds pathetic but what he is saying is probably true. He ignores the comment about the smell. He'd covered himself in cleaning sprays to ensure he didn't reek of the celebratory drink he'd had last night.

"You mean a former drink problem. You're clean now, right?" Gary looks at his son.

"Well, I'm an alcoholic, so I'll always have this illness. It's how I manage it that's important," Dean replies. "Don't worry Dad, I've got it all under control."

Gary slumps in his seat and lowers his eyes as he hands over the cheque and Dean gets out of his car.

In just ten minutes, he has realised two things: his son will end up back in rehab and he's just given ten grand to a self confessed alcoholic.

Chapter 4

It's Sophie's 18th and she's having a big party at the village hall. Her grandfather's position secured them a really good deal. Her grandmother is catering with some outside help. Her grandfather has to keep being reminded that he's not to use this as a photo opportunity for the upcoming local elections.

Grant pops over with a present of a new laptop. Sophie is thrilled. He apologises that he can't make the actual party as he has a football thing. Sophie understands. She's getting on well with her brother these days having followed his advice to stop attending the *Church of the Living Water*. She hasn't really settled anywhere else yet as she still feels confused about the different churches and what they represent. Grant is hoping she will come to his church in due course but doesn't want to rush her as she's been through a lot.

The party is in full flow. People are drinking and dancing and enjoying themselves. The few oldies that Sophie's grandparents have invited are gathered in a corner trying not to cramp the style of the younger people. Gary is parading around as if he owns the place, Sophie doesn't mind as she knows he can't help himself. Janet is busy in the kitchen instructing her team of helpers as they replenish dishes at the buffet.

Sophie looks around. Where is her father? Dean had promised he would come, even if just for half an hour to say hello. She knows he's out of rehab as her grandfather had told her about their awkward car journey. She had asked Gary how her father was and whether he'd asked about her. Gary had looked uncomfortable and hesitated before saying that her dad had been fine and had asked about her as soon as he'd got in the car. She'd known it was a lie but hadn't challenged it. It wasn't as if she had expected any different.

Dean had dropped out of her life the minute her mother had died four years ago and they'd had rocky spells even before that. If her grandparents hadn't stepped in, she would've had to live with friends or gone into foster care. Her dad just doesn't seem capable of dealing with any level of responsibility and more often than not, when she has seen him in recent years, she's ended up looking after him in his sorry, drunken state.

Sophie is fed up with the hope and disappointment cycle though and had been sure he would put in an appearance on her 18th.

Suddenly, there's a loud noise outside, the repeated honking of a horn and what sounds like fireworks exploding in the street. The music inside is paused.

Everyone in the village hall piles towards the door, excited to get a look at what's causing the commotion.

Sophie reaches the door first and steps out. A car transporter carrying a bright red sport's car appears to be the source of the noise, as the driver continues pressing the horn. The car has a giant bow to match and a banner which reads "Happy Birthday, Sophie!" blowing in the wind. The fireworks are being set off by the passenger of the car transporter.

Momentarily stunned, Sophie looks around for answers to the many questions in her mind. *What? Who? How?*

Janet reaches her side. "I think it's from your father, dear…"

"What? Is he here then?" Sophie asks looking towards the two strange men celebrating her birthday.

"I don't think so, honey. I just got an odd message from him saying that he'd sent you a gift which should be arriving very soon and that he'd had to work tonight," Janet says gently.

Gary, who had been in the rest room, joins his wife and granddaughter.

"What the….?" he exclaims as he sees the monstrosity in the street.

"It's a gift from Dean, love. He just sent me a message," Janet says.

Gary doesn't say anything but looks as if he might explode. His face goes red before he turns on his heel and marches back inside.

"What's wrong with Granddad?" Sophie asks.

"Oh, don't worry. I think he ate some curry and it might be messing with him. He'll be fine." Janet pats Sophie's arm. "Perhaps, we should go and talk to these guys or they might stay here all night honking horns and setting off fireworks."

Sophie smiles, "Yes, okay. Wow, Dad is so generous. I had no idea he still had money from Mum's will, I thought he blew it all on drink and gambling. I can't believe he spent so much on me…"

Janet closes her eyes and sighs before following Sophie over to the men to receive the ridiculously extravagant gift that's been purchased for her granddaughter.

She silently asks the question, "Where are you, Dean?"

Chapter 5

Dean sits in the Wild Crown with his mates. He's on his fifth pint and it's going down well.

"Isn't it your daughter's party tonight?" Richard slurs, he's had three beers but isn't a seasoned drinker.

"Yeah, I bought her a sport's car!" Dean boasts.

"Wow! That's amazing. How could you afford that? You're not working at the moment are you?" Richard asks, curious.

"Annie's money. I thought it'd be good to spend some of it on Soph," Dean lies.

"Oh. I thought you said you were nearly out and we'd have to start buying our own drinks again?" Sam laughs.

None of them are really interested in being that friendly with Dean the alcoholic, but he happened to have joined their local when he'd just received a windfall, so….

"I found some more," Dean says vaguely. He doesn't have to explain himself to these guys who sponge off him.

"So, did you see her earlier then? I thought the party was tonight, my wife said our Alice was going to the village hall," Richard says.

"I sent it on the back of a car transporter and paid the guys to deliver it with a big display. Thought it would be a grand entrance," Dean says proudly.

"Would've been even better if you were there…" Richard mutters.

Grand entrance but you didn't enter….. Sam thinks.

Dean says nothing. He isn't going to tell them he's been in rehab for three months and is meant to be sober. It's nothing to do with them. Besides, he's enjoying himself and he doesn't want to ruin his daughter's birthday by gate-crashing the event.

Dean receives a call and stumbles outside to take it.

"I can't believe you spent all the money on a sport's car. What are you going to live on? Do you really think it's good to spoil Sophie with such an extravagant gift?…" The questions come tumbling out of Gary's mouth. He is furious.

"Hold on, hold on," Dean struggles to get his brain functioning and to avoid slurring his words. He moves the phone away from his ear.

"No, I won't hold on. You abdicate responsibility for your child and then pop up out of nowhere with a ridiculous gift and you don't even deliver it yourself! You know she would much rather you'd kept your promise to show up?!" Gary isn't calming down.

"Wait, I can explain everything," Dean says.

"I'm listening," Gary answers, inwardly seething.

"So, I think it'd be better if we spoke about it tomorrow when you've calmed down a bit," Dean hedges. "I'm actually out at the moment with some mates and they're calling me. I have to go now."

"Don't you dare hang up on me! Did you get it on finance? How much are the payments? What about insurance....?" The dial tone sounds loudly in Gary's ear. He swears and smashes his phone against the outside wall of the village hall. A few passer's by stop and stare at him, so he hastily pulls his hood up to cover his face before heading back inside glowering.

Dean hails a taxi and heads home. Gary's call has put a dampener on his evening and abruptly sobered him up. He's jetting out to Spain for a five star package holiday tomorrow morning, so he needs to pack.

Having anonymously collected his LottoMillions jackpot, the world is his oyster; he can go anywhere and do anything. He is somewhat restricted by his desire to keep his good fortune under wraps, and to himself, but that goes with the territory. Alcoholics are used to hiding things so he's sure it won't be too difficult: no more expensive gifts and sticking to a low key life-style locally.

Arriving home, Dean forgets about packing and instead sits down to cheer himself up by planning his new life. After an hour of struggling to focus as the effects of the drink haven't completely worn off, he realises that with Grant still at home and his parents hovering nearby, he'll need some type of explanation for his sudden increase in wealth.

Maybe he could say that extra money has belatedly come from Annie's will? Dean grabs a folder containing Annie's paperwork; he's only kept it because of the will. They'd probably still be suspicious as Annie wasn't rich.

He notices a certificate for some bank or other and pulls it out of the centre of the pile. It's for Premium Bonds. He types the words into Google and learns that they work by individuals investing sums of money and then receiving prizes from a monthly draw. It looks similar to a raffle or even a lottery, although the initial investment can't be lost.

Dean's brain is tired and it's all seeming like a lot of effort. He forces himself to think as he continues reading and sees that the jackpot is a million pounds. Maybe he could tell the family that Annie had won the jackpot and he has received the proceeds as her next of kin. He can even show them this certificate to prove the investment. This would deal with the cover-up of the jackpot from the rehab pool and stop their questions.

Dean relaxes now that he has a plan. He packs a few things and then grabs a beer from the fridge.

Chapter 6

Dean wakes up. He feels a bit groggy and has a slight headache. He glances at the clock on the bedside table. 9am! His flight is in two hours. He jumps out of bed in a panic, tripping over things as he rushes to the bathroom. Staring at himself in the mirror, he notices a slight yellow tinge to his face. He throws water on it and deliberately looks away.

Ten minutes later, he grabs the bag he had started last night and fills it with clothes. His heart racing, he tries to calm himself down as he searches for items that he might need on his two week break to Lanzarote. It all gets too stressful and he sits back down on the bed and groans as his head starts spinning.

Wait a minute. I've just won the lottery! I don't need to take anything with me. I can just buy it all there. The realisation that things will never be the same again is slowly dawning on him. He grabs his phone, wallet and passport, abandons his bag full of old stuff that he no longer needs and runs down the stairs.

He heads for the front door passing Grant who is eating his breakfast.

"Hey Dad, where are you off to in such a rush?" Grant says with a mouthful of cereal.

Dean looks guiltily at him. "Remember, Son. I told you I was going away again."

"No, you didn't, Dad. How long are you going for? You're going to miss the county play-offs!" Grant says with dismay.

"I definitely told you. I'll be back in two weeks and there will be another time. I have to go or I'll miss my flight," Dean is backing out of the front door, away from this uncomfortable conversation.

"But, wait, Dad. Where's your stuff?" Grant is confused. His father's behaviour is becoming increasingly odd in recent months.

"I don't have time, so I'll just buy stuff out there. It's pretty cheap, you know…bye!"

Dean shuts the door firmly before realising he's forgotten his keys. *Never mind, I'll sort that out when I get back.*

He jogs down the street and turns right, then heads across the road to the taxi rank. Perfect, a taxi waiting as if just for him. He jumps in, "Manchester Airport and I'll give you extra if you get me there quickly."

The driver doesn't wait for further instructions and puts his foot firmly on the accelerator.

The doorbell rings and Grant looks at the clock. It's only been fifteen minutes since his dad left. Maybe he's come back for his keys that Grant can see lying on the counter. He walks to the door and opens it.

"Hey, Grant. I really need to see your dad, is he here?" Gary asks.

Grant notices that his grandfather looks totally exhausted. "No, sorry, Granddad. He just left for the airport."

"What!! Which airport and where is he going?" Gary asks, struggling to control his temper.

"Actually, I don't know. He said he was going to Lanzarote for two weeks and I guess Manchester? He rushed out of here pretty fast; I think he was late for his flight. What on earth is wrong?"

"Oh, I'll never catch him now," Gary sighs wearily and leans against the doorpost.

"Come in, I'll make you a cup of tea. I'm only going to the library to meet Louise in a bit anyway." Grant says.

"Okay, I may as well. I can't do any work with this all going round and round in my head. Can't sleep much either." Gary sighs.

"I guessed something must've been wrong for you to appear at this time of the morning as usually you're in meetings, right?" Grant makes conversation.

"I can't focus on any of the council stuff until I sort out your father's mess," Gary mumbles as he gratefully takes the mug of tea handed to him.

"What's he done this time?" Grant says. Nothing would surprise him.

"Didn't you hear about Sophie's present?" Gary asks. "I assumed you would have."

"Oh yeah. Did she like the laptop?" Grant says.

"She did but then it was eclipsed by something much larger and much more expensive!" Gary replies.

"What did he get her? It can't have cost that much as he doesn't have any money. I don't know how he's affording to go on holiday again so soon." Grant is perplexed by his father's seemingly never-ending supply of money that is funding his extravagant life-style.

"Okay, this may hurt but I might as well tell you everything as you'll find out anyway," Gary begins. "His last spell in rehab wasn't exactly voluntary. I bribed him to complete it." Gary isn't going to tell his grandson that his motivation was entirely selfish to protect his reputation.

"Well, that clears one thing up. I couldn't understand why he went back there so cheerfully as he hated it last time." Grant says. "You didn't give him a lot, did you?"

"Apparently enough to buy a sport's car and fund a trip to Lanzarote," Gary realises.

"Wait. What sport's car? I haven't seen any sport's car. He got a taxi home from the pub last night, worse for wear by the sound of it," Grant says. "So much for rehab, heh?"

"Arghhhh. When I get my hands on him, I'll kill him. I really will. He's conned me out of ten grand and I won't be able to get any of it back as it's in that stupid car," Gary fumes. His face is going red as the anger builds.

"TEN GRAND? Woah, that's a lot. I thought you meant a couple of hundred quid and that he'd got the car on finance and paid a deposit or something. Still, ten grand isn't enough to buy a sport's car outright. So, where is it?"

"This is the painful bit. He bought it for Sophie, for her birthday. It's outside our house." Gary comes clean and watches his grandson's expression.

"WHAT!? But he never even remembers my birthday and if he does, I get a CD or a DVD obviously purchased at the last minute from the newsagents around the corner." Grant looks defeated. After a few seconds, he forces himself not to be bitter and tries to remind himself that his father, and indeed, his grandfather aren't Christians. The lavish gift and favouritism still hurt, though.

"I know, I know. It's not fair. It's a nightmare for us too as I have no idea if he's paid the insurance, if there are more payments to make or anything really. Sophie hasn't even passed her test yet, she's still provisional and a sport's car isn't exactly an ideal car to learn in. I tried to talk to him about it but he fobbed me off and now he's gone abroad. I'm so angry!" Gary rants.

"Sophie's sensible enough. What does she say about it?" Grant asks, having got over the initial shock of his father's rash decision.

"I don't think she's thinking clearly. She loves the car so much that she's already planning how she can be driving it as soon as possible. She keeps begging us to insure her on our car and take her out for lessons. The problem is, I now have a company car which is pretty upmarket, a Merc actually, and your gran gave up her car a while back. So, it's not really an option...." Gary finishes. As he is talking it occurs to him that the perfect person to prepare Sophie for the road is probably her brother.

Guessing his granddad's thoughts, Grant says, "Alright, I'll do it. I guess we should all rally round and keep Dad's problems in house as much as possible." Grant is still battling the jealousy that is threatening to rear its ugly head but manages to keep it under wraps.

"I know you have other things going on but I'd really appreciate it. I just can't bear the thought of ruining this for Soph and I can't take the car back even if I wanted to as I have no idea where he got it," Gary says, the redness in his face is reducing as he sees light at the end of the tunnel.

"Try the glove box. Dad usually puts stuff in there," Grant suggests. "I'll pop over later and talk to Soph and we come up with a plan."

"And, I'll have to contain my fury until he gets back from Spain. He won't answer his phone while he's there as he's avoiding me. By rights, I should insist on his paying my ten grand back as he's already been out drinking. You live and learn." Gary gets up and walks to the door. "I'm glad you were here today, you've taken a great weight off my shoulders."

"We're family, Granddad," Grant says simply as he starts getting ready to go out.

Gary leaves and heads back to his car. *Wow, I don't think I would've taken it so well when I was a young guy, if my brother or sister had been given something like that. He's really growing up fast or maybe it's something to do with his religion. He's really into all that again.*

Gary continues pondering the whole situation as he heads home knowing that, thanks to Grant, he should be able to sleep better tonight.

Chapter 7

Dean relaxes in his first class booth. He'd just made the flight and because of his ticket, had been shown straight in past the queue of people waiting. Now, he's making himself comfortable as they've reached altitude and are cruising.

A stewardess appears, "Can I offer you a drink and a snack, Sir?"

"White wine and ...no wait, champagne and chocolates," Dean instructs. He's trying to pretend that he's used to flying first class but he really has no idea how to behave.

Once the drinks are served, the staff gather in the preparation area to discuss their various guests in the more luxurious part of the aircraft. There is a famous singer, a couple of regulars, several who work for the airline and are taking advantage of their perks, a mysterious girl that nobody recognises and Dean.

"I think she's a wealthy widow, married to a millionaire and he's part of an organised crime syndicate," one of the guys says.

"No, it's the other way round. She's the criminal and he's a wealthy widower," suggests the head stewardess.

"Maybe, he's just blown all his money on one first class ticket just to see what it's like. I don't think we've had him before and he's guzzling all the champagne," a junior team member says sounding irritated.

"I reckon, if I give him another drink, I can find out. Care to place a bet?"

"Widower, five quid," says one.

"Criminal, five quid," says another.

"Pretending to be rich, five quid," says a third.

An hour later, Dean has nearly polished off an entire bottle of Champers and is feeling pretty happy...and drunk. A stewardess approaches.

"You certainly seem to be enjoying that drink, Sir. Celebrating something?" She holds her breath as she waits to see if lowering his inhibitions will be enough for him to reveal the personal detail.

"Yeah. Lottery win," Dean slurs. There's no harm in telling these people and it feels great to share his good fortune with someone else, even if she is just a stranger on a plane. "Share a glass?"

"Sorry, Sir. That's forbidden. Congrats on your success and I hope you have a great time in...which resort are you staying in?"

"Santa Rita, I think." Dean hadn't taken that long over the details. He'd just booked the first thing that looked half decent and cost a lot. After all, you get what you pay for.

"Perfect. Thanks!"

The response from the stewardess hadn't been exactly what Dean was expecting. In fact, it seemed a little odd, but not strange enough for Dean to think any more about it.

However, the crafty stewardess, armed with this new information, has headed back to her co-workers.

"You were right, he's just pretending. Sad sort of a life, I reckon," she casually informs them as she hands over her £5 to the winner of the bet.

"Take your seats for landing," the captain's voice, loud and clear.

The plane lands without a fuss and the passengers gather their belongings and slowly head for the exit.

The stewardess, who now has several days off, follows them off the plane. She gets out her phone, switches it on and, smiling to herself, she sends several texts all saying the same thing:

"Lotto winner, Santa Rita, male, 6", mid 40's, blonde hair, unshaven, name of Dean Yale, just left the plane."

Chapter 8

Fortunately, Dean's transport has all been arranged as part of his package holiday, otherwise, he'd be in a real muddle by now. He stumbles through the airport, aware of the disapproving looks from the adults and wide-eyed stares from the children. With the help of a €20 note that had happened to be in his pocket, he is whisked through a short line at Spanish immigration. The tour operator is waiting for him with a sign that he can just about read, bearing his name. He heads towards the few people gathered.

"Where's your luggage, Sir?" A smartly dressed man asks him in English but with a foreign accent.

"I don't have any. I just want to get to my hotel," Dean says curtly. He's fed up with being asked about his belongings as he has been at least five times already. *Surely, the rich don't have to worry about luggage and now I'm one of them, I shouldn't have to either.*

"Righto," the man says as he looks him up and down a little dubiously. This guy doesn't look like the sort of clientèle he usually deals with and he isn't convinced that he will fit in at the hotel either. "Our taxis are over there. They'll take you straight there."

Dean follows the man's finger and sees a waiting vehicle. He heads towards it and falls into the back. He just wants to sleep now.

The driver waits patiently until Dean realises he needs to tip the man. He pulls another €20 from his wallet and hands it over. The driver's eyes light up and he quickly starts the engine.

Arriving at the hotel after about thirty minutes, Dean is fast asleep. A bag boy employed by the hotel has come to collect Dean's luggage. He opens the boot and looks in the back of the vehicle but sees only a body slumped across the seats.

"He's been comatose since we left the airport," the driver says in Spanish.

"Drunk. Disgusting. We'll have to wake him up and help him to his room. I'll get some more people. He can pay us tomorrow. Where's his luggage?"

The driver shrugs. He's done his duty, delivered the intoxicated passenger and been paid well. As the bag boy heads off to get help, he has an idea.

"Wake up, wake up. We're here." He shakes Dean awake and helps him out of the car onto the pavement. He stands next to Dean waiting.

Dean, blurry eyed, looks confused. "What are you waiting for?"

The man looks down.

"Oh, you need paying." Dean fumbles in his wallet and gives the man another €20. The man waits, Dean fishes out another €20 and hands it over.

"Hey, what's going on?" a voice from behind him.

The driver quickly rushes to the door of his cab, jumps in and takes off leaving a bewildered Dean looking after him.

"How much did you give him?" the bag boy asks in halting English.

"I don't know," Dean says, which is the truth.

A couple of other guys appear and they help Dean up the stairs, into the hotel, to the lift and to his room. He can register in the morning.

Grant comes back from visiting the library with his girlfriend, Louise. They are sitting drinking coffee in the lounge and Grant is telling her all about the sport's car and his father's weird behaviour.

Every time Grant spends time with Louise, he is grateful to God. They hadn't had the most conventional beginning to their friendship. Grant had been in a car that had run Louise over and driven from the scene. Louise had had to have part of her leg amputated as a result. Grant had befriended her under false pretences before everything had been exposed and his life had come crashing down around him.

Having begged Louise for forgiveness and returned to his Christian faith, Grant's expectations hadn't been high but Louise had been so affected by the change in his life that she had started her own journey of faith and had recently been baptised. They are taking things slowly but they figure that if they can get through what they've already dealt with, they can probably get through anything!

"I took Sophie out for her first lesson yesterday and saw the sport's car on the drive. The whole thing doesn't make any sense as we found the paperwork and rang the garage who said it's fully paid for. They wouldn't confirm the price but there's no way it'd be anything less than thirty grand and Dad only had ten...."

"And he's just jetted off on a two week holiday," Louise finishes.

"Exactly. There's something not quite right but I can't put my finger on it. When I came home yesterday, I also found a Premium Bond certificate in my mum's name on the floor in the lounge. I don't know why Dad would've had that out. I didn't even know Mum had things like that," Grant explains. He feels like he's involved in solving a mystery which might be a lot of fun if it wasn't for the stakes involved. Deep down, he knows that the whole thing will come back to his father being dishonest.

"Hmm, that is weird. Isn't that like a lottery where you win prizes?" Louise asks.

"I think so, but I guess the money is returned when someone dies." Grant is thinking out loud. "I don't know what's going on, but if it involves money or alcohol, and my dad, it can't be good."

Chapter 9

"Room service!"

Dean wakes up with the mother of all hangovers. He's used to the feeling and knows it'll pass if he can find another drink. He looks around at the unfamiliar surroundings. The bed is very comfy but he is still in his clothes from the day before and suddenly remembers that he doesn't have any others with him.

"Come in," he calls hoping what he needs is already in the process of being supplied.

An immaculately presented waiter enters, pushing a large cart with all manner of delicacies on it.

Dean catches the smell of fried food which makes him feel ill. He holds his nose.

"Just some fruit, toast and coffee," he calls, trying to sound authoritative.

"Of course, Sir. Anything else?" the waiter bows.

"I need some clothes. Find me a personal shopper, they will be well paid." Dean has no idea if they even offer these kind of service in Lanzarote, but he feels sure that the rich and famous have people at their beck and call constantly. Money will free him of the inconvenience of having to deal with trifling matters, like shopping, himself.

The waiter looks baffled by the request. "I'll speak to the manager, Sir and see what can be arranged."

Dean feels compelled to explain, "I know you Spanish are more than capable of finding suitable things for us Brits to wear." Again, Dean has no idea about any of this but it trips easily off his tongue, and causes the waiter to relax a little, as he collects another cart with the requested items of food and makes a hasty exit, bowing as he does so.

Alone again, Dean notices how quiet, and lonely, it is. He heads for the bathroom and scans it for toiletries. Everything that he will need is in place. Perfect. He catches a glimpse of himself in the mirror. He looks awful. Peering into it, Dean takes a closer look at his face. The yellow tinge is still there and is more noticeable in the whites of his eyes. *Everyone gets that with age, don't they?*

He shakes his head and moves towards the mini fridge. He'd clocked it as soon as he'd arrived despite his drunken state. He removes a few small bottles of spirits and tips gin into his orange juice.

That should deal with the headache. He picks up a piece of toast and starts eating it gingerly as his stomach churns. Maybe he's going down with something, he doesn't feel well at all.

He falls asleep again and, a few hours later, is woken by a knocking at the door.

"Yes?" he calls.

A different man, also smartly dressed enters and bows towards Dean.

"I understand you need to purchase some clothing, Sir?" he says in perfect English with only the faint trace of an accent.

Dean rubs his eyes, "Yes. I was in a rush and didn't have time to pack anything. Money isn't an issue."

The man's eyes brighten slightly at the latter comment but he maintains his steady expression. "Of course, Sir. I can help you. I often select clothes for those who can afford my services when they visit this hotel. When will you be ready?"

Dean looks surprised. "Can you not just make a judgement call and decide yourself. I'm on holiday, I want to chill out."

"I understand, Sir. I will bring you a selection of items for you to choose from at your convenience," the man nods and bows as he exits the room.

Dean leans back on his pillows. He feels better from the sleep. He gets up and grabs a small bottle of whisky from the fridge and downs it in one go. He feels the slight burning sensation as it hits his stomach.

"Right, time to enjoy myself," he says to himself. Fortunately, the shorts he had been wearing the day before double as swimming shorts. He grabs a towel and heads downstairs to find the pool.

He registers at reception where, in response to their questions, he makes it clear that no expense should be spared during his holiday. He's more than happy to keep an open tab for personal errands as well as at the various bars. The staff gaze at him with appropriate levels of respect but behind his back they are contemptuous of the rich foreigner who threats them like slaves as he throws his money around.

Chapter 10

Dean heads out to the pool and is led to an allocated sun-bed by an attendant. He is surprised as usually he would be able to pick where he wants to lie but the attendant is insistent that this bed has been reserved for him as it's the best spot in the place. He feels empowered as the conversation is heard by everyone around. In fact, they all stop to look at this mystery man deserving of so much attention.

Dean lies on his towel and enjoys the sun beating down on him. He is aware there is an attractive woman either side of him. He's a single man, of course he notices things like this immediately. One of the women is pointedly ignoring him and has her nose in a book. The other looks at him with open interest and seems to deliberately nudge him as she walks past to go to the pool. They are both wearing very skimpy bikinis but Dean considers them comparatively modest as many of the women sun-bathing are topless.

Dean looks more closely at the book the woman that is left is reading: *The Testament* by John Grisham. Dean has read it before. Annie used to leave novels like this lying around and Dean had been curious and read a couple of them. It had been a page-turner and he had understood why his late-wife had been hooked on this Grisham guy. The memory makes him briefly nostalgic as he thinks back to the good times they had had before all the strife.

Dean's tired brain works overtime to remember some of the detail from the book in order to make some kind of half intelligent conversation about it. He's more intrigued by this woman as she seems less interested. There's something perverse in him that wants to chase and catch something he can't have and he likes a challenge. The other woman would be too easy.

He recalls that the book is about a very rich man with a bunch of spoiled brat relatives. The man decides to take his own life but doesn't want his horrible offspring and their kids getting their hands on his wealth. So, he devises a plan to leave everything to a distant relative working as a missionary in a remote place. Dean can't remember much more than this but it's a good start.

"Good book?" he asks the woman, with a lazy smile.

She pushes her sunglasses up onto her head and looks at him intently.

"Pretty good, have you read it?" she says in a Northern English accent.

"A while back, yes. I don't think I would have wanted to leave my hard earned cash to them either." Dean knows he's gambling when he makes this statement as the woman may have a completely different perspective.

She smiles and turns to face him. "Me, neither. So, you're a Northerner too. I thought I was the only one here."

"Manc," Dean acknowledges.

"Me too. What did you make of the religious stuff in the book?"

Dean thinks the woman is trying to get to know him. He responds carefully, "I don't know. You?"

"I'm Catholic. I think it's interesting how even with all the money in the world, the man in the book ends up killing himself and instead of feeling sad about his death, his relatives are left fighting over his money. Money can't buy love or happiness." As she makes these bold assertions, the woman looks directly at Dean and he thinks he catches a hint of mockery in her eyes, but just as quickly as it was there, it's gone again.

"I reckon, if I had all the money in the world, I'd be enjoying it rather than jumping from a high building. That's what happens, isn't it?" Dean hopes he's remembering the book correctly as it was so long ago. He feels uncomfortable with the direction their conversation has taken and doesn't know exactly how they ended up on the topic of money.

"I think he had a terminal illness, hey, something else money can't buy, health!" the women says, almost triumphantly.

Dean lightly changes the subject, "Well, I know something money can buy, would you like a drink?"

The woman looks at her watch. "It's after midday, sure. I'll have one of those lush looking cocktails if you'll join me." She puts down her book and moves nearer to the table between them.

Dean gets up and is about to head to the bar but a keen waiter sees him and rushes over to take their order. He tells the waiter to put it on his room tab and tips him with some money from his shorts.

"Phew," the woman says. "If you keep tipping like that, you'll be broke in no time."

Dean looks down, embarrassed. He hadn't intended for her to see.

"What's your name, anyway?"

"Danielle, but most call me Dani"

"Okay Dani, I'm Dean. So, are you working out here or just on holiday?"

"Definitely, working," Dani says.

She doesn't volunteer any further information so Dean doesn't ask.

"How about you? You look like a businessman on holiday, right? I'm right, aren't I?" Dani says with a laugh.

"How did you guess?" Dean says smoothly.

"You just have that look about you. Exhausted from the day job and excited to be on holiday and not have to think about work," Dani says confidently.

If only she knew the reality. He's glad she doesn't know the reality that he's an alcoholic, fresh from a failed attempt at rehabilitation and trying to escape his problems in a tropical paradise.

Several hours later, having consumed a few cocktails, Dani decides she needs to go and do some work. They arrange to meet the following day. As Dani turns to leave, she offers him her book.

"I won't have time to read any of this before tomorrow, why don't you refresh your memory and we can chat about it?"

Dean takes the book, intrigued. Then, he also gets up to go back inside the hotel. He feels happy to have met Dani but can't quite work her out. She's guarded and often deflects questions back to him. The whole thing with the book is a little odd as well. He feels like she already knows him and is playing a game, but that's impossible, isn't it?

Annoyingly, Dean also can't stop thinking about the character in the Grisham book who'd had everything but had ended up jumping from a high rise building because he couldn't buy back his health. He doesn't know why this should bother him, but it does.

Alone in his hotel room, having picked a range of clothes from the many options presented by the keen super-shopper, he reads the novel late into the evening. Even before the missionary is found by the well-paid lawyers acting on behalf of the dead billionaire, Dean knows what her response will be. She's going to reject the money in favour of her missionary life serving God.

A Bible text is quoted: *"For what should it profit a man if he gains the whole world but loses his own soul."* The text goes round and round in Dean's muddled brain as he puts the book down and tries to get some sleep.

Chapter 11

The landline rings. Grant stares at it. It's been so long since he's used a landline phone, he'd forgotten they even had one. He decides to ignore it, let the machine get it. It'll be for his dad anyway.

"Hello, Mr Yale. It's just Justin calling from LottoMillions. We just wanted to double-check that you still don't want any publicity. Sometimes, people change their minds when the excitement has worn off and they've had a chance to think about it. We'd also like to talk with you about how you might want to spend some of your winnings. There are some good causes that we like to support. Anyway, I'll wait for your callback. Take care!"

Grant's mouth had dropped open as the overly-enthusiastic caller had continued his pre-prepared speech. Straight away, he grabs his phone and looks up LottoMillions. Then, he looks for the last few weeks jackpot payouts. He jumps back and exclaims as he sees that the jackpot had rolled over for several months leading to a ten million pound payout in the UK. It was the biggest payout for a year. Surely, that can't be what his dad had won?

Grant had been intending to wait until Dean was back in the UK to talk some things through but now, he really can't wait. He checks the time and rings his father's mobile.

Dean answers sleepily and Grant knows he's woken him up.

"Dad, are you okay? Good holiday?" Grant asks. He knows if he starts off in an accusatory tone, his dad will just hang up and switch off his phone for the rest of the holiday. He's surprised he's answered at all.

"Hey Grant, yeah, actually, pretty good. What's up?" Dean asks sounding a bit more alert.

Grant decides to start with something simple and see if his father will fess up, "Dad, I found a certificate for Premium Bonds in Mum's name on the floor in the lounge. Do you know why it's there?" Grant asks.

Dean decides to go with his earlier plan. "Yes, I was going to tell you when I got back from holiday as I needed time to think about everything. I had a call that your mum had won some money and as her next of kin I was able to claim it."

Grant sighs but keeps himself in check, "Oh, so that's how you bought the car for Sophie. I knew it couldn't have been just the ten grand Granddad gave you."

"Oh, so you know about that too. I guess that was inevitable. Look, I didn't pressurise him. He was so worried about his reputation that he practically forced me to take it," Dean explains.

"I've been teaching Soph to drive actually as we didn't think she should start off in that car," Grant says. "She's doing really well."

"That's great. I'll see you when I get back," Dean says.

Grant takes a breath, "So, how much did Mum win anyway?" he asks innocently.

"Oh..a few hundred thousand," Dean says breezily. "You can have some of it when I get back, I promise."

"I wasn't after……." Grant begins but his dad has already hung up.

Having hung up the phone, Dean feels inexplicably anxious. Lying to everyone around him, including his own family, just to protect his wealth, feels wrong. He reminds himself that he's doing it to protect them really — if other people knew the family had won such a large jackpot, they could no longer be sure of their friends and wouldn't be able to trust anyone. At least this way, no one knows so they can all carry on as normal.

Something else had bothered him though; his son hadn't seemed jealous about the gift he had given to Sophie and had even been helping her appreciate it. Dean knows that given the same situation, there's no way that he would have accepted the partiality with grace. He would have stomped and shouted and complained until the benefactor gifted him an equal amount.

Dean senses there's something different about his son now. He'd certainly helped him out of some scrapes in recent years; the hit and run where the girl had been injured, is the one that stands out. But, more recently Grant has changed and Dean can't shake the feeling that it's something to do with that church he's involved with again. The whole thing makes him extremely discomforted as he doesn't understand it and would rather his boy behaved like normal boys of his age; chasing women, boozing a bit and playing sport.

Well, at least he's into football and good at it. Dean can be proud of that. Even as the thoughts float through his mind, Dean realises that Grant hadn't said anything about the play-offs and how his team had done and Dean had been so wrapped up in his own life that he had forgotten to ask.

He grabs a bottle from the mini fridge and downs it, pushing the guilty feelings far away.

Chapter 12

Dean grabs the John Grisham book, dresses casually, avoiding looking at his face in the mirror and heads down to the pool. He's escorted to his allocated sun-bed again and sees that Dani is already there. The other woman is nowhere to be seen today, Dean feels relieved.

Dani gives him a big smile and they immediately start talking about the book. They have different conclusions, Dean still feels that having all the money in the world is a desirable position to be in and that he would make the most of it. Dani seems more down to earth and realistic.

The discussion ends when she says, "Well, as neither of us are likely to become millionaires any time soon, I guess we'll never know."

Dean can't help the flush that immediately warms his face. He jumps up and quickly heads for the pool stating that he needs to cool down. He dives in and swims a few lengths.

Dani watches him curiously from the sun-bed. She knows she's taunting him but she can't help herself and she enjoys it. It's all part of her "job". It's fun to bring down the hoity-toity rich who think they're invincible, stepping on those they consider beneath them, and believing they can buy everything they've ever dreamed of. Plus, as a single mum, she has three mouths to feed. Her conscience is clear.

Since receiving her friend's text that Dean Yale, the lotto winner, was getting off the plane, she's been waiting for her opportunity to fleece him. Slow and steady wins the race and she knows she mustn't pounce too soon or he'll guess her secret and the game will be over.

Dean is largely oblivious to the behind the scenes activities that have been triggered by the fact of his wealth reaching the eyes and ears of the public domain. Whilst sitting at the pool, he's been offered time-share apartments, a round the world tour, cruises in various exotic locations and day-trip excursions galore. He hasn't noticed other holiday makers being pestered so persistently, but he thinks that maybe he just hasn't been watching closely enough. They always appear when Dani is in the bathroom or has gone off to do some work, which he does find a little strange. He buys a time-share apartment and pays a deposit on a cruise for later in the year. Money well spent, he's sure of it.

He spends much of the first week at the pool with Dani, but quickly finds that other than the book, they don't have much to talk about. She's withdrawing and clearly isn't interested in him romantically. He is beginning to feel that maybe she has another agenda but she remains friendly enough. They still chat, share drinks and keep an eye on each other's things including wallets and phone.

Then, one afternoon, she says goodbye and doesn't return.

After a few days, he asks the bar and hotel staff about her, but they deny having a guest by the name of Dani and act as if she's a figment of his imagination. The whole thing is so bizarre that Dean begins to wonder if he has invented a mystery woman, but then he remembers the book which is still very much in his possession.

Finally, he sees the woman who had been interested in him on the first day and asks her about Dani. The jilted lady is annoyed at being asked about a rival and clearly doesn't want to engage with him on the topic. Of course she remembers the woman, though. She's seen her hanging around other pools of nearby hotels and she's heard her speaking a number of languages with different accents.

Alarm bells are ringing in Dean's head. He is pretty naive but even he can see the red flags now. He heads straight for the hotel reception with his debit card. He asks for the bill to date and is shocked that it has reached five thousand pounds. He asks for itemised expenditure but they don't understand and it would take too long to try and explain. He offers his debit card to clear the debt.

There is a beep as the card declines.

He puts it into their machine, types in the pin and waits. Another beep.

"Sorry, Sir. It is unauthorised. Do you have another card?" the clerk asks, as he discreetly summons the hotel manager.

"I'll need to ring my bank," Dean says. He hadn't thought to sort out another card just in case. He'd just chucked a hundred grand in this account for the holiday and decided to sort the rest out later.

The manager comes over and gestures for him to go into a private office. He hands Dean a phone and tells him the country code for England. Dean dials, he is starting to sweat as he already knows what they are going to tell him.

After thirty minutes going through security, Dean eventually learns the truth. His account is empty. He rushes into a toilet cubicle and is violently sick.

Chapter 13

After some negotiations with his bank and a bit of back and forth, they refuse to assist, and Dean is detained by the Spanish police. He makes a frantic call to Grant who quickly contacts Gary. Between them, they pay the hotel bill and at Dean's request, book him a flight home.

Back in his hotel room after his horrid debacle, Dean paces the floor. The yellowing of his skin is more prominent and he feels wretched. He started off feeling angry with Dani, then foolish as he realised he had been targeted from the outset. Now, he's hurt as he had trusted her with details of his life but she had been lying to him all along.

Dean hasn't realised the hypocrisy and double standards in his own life or seen any parallels. He is a victim of fraud and the actions of a con-woman and he is justly hurt and angry. He wants revenge but as no one really knows who the woman is and she has now vanished, he's unlikely to be able to do anything about it.

Dean heads back to the UK with his tail between his legs. Grant picks him up at the airport.

"Dad, you really look terrible. The Spanish police didn't do anything to you, did they?" Grant asks, concerned.

"No, I just don't feel well. I've been feeling rough for a while now," Dean admits.

"I'll take you to the doctor tomorrow?" Grant offers.

"Maybe, but they'll just tell me to quit drinking," Dean sighs. "That's what they always do." Dean doesn't tell him that when he'd last seen a doctor in rehab, on seeing his test results, the doctor had expressed concerns about the state of his liver. He'd been warned that any further drinking might result in deterioration and cirrhosis, which would be irreversible.

"Well, if that's what you need to do, then you need to do it, Dad. Even if it's hard. We'll all help you." Grant tries his best to sound reassuring but he knows that only his dad can make the decision that needs to be made.

"I just need to sleep and sort my money out," Dean mumbles wearily. The stress of keeping track of the large payout and keeping the size of it hidden from everyone is getting to him.

Grant looks at him sideways. It's time. "About that…"

"Don't worry, I'll pay you both back," Dean says sharply.

"It's not that, Dad. It's just….you received a call from LottoMillions whilst you were away…." Grant waits for an explanation.

Dean realises the game is up and he's had enough anyway. He hangs his head. "I was going to tell you the truth." He knows he sounds pathetic and he doesn't want to look at his son as he admits his deception. "I won the jackpot. I was told just as I was coming out of rehab. It was a roll-over, a life changing amount of money."

"Ten million, right?" Grant says. He doesn't sound annoyed, just sad. "So, I guess the Premium Bonds thing was just a cover to make us think you'd won less. Why would you do that, though? You know I don't really care about money."

Dean glances at him. "It was a stupid idea. I just panicked and, after I told them I didn't want publicity, I decided the best thing would be to keep it from everyone," Dean admits.

He doesn't tell Grant about the rehab pool and the agreement he'd made with the others. If he'd split the jackpot as he had promised, he'd only have two million which wouldn't be enough to do the things he has planned.

"It's good that you know actually. I want to extend the house or move to somewhere bigger and buy a chain of pubs as an investment. I know how to make them work as I've practically lived in my local. Also, I want to get you a car to match your sister's. I'm sorry about that by the way. It just happened to be her birthday at the right time." Dean's enthusiasm is returning as he thinks of his big projects. It'll be so much easier now that Grant knows the truth.

"Thanks for offering, Dad but I don't want a sport's car. From what I've seen, possessing things like that affects people in negative ways. Do you really think a chain of pubs is a good idea for you?" Grant looks aghast at the very idea of his father owning and managing pubs for a living. "What about a health spa or rehab centre?"

"You're kidding, right? You think I want to be reminded of that horrible place. I'd probably get PTSD every time I went through the door. And when have you ever seen me exercising? Definitely pubs, you'll see me make something of myself, I just need to get started…"

Chapter 14

2 years later....

Everyone is assembled in the packed church. Grant stands at the front looking nervous and throwing an occasional glance towards the massive front doors. Dean, Gary, Janet and Sophie are all wearing their smartest clothes and are sitting at the front on one side. Church music is playing.

"All stand for the bride," announces the pastor.

The huge body of people rise *en masse* and collectively turn their heads to see the bride, on the arm of her father, walking slowly down the aisle. She is still getting used to her prosthetic which isn't visible today.

Grant smiles as he sees Louise. She is beautiful. She reaches the front and smiles at him as they take each other's hands and the wedding service begins.

Dean is sweating profusely. He had seen the giant sign on the wall of the church as soon as he entered: *"For what shall it profit a man if he gains the whole world yet loses his own soul."* He remembers it from the Grisham novel. He feels really unwell. He coughs a few times. Gary stares at him, noticing again the yellow tinge in his eyes and now on his skin, and hands him a handkerchief.

"Pull yourself together," he growls. He's had years of dealing with his wayward son and has had enough. If they can just get through this day...

Gary had found out about the jackpot win after six months when Dean had started buying up pubs locally. Being a councillor he'd heard about it through the grapevine and gossip-mill. People had been saying that Dean had won and had won big. It certainly went some way to explaining the massive extension to Dean's house. The expensive cars now on the drive. The frequent luxurious vacations and the latest gadgets and gismos that kept turning up on his doorstep without request.

Dean had learned that the best way to silence his suspicious father was to give him something expensive or to make large donations to his political party. He couldn't really complain then, well not for a while anyway. Then, there were the local issues that Gary had been desperately fund-raising for. Dean could make problems disappear with the click of a button and he was more than willing to do so to keep Gary on side and stop him nagging about his drinking.

"I now pronounce you husband and wife...." the pastor says. His eyes are twinkling. He's seen this couple through a lot, beginning with the aftermath of the terrible accident where Louise had been injured.

Everyone cheers and claps. There is a loud groan as Dean sinks to the floor, crashing into several chairs and ending up flat on his back, unconscious. Guests move out of the way. Grant's attention is drawn and looking at Louise, who gives him a nod, he rushes to his father's side.

Dean can't be roused. An ambulance is called. People are shocked. None more so than Janet who remarks to no one in particular, "He looks really jaundiced. Why didn't I notice it before?"

Gary agrees to go with the ambulance. Grant can hardly abandon his wedding. Everyone is sure that this is just another one of Dean's dramas, an extra bad hangover from the previous night, perhaps. Although, he's never been carted off in an ambulance before, that is new.

The ambulance departs. The wedding continues, slightly more subdued than before. Grant is desperately trying to maintain focus for the sake of his wife. Janet and Sophie are upset but cover it well. They are all hoping that Dean and Gary will reappear by the end of the day and everything will be back to normal.

The wedding dinner proceeds as planned and the evening event has just started when word comes from the hospital: Dean is dying. Years of alcohol abuse have taken their toll. He has cirrhosis of the liver and needs an immediate transplant to save his life.

Chapter 15

What on earth are they to do? Grant and Louise are due to set off on a two week honeymoon to Greece tonight. But this is Grant's father who, without the transplant, may only have weeks to live.

Louise comes to the rescue and says that of course Grant needs to be with his dad. The whole family should be there and she is part of their family now, so she will be there too. Grant loves her even more as he realises her sacrificial nature.

After agreeing to postpone the honeymoon for a few weeks, they change and then all traipse to the hospital.

Dean is lying in bed hooked up to a bunch of machines. Eyes closed, he is deathly pale, but, contrasted with the crisp, white sheets the yellowing of his skin is more prominent.

Gary is sitting by his side. He looks like he has aged ten years in the last few hours. He explains the situation in a whisper. They need a donor and quickly. Living donor family members are best, otherwise the waiting list for a stranger is very long and would probably be too late. Dean must've been enduring agonising pain for a long time for things to have got to this stage. To no ones surprise, the evidence suggests he is obviously still drinking heavily.

Dean's eyes flicker open as he hears voices and senses the gathering crowd of people. He looks like a small child and the fear in his eyes is palpable. He looks at his family one by one and stops at Grant.

"I didn't think you'd be here. What about Greece?" he says in a tiny voice.

"You're my dad!" Grant says.

"We're all here for you," Louise says gently, stepping forward.

Dean's eyes tear up and he brushes a hand across his face. "They say I need a donor…" he looks at his father hopefully.

"I'm sorry Son, they've said I'm too old. Has to be someone under 60," Gary says apologetically although secretly he's relieved. He doesn't fancy such a major operation at his age and the recovery would be painful.

"I'll get tested to see if I'm the same blood group," Grant says firmly.

"Me too, I guess," Sophie offers hesitantly. She can't think of anything worse and the very idea petrifies her but she wants to show willing so she tries to be brave.

Grant and Louise head off to find a nurse or doctor.

"Are you sure about this?" Louise asks. "I mean, I think it's great if you're willing but you know you'll miss the football final and then, there's our honeymoon, we'd need to postpone it for longer...."

"I hadn't even thought about the football," Grant admits. His county have been trying to reach the final for years and have made it at last. "I'll be sorry to let them all down, but I know they'll understand. The honeymoon is different. If you want me to go, I'll go, you're my priority now."

"No. There's no way you'll be able to enjoy it if your dad might die whilst you're away. Of course, you need to do this and I really don't think Sophie would be the right person, poor little thing, she looked scared out of her mind," Louise says.

"There's no way I'd let my little sister do it, if I have a choice. It's my responsibility. Let's pray I am a match," Grant says.

"I'll update our pastor and get the church praying," Louise offers.

Grant heads off to get tested.

Sophie agrees to have the test as well, just in case, but she's relieved that Grant seems set on being the one to donate.

A doctor from the transplant team has asked the family to wait outside and is having a strong word with Dean.

"You do realise that if you receive this transplant, you'll have to give up drinking completely. If you end up back in here with further problems as a result of continuing to drink, we won't be able to help you because other people will be prioritised."

The doctor has seen so many of these cases and he knows that his words are probably falling on deaf ears but he has to at least try. He has a flash of inspiration. "I've heard that your 22 year old son is keen to donate but he will be missing both his honeymoon and the final of his county football if he's a match."

"Oh, no!" Dean is crestfallen. "There must be another way." For once he's thinking of someone other than himself and is horrified at the scale of the sacrifice his son will be making for his recklessness.

"It's the only way, I'm afraid but if I was in your shoes, I'd determine never to put anyone I cared about in a similar position in future," the doctor prompts. His words have had the desired effect.

"Do you know, doc. I won the lottery a few years ago, a huge sum. Yet, all the money in the world can't deal with this. It all feels meaningless when staring death in the face," Dean says sadly.

"Money can't buy everything."

"Dani was right," Dean says softly as the doctor leaves the ward.

Chapter 16

The news is in. Grant is a match. The surgery has been scheduled and in the nick of tim,e as Dean is looking more and more unwell. The doctors had been starting to worry that he wouldn't be strong enough for surgery, but the family have convinced them to at least give him a shot.

The football team had been disappointed but have agreed to bring the trophy to the hospital for Grant to get a look if they should win.

The honeymoon has been re-arranged for six months time. Something Dean could pay for.

Gary and Janet have taken over the running of Dean's pub network in his absence. It had all been going surprisingly well and they thought it would be a shame to let it all fall to pieces.

Dean has completely re-evaluated his priorities and is determined that, should the surgery be a success, he will never drink again. He plans to sell the pub chain to avoid the temptation to drink, it had been a crazy idea in the first place. Perhaps, he will buy a health spa or a football club instead.

For now, though, he's concentrating on the major surgery that, thanks to his foolishness, both he and his son are now facing. He hasn't a clue how he will even begin to repay Grant for his generosity or Louise for allowing their time as newly-weds to be ruined. Somehow, he knows that money won't help with this either.

As Dean is wheeled into surgery, his last thought before the anaesthetic takes effect is the text that he's now seen twice: *"For what shall it profit a man if he gains the whole world, yet loses his own soul."*

Nearby, Grant too is taken to surgery. He is praying for his father, that he will understand that he's not just made these sacrifices out of love, but because he knows his dad isn't ready to meet God. He, Louise and the whole church are praying that these experiences will humble Dean and that he will realise his need not just of his family's forgiveness, but of God's. As Grant goes under, he's thinking about his wife and her willingness to support him on this crazy journey of faith.

Dean wakes up. He's in a recovery ward. He's in pain but it's not unbearable. He needs a strong drink, but is only allowed water. He's handed a cup by a nurse and told not to try and speak.

Grant wakes up. He's in pain but he'd been warned that would be the case. It will take a few months for his liver to regrow and he needs to avoid alcohol and certain foods for a year. He will be weak for a few months.

A doctor comes and addresses them both. They then realise they are next to each other in the ward.

"The surgery was a success. You'll both be able to go home in a week. The nurses will look after you. Your family can visit from tomorrow," a brisk but clear summary from the busy transplant doctor who's already moved on to the next patient.

Over the next few days, Dean and Grant chat a lot, partly as they've never really done this before and partly because there's no one else to talk to.

When they win the trophy, Grant's county football team arrive as promised to celebrate with him. They excite all the patients in the ward by posing for photos and the story makes the front page of the local paper. Dean feels immensely proud of his son. The feeling almost assuages the underlying guilt that he's doing his best to ignore.

Dean realises that he has to show his family that he can change rather than just talking about it. He isn't confident of success but at least he has money that can help to distract him with other projects.

Now that he's out of danger, his priorities are already shifting again. He's thinking of how to expand his empire. He might still sell the pub chain but he plans to replace it with something bigger and better. He's also decided he needs a new car as he's bored of the others crowding his driveway.

Although he knows Grant and Louise aren't interested in expensive gifts, he has to get them something to thank them; he's thinking about buying them their first house together. Sophie will need something bigger than last year as well and then there's his parents.

Dean has thought a lot about the text that seems to pop up everywhere, he knows it's from the Bible. He's decided that it means that now that his soul is no longer at risk of death, it's okay for him to get as much out of the world as he can. The verse only warns people that it won't help them to have everything when they die. Dean isn't planning to die for many years, therefore he can live it up and enjoy his winnings.

He decides to find the verse in the Bible but he doesn't have one. He won't ask his son as it would likely produce a ten minute sermon or in the very least would make his son hopeful of a conversion.

Then, he remembers that hospitals and similar places often have Bibles in their drawers. He reaches into the drawer at his bedside table and pulls out something that has the words New Testament and Psalms on the cover. He glances at Grant who is sleeping soundly. He opens the small book at a random page and begins to read at Luke 12:13:

"Someone in the crowd said to him, :"Teacher, tell my brother to divide the inheritance with me."

Jesus replied, "Man, who appointed me a judge or an arbiter between you?"

Then he said to them, "Watch out! Be on your guard against all kinds of greed; life does not consist in an abundance of possessions."

And he told them this parable: "The ground of a certain rich man yielded an abundant harvest. He thought to himself, 'What shall I do? I have no place to store my crops.'

Then he said, "This is what I'll do. I will tear down my barns and build bigger ones, and there I will store my surplus grain. And I'll say to myself, 'You have plenty of grain laid up for many years. Take life easy; eat, drink and be merry.'"

But God said to him, "You fool! This very night your life will be demanded from you. Then who will get what you have prepared for yourself?"

This is how it will be with whoever stores up things for themselves but is not rich toward God."

Note To Reader

In this final book about the Yale family, we take a closer look at the life of Dean, the husband, son and father.

Dean has suffered the loss of his wife Annie, but instead of grieving then trying to create a life for his teenage children, he becomes reckless and foolhardy.

He has been drinking excessively for years and has now become an alcoholic, ending up in rehab where he blames others for his misfortunes.

Having blown all of the money from Annie's will, he then wins a huge lottery jackpot which should, by rights, have been shared with others in the betting pool, but Dean keeps it to himself.

He goes on expensive holidays, extends his house, buys a ridiculously over the top gift for his teenage daughter and sets about creating a pub chain business, all the while allowing his drinking to get worse, despite a doctor's health warning.

In the end, everything comes crashing down around him. He collapses at his son's wedding and ends up needing an urgent liver transplant to keep him alive.

His Christian son, Grant steps up knowing that he will have to delay his own honeymoon and miss his county football final. His new wife, also a Christian, supports him every step of the way also making huge sacrifices for her new father-in-law.

Dean ultimately ignores the warnings and, having received the donation and now out of danger, he makes plans to expand his empire once again.

It is only then that he is confronted with the parable in the Bible about *The Rich Fool*. This man decided that as he had plenty of wealth, he would tear down his barns and build bigger ones to store it all. However, God told him that he was foolish because he would die that night and his money would pass to others.

The parable warns us about greed and reminds us that a person's life is not measured by what he owns. It's worth noting that the problem was his attitude towards his wealth, he was relying on and occupying himself with it. He wasn't right with God. Being rich isn't necessarily sinful.

The man was helpless in the face of death. Dean too, was helpless when facing death and although he was given another chance, he didn't initially mend his ways. We don't know how he responded when reading the parable in his hospital bed or whether it was the wake up call he needed.

We can learn lessons from this story as we often behave like Dean and the man in the story. We are greedy and selfish by nature instead of thinking of others as more important than ourselves. We hoard possessions and think that throwing money at things can solve problems. We may have an earthly perspective instead of a heavenly, eternal one. We may even believe that God has promised us health, wealth and happiness, when actually He says that Christians will have trouble in this world.

If we have been blessed financially, we should use our money and possessions for God. God owns everything anyway and can easily strip it all away with a simple word or usher us into eternity when we are least expecting it. We need to be ready for both of these scenarios and hold earthly things loosely so that we can respond biblically when called to do so.

The text, *"For what shall is profit a man if he gains the whole world yet loses his own soul,"* is a good reminder of what is at stake.

ABOUT THE AUTHOR

Natalie Vellacott spent a decade as a police officer in England before swapping her badge for a Bible and heading for South East Asia as a Christian missionary. She volunteered on Logos Hope, a giant ship, for two years with 400 people from 65 other countries, enduring the cultural catastrophes in order to enjoy the exciting adventures.

Natalie began writing in the Philippines when she fell in love with a group of street children addicted to a solvent called Rugby. Having founded a charity to help the boys and draw attention to their plight, she naively entitled her first book and has been trying to get it out of the Rugby Union chart ever since!

Natalie has also dabbled in Christian fiction for children, in the 'choose your own adventure' style, mostly for the benefit of her nephew Reuben, who is pleased that he takes centre stage. She has also written a fictional series of short stories for a contemporary audience based on some of the parables of Jesus. The first book is entitled *I Did It My Way*.

For the last few years, Natalie has been involved in full-time evangelism in the UK. Through her latest book, *Evangelism is Exciting!*, she wants to encourage all Christians, especially in the UK, to get involved in fulfilling the Great Commission in whatever way they can and to show that there really is something for everyone.

Please feel free to contact the author at natalie.vellacott@gmail.com. The author is always grateful for reviews at Amazon UK, Amazon US and Goodreads. Thankyou!

NATALIE'S STORY

I became a Christian at a young age primarily due to having been raised in a Christian home and being surrounded by Christianity. As a teenager there were times when I was really serious about my faith but I often became distracted. During a more serious faith phase at the age of seventeen, I was baptised, but just six weeks later fell away from God in dramatic fashion.

I subsequently spent six years immersed in the "party lifestyle", succumbing to many activities and bad habits that sought to replace God, including an abundance of alcohol, cigarettes and gambling. I moved from one non-Christian relationship to another in an attempt to find the happiness that eluded me. I became more and more miserable, attempting to ignore God but knowing deep down that He was there and that I was under His judgement because of my lifestyle choices.

In the year 2000, I began a degree course in Law and Criminology, but dropped out after just six weeks to join the police, thereby fulfilling a childhood dream. In 2002, my younger brother James (who was a Christian) was tragically killed in a car accident at the age of just eighteen. My parents clung to their Christian faith at this time, but I became angry with God for allowing this to happen and resented Christians for judging my lifestyle.

In April 2005, after many other problems and a long struggle, I faced up to the fact that I was miserable and that my life was a total mess. I had recently witnessed my younger sister, Lauren, going through some of the same struggles. I then saw the resulting contentment when she turned back to God. I knew that I was carrying the heavy weight of my many sins around on my shoulders. I sometimes woke up at night in a terrified state, believing I was going to hell because of the things I had done. I knew that God was waiting for me to repent of my sins and turn back to Him, and that He had been patiently waiting for a long time. I lived in constant fear that time would run out and that I may have tested God one too many times.

Eventually, like the prodigal son in Luke chapter 15, I realised I couldn't continue as I was and I came to my senses. I said sorry to God for my many sins and asked for His help. I believed the promise that "everyone who calls on the name of the Lord will be saved."

I abandoned my sinful vices immediately and began regularly

attending my former church, Worthing Tabernacle. Two Bible verses became very important to me as a result of my experiences. The first is found in John 6:67-68: "'You do not want to leave too, do you?' Jesus asked the Twelve. Simon Peter answered him, 'Lord, to whom shall we go? You have the words of eternal life.'" (NIV) These verses remind me that seeking anyone other than Jesus is a total waste of time because He is the only one with the words of eternal life that can offer hope for the future. The second verse is from Mark 8:36: "For what shall it profit a man, if he shall gain the whole world, and lose his own soul?" (KJV) This sums up my life experience as I tried seeking happiness in the world but foolishly risked losing my soul in the process.

God already had His hand on my life, due to my Christian upbringing, former beliefs and the fact that many people were praying for me regularly. All of the glory for the change in my life goes to God as I wasn't capable of turning my own life around having tried and failed many times.

THE WORDLESS BOOK

Just in case there are any non-believers reading this, I would like to explain how to become a Christian and how you too can be free of your sin and reconciled to God to spend eternity in heaven with Him one day.

During my few years of missionary service, I was taught a tool to explain the Gospel. It has been effectively used by millions of people around the world. It's called the *Wordless Book* and consists simply of five coloured sheets of paper or material each representing part of the message of salvation found in the Bible:

YELLOW

This represents heaven. Do you want everlasting life in heaven? The Bible tells us that the streets in heaven are paved with gold. It also tells us that God is light and that in Him there is no darkness and that Jesus (God's only Son) is the light of the world. heaven is God's dwelling place and the Bible also tells us that no man has ever imagined the wonderful things that God has prepared in heaven for those that love Him. heaven is forever.

BLACK

This represents sin. What is wrong with the world? More importantly, what is wrong with me? Being honest, we need to face the bad news in order to see the value of the Good News. The Bible says that all people have sinned and fall short of the glory of God and that the wages of sin is death. God is holy and cannot have anything to do with sin. God is righteous and just and, therefore, cannot just overlook our sin and forgive us because this would make Him unjust. Our sin separates us from God's love permanently. All sinners are destined to spend an eternity in hell under the wrath of God. hell is a truly terrible place where people will long to die because of their torment but will be unable to do so. hell is forever. This is the bad news.

RED

This represents the blood of Jesus. Why did Jesus need to die?

God loved us so much that He provided a way of for us to be reconciled to Him and to escape the torments of hell. He sent Jesus, His only son, to live a perfect life here on Earth. It was necessary for a penalty to be paid for our sin. Jesus' purpose in coming was to die for the sins of the world so that anyone who who believes in Him can get to heaven. He died instead of us so that we could be free from the guilty sentence hanging over us because of our sin. He died on that cross and then rose from the grave just three days later, proving that He had defeated sin and death once and for all. Jesus' death acted as a bridge between guilty sinners and God, allowing all who trust in Him to be forgiven of their sins and to live in heaven forever with God.

WHITE

This represents being washed clean from sin. How can be we sure of God's acceptance? Think of your life as a white sheet. Every time you sin, even in a small way, a black stain is left on the sheet. When a person becomes a Christian and turns away from their sin, God promises them a new start. He says that he will remember their sins no more. When God looks at the life of a Christian, he sees only Jesus and His righteousness instead of the sin.

GREEN

This represents growth. How should this change my life? All true Christians will grow spiritually over time. In order to grow, Christians should regularly read the word of God (the Bible), pray, attend a church, spend time with other Christians, and tell other people about Jesus and His sacrifice for them. These things do not save people. There are no "divine scales" weighing good and bad deeds as a determining factor for entry to heaven or hell. No human can ever do enough good things to get to heaven, as the standard required is perfection; this is why Jesus had to die. The things described here are the grateful response of a Christian who has been rescued from a life of sin and death and has been reconciled to God for a life of hope and an eternal future in heaven.

New Book

Catch the Vision and Share the Good News of Jesus

NATALIE VELLACOTT

EVANGELISM IS EXCITING!

True Stories

PLANET POLICE
NEVER A DULL MOMENT
POLICING THE STREETS OF BRITAIN
Natalie Vellacott

The LOGOS Life
Natalie Vellacott

Street Kids, Solvents & Salvation
Bringing hope to the hopeless in the Philippines
Natalie Vellacott

A Missionary in Manila

Christian Choose Your Own Adventure